The Last Year
of Confusion

The Last Year of Confusion

Janet Turpin Myers

Seraphim
EDITIONS

The publisher gratefully acknowledges the financial assistance of the Canada Council for the Arts and the Ontario Arts Council.

 Canada Council   Conseil des arts
for the Arts   du Canada

 ONTARIO ARTS COUNCIL
CONSEIL DES ARTS DE L'ONTARIO
an Ontario government agency
un organisme du gouvernement de l'Ontario

Library and Archives Canada Cataloguing in Publication

Turpin Myers, Janet, 1958-, author
    The last year of confusion / Janet Turpin Myers.

ISBN 978-1-927079-35-5 (pbk.)

    I. Title.

PS8639.U774L37 2015   C813'.6   C2015-901779-3

Editor: George Down
Cover and book design: Rolf Busch

Published in 2015 by
Seraphim Editions
4456 Park Street
Niagara Falls, ON
L2E 2P6

Printed and bound in Canada

For my bright and beautiful –

Stephanie, Ella, Steven, Rhett

Thank you for keeping me heading forward

All my love, Mum/J

"What will happen when the secret corners of the forest are heavy with the scent of many men and the view of the ripe hills is blotted with talking wires? Where will the thicket be? Gone?"

– *Chief Seattle*

CHAPTER 1

Geezer Positioning System (GPS) & the World Wise Web

Villis spotted a diaper, the biodegradable kind, flattening a tuft of road-side phlox. He pinched the diaper with his chopsticks and dumped it in the green garbage bag that was hitched through the loop on his belt. The driver of a car going by lobbed a takeout coffee cup out the window. It hit Villis in the chest. Things like that happened all too often.

Villis shouted at the disappearing car – "*Govniuk!*" – and gave the driver the finger. It bothered him, the speeding of drivers, but that was peanuts compared to how he felt about their garbage. Especially when it ended up in The Pearl.

He shoved his chopsticks into his back pocket. He only needed them for garbage with germs; otherwise, he used his fingers. He continued hunting for litter, his eyesight much better since he'd increased his vitamin intake – keen as a red-tailed hawk's, he liked to think – scanning for telltale glints of corporate logos snagged on fountaining tiger lilies; dregs of consumer goods tossed from zooming cars by fools. Cheap stuff. Made in China, mostly. Stuff, Villis believed, was the opium of the masses.

The road itself started out straight enough, kilometres away, though not as far as China. Thank God, Villis thought, though he didn't believe in God. The road was a spear of asphalt cutting across what used to be a lake bottom pressed to flatness eons ago by the weight of prehistoric waters. Several metres beneath this road, which seemed to Villis brittle like a finger bone, were other sorts of bones, though none of those pointed with the advancing resolve of the road; rather, they lay as if carelessly buried here and there by the hands of time. Villis had a list of them in his head like a kiddie verse: verteBRAE, scapuLAE, ribs-AND-fe-murs, all from woolly mammoths, beasts like elephants wearing shag carpets who had once munched grass that had danced green light across this land.

Munching, commingling and minding their mammoth business – until, that is, spindly men, too smart by half, had charged at them with arrows and hunted them to extinction.

What wouldn't Villis give to have seen a woolly mammoth?

In any case, the road had no business coming anywhere near The Pearl.

Villis felt duty-bound to check the road for litter once a week, doing the rounds, as he understood it, trolling for garbage along its hard edges as it zipped along the western side of The Pearl.

What did he find?

Empties, mostly.

When he had started doing the rounds twenty-five years ago, he had found mainly mickeys of rum and bottles of Mateus. But people were health-conscious now, and so the booze bottles had been replaced by plastic water bottles, lately fortified with vitamins. In the old days he'd often found collapsed condoms, which were slippery like egg noodles and had been the initial reason for the chopsticks. If he'd had a loonie for all the slack condoms he had twiddled between the tips of those chopsticks, cursing smug Romeos who had ejaculated their pods of spent manhood through the windows of their speeding cars, ignorant *duraks*, why, with all that coinage he could have bought a ticket to Easter Island for himself and Bipin.

Still, nowadays, being honest about it, he was more apt to find spent bottles of Viagra.

He held a secret hope that, amidst the condoms, the takeout coffee cups and the plastic tips of cigarillos that erupted like a pox along the roadside, he might someday find a bifacial tip from the spear of an Old Stone Age hunter, or, even better, a fragment of bone from a woolly mammoth.

Sometimes, while walking in the woods of The Pearl, Villis felt a prehistoric hunter slipping through the green shadows beside him on the path, the hunter's Palaeolithic senses riding the musky scent of game the way a surfer rides a wave.

Or not.

Villis knew the difference between wishful thinking and delusion.

His GPS beeped. He glanced down at it, also fastened to his belt loop. A GPS 90Zx with capacity to enable the Wide Area Augmentation System in adherence to the Minimum Operational Performance Standard for global, satellite-based augmentation systems. You could also play Lizard Whack and Beast Hunt on it, though Villis seldom did.

At first, Villis had refused to wear the GPS, along with its homing transmitter. Bipin, who had nicknamed the GPS "Geezer Positioning System", had presented it to him on his last birthday. It was the kind people used to locate lost dogs and teenagers at malls.

"My dearest friend, Villis," Bipin had said in his singsong Indian accent, "you're ninety years young. A geezer of such ripe vintage cannot be traipsing around the woods without some sort of communication device. What if something calamitous were to transpire?"

"You're no spring chicken yourself," he had said. "What if something should transpire to you?"

Bipin had chuckled. "My thoughts precisely, my old-growth companion. Therefore, though it is true that I am fitter than your usual fiddle, I have nonetheless purchased a GPS for yours truly. Thus when we are out and about in The Pearl our respective devices will allow us to locate each other, willy-nilly and hunky-dory. Give or take."

"Give or take what?"

"Give or take you remembering to turn yours on."

Villis had agreed to wear the GPS if only to stop Bipin from nagging. But did he really care what could or could not happen to him while traipsing in the woods of The Pearl? So what if he fell, bashed his head on a rock?

Then I'll be dead. And good riddance to me.

Fact: Villis thought about death every day. For about a minute. He thought, Is today the day? Is *this* the last one? Then he would invariably look around and pick out something lovely in the woods. If today's the day I kick the bucket, he might think, then at least I will have enjoyed the smell of that wild ginseng. And then he would shrug and live the rest of his day. Resigned.

The GPS beeped again.

Bipin? Who else?

Villis beeped a response, letting Bipin know he was on his way. He wondered, what would Palaeolithic man have made of a device that allowed you to navigate the bush not by noticing broken twigs and moss on rocks but by receiving radio waves from outer space? He'd probably think it was overkill.

Nonetheless, Palaeolithic man would appreciate the device's Fish and Hunt app, which told you when the best time for hunting and fishing were for your current location and, even better, predicted what kind of animal-killing day you could expect.

The GPS was indicating that Bipin was waiting for him on the Second Bridge.

There were three weathered wooden bridges on The Pearl that crossed the creek at different places. Bipin and Villis had agreed to call the middle of the three bridges the Second Bridge, but they disagreed about the other two. What Bipin called the First Bridge, Villis called the Third. And vice versa. This was because they came onto The Pearl from opposite directions, Bipin walking west from the back of his property, and Villis walking east from his.

"Our splendiferous Second Bridge," Bipin had once told Villis, "is the physical manifestation of what the Ancient Greeks taught – you know what I'm getting at, my esteemed friend – 'seek the middle way in all things.'"

"Yes," Villis had said. Except sometimes. He had been thinking of extremists. Sometimes, the only response to extremists was to be extreme right back at them, only in the opposite direction.

Villis made a knot in the garbage bag and turned away from the road toward The Pearl. He made sure his homing transmitter was switched on so that Bipin could track his progress through the woods. Not that either of them worried about getting lost. Both men moved within the woods like thoughts inside the green mind of The Pearl.

It was spring. Villis's favourite time. At least until summer came along. Then that was his favourite. Until the fall. Then, of course, there was winter. Nothing was more beautiful than the woods in winter, especially when the trees, coated in ice, became crystal. In winter, with the leaves off the trees, the sky filled in the spaces between the reaching black fingers of the branches and came so close that Villis had only to put up his hand and pull the blue down upon himself like a blanket.

Villis located Bipin on the Second Bridge, doing a Downward Dog. Villis marvelled, as he often did, at how young his old friend looked, his eighty-eight-year-old body as lean and muscled as that of a man half his age. And what a wonder – Bipin's Ray-Bans never fell off, even when he was doing Downward Dog.

Villis had found the Ray-Bans alongside the road a few years ago. They were a retro pair from the 1960s, called Wayfarers, with thick black frames that looked like old-fashioned TV sets sitting on your face – young counterculture types used to favour them. He had given the sunglasses to Bipin because Bipin had been a follower of Mahatma Gandhi. In fact, at the age of eight, Bipin had walked behind Gandhi the entire four hundred kilometres of the famous Salt March to Dandi, where they'd sifted salt from seawater in defiance of British taxes. "In honour of your activist days," Villis had said to Bipin, handing over the Ray-Bans.

Bipin followed his Downward Dog with a forward bend and a "*Namaste*" to the World Wise Web, then he turned to Villis.

"Listen to this, my dear fellow. I got the load-down last night," Bipin said, snugging the Ray-Bans on his nose.

"You mean download."

"Right, right. I have it here." Bipin pulled a sheet of paper from his fanny pack and read: "'Welcome to the *So You Think You Can Think* Contest Homepage. Contestant hopefuls' – that would be us –

'must answer three of the most pressing questions challenging people everywhere. If your answer is the BEST ANSWER, EVER then you will appear on an episode of *So You Think You Can Think*. Answers must be Tweet sized.' ... Holy cow, what's that?" Bipin stopped reading.

"One hundred and forty characters. No more."

Bipin's eyes went buggy beneath the Ray-Bans. "One hundred and forty words! What can a contestant say with that? Why, the ingredients list on my hair conditioner is ten times ten longer."

Villis decided against correcting Bipin. It was one hundred and forty characters, which was even less than one hundred and forty words. But what was the point? He wasn't sure he wanted to enter the idiotic contest. Even supposing they had the best answer, EVER, who would put two old geezers on a reality TV show? Reality, schmeality. You want reality, try waking up each day in a ninety-year-old body.

Still, Villis knew Bipin was doing it mostly for him. Though it was true that Bipin wanted to go to Easter Island as much as anyone.

Bipin and Villis had watched *So You Think You Can Think* together many times. If you made it "all the way", surviving Being Expelled or having to Drink the Hemlock, then you won $150,000 – which, even with the highway-robbery cost of travel insurance for geezers, was still more than enough to get the two of them to Easter Island for a long stay.

Villis, who had managed to complete his postgraduate degree in anthropology in his home country of Latvia before World War II interrupted, was captivated by the mystery of the famous stone statues – the moai – that lay toppled across the stark terrain of Easter Island like sickened gods. Over the decades of his academic career he had carefully assessed all theories about the island and its statues – some concocted by morons who suggested that the massive monuments had been moved from a quarry to the hillside by extraterrestrials – but the current understanding of what had happened on Easter Island seemed to him supported by the evidence. And for Villis, these facts were a grim warning.

Fact: Easter Island, a lush Eden where giant palm trees had once tickled the sky and green things and flowers and sweet fruits had grown, had been rendered barren by two-legged creatures wielding axes, who had felled every last tree on the island. The cylindrical shape of the felled tree trunks, so the islanders had discovered, made them perfect for rolling moai. "That's how the islanders did it," Villis had explained to Bipin. "Not aliens, but ordinary islanders using tree trunks functioning as roller-wheels beneath those massive stones. And what was the result?"

Bipin had shaken his head, looking sad. "I'm afraid to utter it, my friend."

Villis snorted. "Deforestation. Complete. Leading to erosion by winds and rain, leading to loss of soil, loss of crops, famine, war, and of course – the final irony – there was no wood for boat-making, meaning those idiot islanders were trapped, fighting and starving, on their depleted land."

The theory went on. The statues were then pushed over by disillusioned islanders after their prayers for new forests had fallen on stone ears, though Villis couldn't help thinking that the gods, if there were gods, had toppled of their own accord, sickened by the devastation of this once-upon-a-time paradise.

"What happened there could happen to us," he had said to Bipin.

"Are you referring to VC – *Man's Degradation of Our Earth*?"

Villis nodded. There was no point in saying more on the subject. Over the forty years of their friendship Bipin had heard the details of Villis's worries so many times that Bipin had categorized them under the acronym VC, which stood for *Villis's Concerns*, followed by a subtitle denoting the particular issue.

VC – *Man's Degradation of Our Earth* was Villis's second most concerning concern, after VC – *Abuse of Power by Uniformed Men with Guns and the Oppression of Citizens*. *Man's Degradation of Our Earth* had numerous subcategories such as: what will happen to coastal regions when the ocean levels rise; why it's too late to stop the ice caps from melting; what will happen to Canada when thirst-stricken Americans stampede north; the extinction of honeybees and a world without pollinators; and so on.

As an addendum to *Villis's Concerns*, Bipin had a section for *Villis's Phobias*, which included police in general, and incarceration particularly. But, as Bipin had often said, given Villis's intense experience as a Forest Brother guerrilla fighter hunted by Stalin's secret police, and his subsequent brutal imprisonment in a GULAG work camp, his acute fear of police and imprisonment etcetera was to be expected.

And it didn't help that Villis had killed two secret police with his stolen German Mauser K98 while defending his Forest Brothers' hideout, which (and Bipin said this only once in forty years) had stirred into Villis's brew of fears the leaden sludge of shame.

Bipin had *not* made a list of Villis's reasons for optimism, because there were so few of them. But if there were such a list – entitled, for the sake of argument, *Villis's Optimisms* or VOs – then The Pearl would be at the top of it. As Villis had remarked with relief on many occasions, at least The Pearl was pristine. At least in The Pearl, men were not mucking things up.

"No," Bipin had agreed. "In The Pearl it's just you, me and the gods."

"I don't believe in gods."

"I know, my friend. That's VC – *Is This All There Is?*"

Villis had waved his hand, indicating the woods. "*If* this is all there is, it should be good enough for any of us."

Bipin picked an inchworm off his shirt and set it on a leaf. "Blessings to you, little fellow," he said. Then he sat cross-legged in Full Lotus pose on the Second Bridge beside Villis. "Are you ready to answer the *So You Think You Can Think* Three Challenging Questions?"

"Shoot."

"Challenging Question Number One: Why do people like having their pictures taken with celebrities?"

"What?"

"Challenging Question Number Two: Why do people like to tan? ... Holy cow, I'm permanently tanned." Bipin waggled his arm to demonstrate.

"Tan?"

"Challenging Question Number Three: Why do people shop?"

"For what?"

Bipin shrugged. "Unhappily, it doesn't say."

Villis held out the garbage bag for the sheet of contest questions.

"Toss it in."

Bipin chuckled. "You always make me laugh, my high-quality friend. Why, that can be Number 13,992!" Bipin nodded in a satisfied way and unzipped his fanny pack.

Villis knew what was coming next. Bipin's "List of Blessings". Bipin had been making his list since his fiftieth birthday – every day for the past thirty-eight years. He had told Villis that when he'd turned fifty he had faced a crisis. He had been spending so much time thanking the World Wise Web for the goodness in his life that he had no time left to actually live. "Can you imagine?" Bipin had explained. "I had fifty years of goodness piled up behind me like a mountain of marshmallows reaching to the heavens. Each morning in my meditations I would start picking at those marshmallows, one at a time, and saying my thank-you's. Thank you for the sweet brown honesty in my dog's eyes; thank you for my hips that are still working despite twisting them into Full Lotus; thank you for the tip of my tongue that tastes honey; thank you for the bees ... And of course, even though I gave thanks for all those things on Monday, come Tuesday they were all still there and I had to give thanks all over again. My morning meditation stretched to nearly suppertime."

Bipin's solution – which was suggested to him in a dream by a blonde – was to start a numbered list, writing down one new blessing per day. By writing the blessings down, he was apparently covered; he didn't have to give thanks for that particular blessing ever again. "And Time *isn't*, really," the blonde had said, almost as an afterthought, "so it doesn't matter if you take a lifetime to count all your blessings. Just so long as you do it – one per day is good enough."

Villis didn't believe in blessings. They implied the bestowal of divine favour. "A blessing," he had said to Bipin on more than one occasion, "requires a god to dish it out."

"Or some sort of benevolent, prospering power," Bipin had agreed. "But you can still count them, my friend, even if you're an atheist. You believing or not believing doesn't change the fact that the world is full of them."

Bipin's notebook had a big, red #39 on the front in nail polish.

Thirty-nine for the thirty-ninth year of counting blessings. Bipin received a new notebook from the World Wise Web every year around the time of his birthday – usually a few days before. Though Villis knew that his friend was incapable of bragging, Bipin couldn't help sounding prideful whenever he talked about how he came to acquire his notebooks.

"Not once, my friend, have I purchased one, or even directly sought it out. But every year, a new one comes to me. Like magic. Why, didn't you yourself find #27 alongside the road and give it to me? And then there are the real estate agents, the insurance persons, the Recycling Commission, the dairy farmers, the Conservative Party – all of whom have sent me notebooks in the mail, or given them to me at public information booths ..."

Bipin flipped the pages in #39 and scribbled with a pencil. "Blessing Number 13,992 – *Villis causes me to laugh.*" Bipin looked up from his notebook at Villis. "Such is the dilemma of the atheist. Who to thank? It's a terrible condition, to feel one's heart swelling with the wonders of our world and yet have nobody to thank for it. It makes a man feel thwarted."

Villis sighed. Bipin was right. So many times Villis had felt moved by the beauty of The Pearl: the way trees cast giant shadows up the sides of hills, doubling the depths of the forest; or how a single strand of ice could dangle from a thistle like a piece of Christmas tinsel; or finding Frog, year after year. At those times he had felt his blood replaced by a golden light and his feet plugged into the earth while his mind floated above the canopy of The Pearl that was a sea of green bubbles. He had wanted to give thanks for all of that. He had even tried, many times, thanking in the style of Bipin – thank you for this wild leek which tastes better than store-bought – but he always felt silly. Thank *you*. Who was "you"?

Bipin tapped his notebook with the pencil and smiled at Villis. "You are written down in here a lot, my friend."

Villis tapped the place over his own heart. "And *you* are in here."

CHAPTER 2

Answers to the Three Most Challenging Questions (EVER)

Villis and Bipin were stopped at the dip in Roller-coaster Hill. Bipin had said he wanted to check the fiddleheads but Villis knew better. Bipin always made up an excuse to stop whenever Villis's knees acted up.

This was a mystery to Villis. How did Bipin know at exactly which moment the slight space between his femur and tibia would collapse just enough to let bone nudge bone, causing his knee to burn? Villis never complained about his knees; he was afraid his doctor would insist he have them replaced with Teflon ones. At his age it was a miracle to still have original knees, even though he didn't believe in miracles. Nonetheless, if miracles did exist, surely the longevity of his knees could be counted as one.

They were walking the trails, looking for a place of resonating nexus somewhere in The Pearl. This had been Bipin's idea.

"A resonating nexus is the best spot for inspired thought. This will give us a competitive edge over the other *So You Think You Can Think* contestants. Consider India and China. What is the competitive edge there? Why, the Indians are a brouhaha and the Chinese are organized. Organization is good for making cheap and unnecessary items, but it quashes inspiration."

Villis wasn't clear on the connection between Asian societal structures and nexuses, but he had to agree with Bipin – there were places in The Pearl where life seemed to resonate with a particular intention. In fact, he had in mind such a location. He had come across it only once while wandering in the woods, but reaching it now would require a scrabbling climb up the trio of Lopsided Ridges that bucked upwards like an unruly set of stairs. He took a deep breath, just as Bipin had taught him to do, easing air down through his body into the space between his tibia and femur. The burning let up. A little. Perhaps if they took the ridges slowly ...

"I know a place," he said to Bipin. "There is something about it. Not sure if it's one of your resonating nexuses but, well ..."

Bipin grinned, gave one of his Indian head bobs. "Say no more. You have found it, I'm certain! Lead the way, please. But not too fast. I am in no mood for velocity."

On the way to the Lopsided Ridges, they stopped to call on Frog. This was something they did every day, in season, spring and summer, when Frog was not hibernating in silt but receiving visitors, as Bipin put it, in his bend in the creek.

Frog was old too – Bipin and Villis had been watching him for six seasons now – and the size of an English muffin. He could usually be found at three in the afternoon, bobbing in the creek a few inches out, one front foot resting nonchalantly on a submerged log, his black eyes, like tiny planets of hematite, shining up.

Villis bent over the bend in the creek and focused on the area near the submerged log, searching for the frog's eyes, which were usually the first things he spotted. He shook his head. "Not here."

Bipin shuffled up behind him, carefully, so as not to step on anybody. Then he whistled. *Woo-hoo-hoo-hooooo* – the opening notes of Beethoven's Fifth Symphony. They waited. Nothing. Villis joined in the whistling. *WOO-HOO-HOO-HOOOOO.* Then came a rustle from behind Bipin's sandals, followed by a *kerplop* into the creek.

"He's fast for an old fellow," Villis said, not without a touch of envy.

Bipin, whistling more softly now, bent over and stroked Frog's back beneath the water. "Blessings to you, my friend. It's good to see you are still with us." Bipin turned to Villis. "You know, his eyes remind me of Gandhiji's. They have the same playful wisdom. I think I will call him Mahatma Frog."

Villis rolled his eyes, and then stooped to take a turn stroking the frog's back. "I don't think you should name him after a man. What's wrong with Frog? Did you ever stop to consider that giving him a human name is an act of species-arrogance? Even if the name does belong to one of the greatest humans who ever lived – still, it implies there is something lesser about being a frog."

"Mahatma is not a name. It's a Sanskrit word meaning *great soul*. If you prefer, I will call him Frog Akbar, which also means great, only in Arabic."

Just at that moment the frog propelled himself out of the water, landing on Villis's running shoe.

"Ah – so that's how it is," Bipin said. "He has made his opinion squeaky clear. He agrees with you, my friend, about his name. Frog it is. Frog it shall remain."

Villis nodded, studying the splotched pattern of greens and golds that decorated the frog's back. He was hoping Frog would jump again. He wanted to see if Frog had knees. If he did, Villis wondered if they ever ached.

The climb up the Lopsided Ridges took as long as Villis had expected it would, given his knees. How interesting, he thought as he plodded upward, that such a minor space – that place between his tibia and femur – could cause such a commotion. A brouhaha. Nonetheless, he was enjoying the walk, which took them into the final scenes of the afternoon – his favourite time of day. At one point along the way, he said to Bipin (and, to tell the truth, Bipin was the only person he could talk to in this way) that the last part of the afternoon reminded him of a girl with long golden hair, lying down for a nap.

"Super-duper metaphor," Bipin said. "The golden strands of the girl's hair spreading across her pillow are the same as the late-afternoon sunbeams, slanting across The Pearl. *Thank you for metaphors because they connect us directly to the gods* – that's Blessing Number 17, from 1972."

When they arrived at the spot that Villis thought might be a resonating nexus, he took a deep breath and eased himself down on a fallen tree trunk.

Bipin cocked his head. "I've never been to this place before. How astonishing! An undiscovered realm of The Pearl."

Villis stretched his legs in the general direction of the nexus. "That's because it's hard to get to. It's far off the trails. But forget about that, do you notice anything?"

"Besides exquisite tranquillity and unrelenting beauty?"

"Besides those."

Bipin took a few steps in the direction indicated by Villis's legs, patting his fanny pack, which was something he tended to do when he was excited. "Holy cow! It's flat. Very, very flat." Bipin peered across the ground. "It's so flat, it's as if a hand has descended from the clouds and squashed it."

"Good. What else?"

Bipin took a few more steps and touched the trunk of a tree.

"Endangered butternut trees. One, two, three ... why, eight of them. Does the Ministry of the Environment know about this? Why, this constitutes positively a butternut comeback. And ho ho ho – these butternuts are forming a *circle*! In the woods?"

"Excellent."

Bipin was shaking his head. "Not a perfect circle, but all the same, holy cow, a bloody respectable one."

"An odd phenomenon in nature."

Bipin grinned. "A mandala."

"There's one more thing. Notice the trout lilies?"

Bipin threw up his hands. "Not the trout lilies, too!" He rubbernecked, as if trying to take in all the trout lilies at once. There were, in Villis's estimation, hundreds of the flowers, lighting up the spaces between the trunks of the butternut trees like tiny yellow lanterns dangling from green stems.

"I don't see anything unusual about the trout lilies. Unless you mean that they all seem to be dangling in the same direction."

"Have you ever seen that before?"

"Come to think of it, no! Emphatically not. And they're dangling *into* the circle. Something is sucking them in! Gently, but still, nevertheless, sucking."

Yes, Villis thought, and there seemed to be significantly more birds singing from the branches of the butternuts than he normally observed, but he kept this to himself, since he couldn't be certain. When Villis had first found this place he had tried to make sense of things. He had had crazy ideas – zany stuff that would never have entered his mind when he was younger. What if the flat spot had been stamped down eons ago by a herd of mammoths? Or better, what if it had been the sacred ritual place of Palaeolithic peoples? He had even spent an hour there rummaging for bifacial arrowheads.

And then he had come to his senses and worried – how was it that as he aged he was thinking more like a child?

"There must be a rational explanation for this," Villis said. "Maybe the ground is perfectly flat because it just *is* ..."

"And maybe there is a swirling force of life rising up from the earth that is drawing the trout lilies in, in the same way dawn draws songs out of birds' throats."

"Super-duper metaphor," Villis said.

Bipin unzipped his fanny pack and pulled out the question sheet from the *So You Think You Can Think* contest. "We are sure to get the best answers, EVER, if we stay in this nexus and discuss these questions. And then, it's Easter Island or bust! Listen up, my friend. Put on your thinking cap. Start your engines. Spin your chakras. Show us your jazz fingers–"

"Question Number One," Villis interrupted, "is ... I forget."

"Why do people like to have their pictures taken with celebrities?"

"You tell me," Villis said.

"Me?"

"You've met a lot of celebrities."

"Oodles. But never once have I had my picture taken. Unless, of course, you count the time with Brando, but that was his idea, not mine."

Over the years, meandering through The Pearl, Bipin had told

Villis many stories about his experiences with famous people. Bipin, retired now for eighteen years, had worked all his life as a set builder for major stage and film productions, making, among other things, Merlin's magical oak tree in a production of *Camelot*, starring Richard Burton; Jesus's cross in *Jesus Christ Superstar*, which was tricky because it had to support Jesus while still giving the impression of crucifixion; and the barricade in *Les Misérables*, which he had constructed so many times that he kept a stash of bricks and barrels in a prop warehouse ready to go.

Bipin took his sandals off and started to massage one foot. "Follow my example, my friend. There's a pressure point on the big toe for relief of pain. Give that one a good going-over."

Villis reluctantly obeyed, removing his runners and sports socks and bending his right leg across his left. He winced a little as his right knee complained, and he began squeezing his big toe until it hurt. Then he said, "So, why do people like to have their pictures taken with celebrities?"

"People like to have their pictures taken with celebrities because celebrities are better-looking than they are."

"So–?"

"Standing next to a better-looking person makes you look more ordinary."

"Why would I want that?"

"Looking more ordinary means you can slip through the city without being noticed."

"I don't follow."

"Slipping through the city without being noticed is vital to the survival of activists."

Villis didn't know what to say to this. He tried wriggling his big toe in little circles.

"Survival of activists will be critical when it comes time for pulling the carpeting out from beneath the hierarchical set-up of our civilization and shaking out the stacks and stacks of money that are hoarded at the very tip-top and squandered on extravagant things such as doggie spas, and $39,000 backpacks made from dead crocodiles, and personal whole-genome sequencing as if there is no tomorrow by those very celebrities who prosper by making people feel inferior because they aren't as good-looking as the celebrities are. After that happens, people will feel better about themselves and each other. You should be writing this down. Here." Bipin pulled his blessing notebook and a pencil out of his fanny pack and handed these to Villis.

"The answer is supposed to be tweet-sized," Villis reminded him.

"Very well, just say this: People like to have their pictures taken with celebrities because it makes them feel better about themselves."

Villis wrote it down, counting the characters – 92 or 109, depending on whether or not you counted spaces and punctuation. Either way they were good to go – less than 140. But surely it was too simple an answer? Not that he cared. He had decided to humour Bipin.

"Next question," Villis said. "Why do people tan?"

"Why do people tan? That *is* a particularly tough one. Especially for someone such as yours truly who is quite naturally a scrumptious honey colour and has no need for tanning. But I will give it my best jab."

Villis poised the pencil.

"People like to tan because dark skin is more beautiful than fair skin."

"You can't say that. That's racist."

"Dark skin *is* more beautiful because you can't see those blue veins just under the surface like you can with fair skin."

Villis wasn't going to write that down, but he had to agree with Bipin about the veins.

Bipin continued, "Seeing blue veins upsets people because they are reminded that those veins are full of blood."

"Blood schmood, what's wrong with that?"

"Nothing, until it ceases to whoosh inside you. When that happens, people are kaput. Seeing veins reminds people that they will someday bite the big one, maybe before their mutual funds mature, which forces them to wonder what will happen after they push up daisies, which is a prickly question because there is no evidence that we persist after our bodies have putrefied in coffins, and so people prefer not to think of kaputting and concentrate instead on imagining themselves as healthy and far from you-know-what."

Villis switched his legs around so that he could work on his left foot. The toe-massaging seemed to be working. His one knee was feeling better.

"Tweet-sized, please."

"Mark these words, my pale friend. People tan to imagine themselves as healthy."

Villis took note of how white his own skin was. And sure enough, there were blue veins of blood crawling just beneath the white like lines on a map. He didn't mind. Blood meant life.

"Ouch," Villis said, coming across an especially tender spot on his toe. "I bet Palaeolithic man never did this."

"An insightful observation, certainly. And I am wagering he never shopped, either. I confess, I am dreading this third question. Why do people shop? Bloody hell if I know. That one's a tough biscuit."

"People shop because they're greedy. They want more more more."

"More of what?"

"It doesn't matter. Just more."

"Hmm. Bizarre. Personally, I want less. Less to clean. Less to fix. Fewer shelving units to assemble." Bipin looked dejected. "But saying that people are greedy is a Debbie Downer. I don't think the contest producers will embrace such a negatory conclusion."

"It's a chance we'll have to take."

Bipin nodded, though sadly. "Then write it down, my friend, but I'm afraid that particular tweet will snuff out our dreams of Easter Island like a candle in the breeze."

CHAPTER 3

An Energy Blockage in the Balls

After they left the place of Resonating Nexus, Villis unhooked his GPS and punched some buttons to do a calculation.

"We've walked a long way today. Five kilometres. A lot of it uphill."

Bipin pulled something out of his fanny pack. "Take a power bar. They absolutely work. One or two bites and I'm all geared up to party." He unwrapped the power bar and handed it to Villis. Then he unwrapped one for himself.

Villis bit tentatively into his. He wasn't the partying sort. Never had been. Fact: anthropologists are not very exciting. Nonetheless, he was hoping the power bar might rev him up, perhaps as did the shot of espresso he had once tried at a symposium on Neanderthals.

Villis adored Neanderthals, almost as much as he loved Easter Island and Palaeolithic peoples. He felt a kinship with them because they had been northerners like himself, and they suffered from arthritis. He had recently read a magazine article making a case for Neanderthals having painted cockleshells and strung them on leather strings around their necks. Villis had always suspected the Neanderthals were not the thick-headed thugs of common stereotype; the cockleshell necklaces were clearly evidence of a nobler disposition.

"The cockleshells were most likely for adornment purposes," he had told Bipin. "Which is highly significant because it means the Neanderthals appreciated beauty."

"Or else they used the shells to pick up girls."

"Neanderthals," Villis had continued, "co-existed with Cro-Magnon men for ten thousand years. During that time those two early hominids were at war, throwing stones and spears at each other. Eventually, the Neanderthals died out, probably annihilated by the Cro-Magnons—"

Bipin had waved one hand, cutting him off. "Spare me the gory details. I cannot bear it. It suggests that one sort has been killing off another sort since the Very Beginning. Clearly, we have not evolved where it matters most, even though we load-down things."

"Download."

"You know what I feel like doing now, my friend?" Bipin asked between chomps on his power bar. "I am feeling the luck after finding the Nexus. Why don't we pander to your favourite pastime and search for mammoth bones or arrowheads? Maybe today is the day we stumble upon something." Bipin bent his head like a terrier and began scanning the ground. He kicked at some dead leaves and then squatted to turn over a rock.

Villis sighed. It was no good looking for artifacts that way. The chances against finding anything lying around in the woods were a million to one.

Bipin straightened and paddled his hands on his trousers. "Zowie, my friend, this is bringing me down. I just realized something excruciatingly sad about arrowheads."

"They're impossible to find?"

Bipin looked up to the sky. "What would Gandhiji say? Arrowheads are for killing. Why does it have to be so – that the most common artifacts remaining from the days of our primordial ancestors are weapons of mass destruction?"

"Killing is in our nature."

"Do you really believe that, my friend?"

"Last one hundred years of so-called human civilization alone proves it. Armenians, European Jews, Kurds in Iraq, Mayans in Guatemala, to name only a few. About thirty-two million corpses rotting in the belly of the twentieth century, give or take."

Bipin rubbed his eyes. "And before that, human sacrifices. Witch hunts. Crusades. And Genghis Khan, alone, stopped forty million beating hearts before toppling off his horse and dying himself."

Villis picked power bar out of his teeth. "If not in our natures, then what?"

Bipin brightened. "I'm getting it crystal clear! Remember what you told me about those Neanderthals guys, how they wore cockleshell necklaces? Since the beginning, then, it's been arrowheads *and* cockleshells. Killing *and* beauty. The problem is not with our natures – it's with our choosings. Cockleshells and arrowheads, and we've mostly gone with the arrowheads. Why not choose the cockleshells? It's simply a matter of selecting that instead of this."

Villis hoped so. But he doubted it. Hope and doubt. Back and forth – he was always going back and forth between those two. Hope was for the future, but doubt came from past experiences. Fact: he was too long in the tooth for the future and too jam-packed with the past. Where was the splendiferous Second Bridge between those two where he could rest and not think about either?

His GPS beeped. "It's saying we're at an exceptional time for hunting."

"Dear me," Bipin sighed. "Even the GPS is choosing the arrowheads."

They walked on toward the Second Bridge, where they would part and make their way to their respective homes, Bipin heading east, Villis west. Since it was getting late they decided to take the short trail – through a boggy patch where the mosquitoes drilled like dentists. Villis's knees were still acting up and Bipin was eager to get home to his laptop and start typing up their application for the *So You Think You Can Think* contest.

"But I'm not satisfied with our answer to the shopping question. I refuse to submit a gloomy response. We must return to the Resonating Nexus and try harder. Maybe if we sit in the middle of the circle of butternut trees. What to do, what to do? If I had a beard I could tug on it and help myself think." Bipin demonstrated by pinching his chin. "But not to worry, my friend–"

"I always worry."

Bipin gave him a serious glance. "I know you do. That is why I am telling you. Not to worry, I'll figure something out."

Villis didn't say so, but Bipin figuring something out was exactly what he was worried about.

They walked on. This part of the trail was easy going, worn soft by years of their padding along. Villis and Bipin had created all the trails in The Pearl. The touch of their footsteps, like slow-motion raindrops, had gently nudged the woodland, just enough and no more, to pat pathways that wriggled unremarkably through The Pearl. If they missed walking a trail for a while, it vanished, the woods brushing it out with breezes. Villis liked this – that The Pearl could erase the signs of their passing. And he didn't like it. After he and Bipin were dead their trails would cease to exist, along with their conversations and silent moments of affection.

"What's that?" Villis stopped abruptly and pointed a few feet up the trail. "Do you see that?"

Bipin squinted. "Something has slashed the trail. Not coyotes."

They took a few more steps and stared down at the ground. They were at a place that was damp from a spring that burbled across the trail. In the soft, damp earth there was an imprint: four parallel gouges, evenly spaced and curved. If Villis had seen such an imprint on the shoulder of the road, or in a field beside a barn, he would have recognized it immediately for what it was, but here in The Pearl it was so out of place, so unexpected, so offensive and therefore impossible to accept, that his brain could not name what it was.

But he knew. In his gut he knew. Were these not the markings of his greatest worry, like the telltale scat of a wild beast?

"Who did this?" he said, teeth gritted.

Bipin bent for a close-up inspection. "It's from a tire. An ATV. No doubting about it."

"What the hell is an ATV doing in here?"

"All-terrain vehicles can travel on all terrains."

Villis roared. "Not in The Pearl they can't." He stomped on the wheel-print, wiping it out. Then he whirled around, slowly, suspiciously, scanning for more prints. There, farther up the trail, he spotted another gouge, this one longer, deeper, with a glimmer of water trapped in its ruts. "Erosion," Villis bellowed. "This is the beginning of it. Some moron has been in the woods with his stupid machine and he's made a rut and the water is now pooling in his rut and this water will make the rut bigger and the trail will start to wash away and the roots of trees along the edge of the trail will become exposed and the trees will be compromised–"

Bipin put his hand on Villis's arm. "I know. It's an unmistakable example of VC – *Man's Misuse of Technology*. But lend an ear to my proposal. We shall soon hit upon this moron and forbid him to drive around here on his machine."

"He won't listen. Those kinds of guys never listen. They like the noise. They want the speed. They do it for the thrill, bombing around, squashing, killing."

"Assholes?"

"Assholes!"

Bipin nodded. "As I understand it, it's a problem not with the anus but with the testicles. An energy blockage in the balls resulting in a buildup of toxins. Like the water in that rut, everything is congealing in that one place. It makes for very poor judgment. The only correction is long and arduous repetitions of the Sage Twist pose. Or else – a swift kick to the goolies. If the moron doesn't listen, then that will be Plan B. Like so!" Bipin snapped his left leg in a quick-as-lightning forward kick.

Villis narrowed his eyes, peering into the woods, as if expecting the ATV man to rumble from within a grove of trembling birch. "How will we find him?"

"We will hunt him down, evaluating the signs of his destructive passing as we come upon them in the woods. Just as your Palaeolithic man went after his mammoth, so too will we track our asshole."

Villis tapped his GPS. "It *is* an exceptional time for hunting." He smiled, but not happily. Rather, it was the iron-grey smile of a man suffering the satisfaction of being correct in his dire predictions.

CHAPTER 4

Bipin's Thought-flocking Principle

Over the next few weeks, Bipin and Villis stalked the ATV asshole, sometimes tracking him single file on the trails, bolstering each other's spirits, and sometimes splitting up to cover more territory. When they split up, they switched on their homing devices, monitoring by GPS each other's progress through The Pearl. If Villis, for example, discovered something – more tire gouges, snapped saplings, churned-up bagels of mud – then he would beep a distress signal and wait for Bipin to come. Together they would repair the damage as best they could, smoothing ruts, reshaping the trail – though there was nothing they could do about the saplings – while Villis ranted and Bipin considered the bigger picture.

"Have you stopped to think, my friend, that you have most likely summoned the ATV fellow into The Pearl in accordance with the principle of Birds of A Feather Flock Together?"

Yes, he had thought *that*, not because he believed in Bipin's Flock Together Principle but because he knew that sooner or later Bipin would bring the confounded thing up, and he wanted to be ready with a snappy rebuttal.

"People aren't birds, so your principle doesn't apply." That was the best he could manage; embarrassing, given his standing as an intellectual. He realized, again, as he had so many times, that he wasn't as sharp as he'd once been. This used to frighten him, say, when he was seventy-five, this sense that his brain was an old-fashioned telephone switchboard with some of the circuit plugs dangling disconnected. But now he shrugged it off. At least some of the calls were still getting through.

And none of this changed the fact that the Flock Together Principle was unverifiable, and therefore unacceptable. It had been taught to Bipin in a dream by the same blonde who had ordered him to make the list of blessings.

"It goes like this," the blonde had declared in her crisp manner. "We get *who* and *what* we think. Thoughts of like-thinking are attracted, one to the other. Birds of a feather flock together."

Bipin had expanded on the concept. "Every thought that leaves our heads is a beggar with a rope tied around his waist; the other end of the beggar's rope is tied to our minds, keeping him tethered so he can find his way back to us. He's wearing a trench coat and carrying an empty cup in his outstretched hand. The cup is for filling with whatever it is the beggar is begging for. And here is the vital bit – what *is* he begging for? It's obvious, my friend, the answer, so palpable I can roll it between my fingers like a dollop of *saag paneer* – the beggar is begging for whatever it is *your* mind has ordered him to find. If you are thinking fear, then that is what he wants in his cup. If you are thinking sex, then off he goes to make his cup runneth over with lusty babes."

Of course Villis knew that thoughts were not tethered beggars but electrical epiphenomena spitting like lightning bolts across the interstitial spaces in his brain. This was a sound idea, proven by science and clearly preferable to Bipin's principle because it let the thinker off the hook. What sensible man wanted his thoughts sprinting back to him bearing cupfuls of consequence?

Although, Villis sometimes thought, supposing for argument's sake that Bipin's flaky theory *was* true, then it would have come in handy during those frozen years when Villis was a prisoner in Perm-36, one of Stalin's GULAG prisons on the border with Siberia. Then he would have sent his beggar out to find food, specifically *piragi* the way his mother had made them – baked buns plump with bacon – and Kashmir socks and an overcoat and scarves to protect his face from the sadistic winds that scraped the Ural Mountains. Come to think of it, he could have sent the beggar out to assassinate Stalin and his secret police, the NKVD, and while he was at it, assholes everywhere who tricked up their fears in acronyms.

Bipin tapped his temple with an organic banana and continued. "When a person becomes an improved thinker, the beggar is replaced with a pilgrim who beams a light into dark places and brings back truth. And if that thinker continues to evolve – shall we say, he takes up meditation, becomes a veggie, stops listening to smooth jazz – then the pilgrim is replaced with a musician whose delicate long fingers play the strings of the World Wise Web like a master." Bipin sighed. "To be a musician strumming the Web, such is my supreme goal, though, frustratingly, I am predominantly still a beggar."

Villis couldn't in good conscience sympathize with Bipin's frustration, since the beggar-pilgrim-musician thing was an irrational fantasy – and yet, there was something familiar in Bipin's longing, like wisps of a dream that is forgotten upon waking. Was it a longing to evolve into a better man, even though, it was a fact, they were both running out of time?

"What does the musician play on the Web?" Villis asked, to be kind.

"Bliss." Bipin sighed again and then sat silently for a few minutes.

To cheer Bipin up, Villis handed him a Ziploc bag full of cherries. "These are good for spitting," he said. "Off the bridge."

They were eating lunch. Since tracking the ATV asshole they had been spending whole days in The Pearl, beginning just after breakfast and continuing until supper. Villis enjoyed munching lunch on the First/Third Bridge, unwrapping the wax paper from his sandwich, sniffing the pickle in the egg salad, dangling his legs over the creek – though it was a challenge to stand up again after sitting for so long.

Bipin spat a pit and then poked Villis in the arm. "My friend, you have spent so much time thinking about those cars zooming along the road, hating them, worrying about the garbage, that your beggar has gone searching for them. It is *your* obsessive car thoughts that have called the all-terrain vehicle into The Pearl."

Villis plucked back the cherries and popped one into his mouth. A bit sour this one was, like Bipin's dumb idea.

"Baloney."

"And further, aren't you an expert in wheels? Haven't you spent most of your life studying them, writing papers, thinking thinking thinking, always about wheels? And now, look what you have done – you have attracted wheels into The Pearl."

Wheels? Fact: he was an expert. If you were an academic you had to specialize in something, so for his postgraduate work he had focused on prehistoric anthropology, especially the evolution of tools, with a particular interest in the development and applications of the wheel.

His interest in wheels had come in handy during his days with the Forest Brothers, just after the end of World War II and before Stalin's labour camp. At that time Villis had joined a band of guerrilla fighters attacking the NKVD and then retreating to hideouts in the forests of northern Latvia. He had become a hero among the Brothers by cobbling together an elevator out of old wheels and ropes. It was this elevator that allowed a Forest Brother to hoist himself on a plank platform to the top of a tall pine in order to scout for sneak attacks by the secret police. And it was while hidden in this perch in the pines that Villis, alone and on guard, had shot two NKVD who had discovered the Forest Brothers' hideout. Shot them dead, and glad to have done it, though he never forgot the double bang-bang of the gunshot and the surprise in their eyes as they died.

Damn crapola bad luck, as Villis generally described it, that's what it was when one day the rope broke on the elevator, leaving no scout in the high pine. And wouldn't you know it, it was on *that* particular day that the NKVD exploded into the secret of their forest hideout, guns cracking like splintering wood.

And damn crapola bad luck, but his expertise in wheels was of no use after the NKVD skewered him at the end of a gun, like an entomological bug sample, and dumped him into Camp TTK-6 (it was 1946) where he toiled seven years – seven years, nine hours a day, felling trees with a dull handsaw. Rolling the logs to the river. And though Villis knew that there was no God, no Destiny, no Fate, he had come to believe in a force of omnipresent irony that had left him chuckling in a dark way despite the desperation of his prison circumstances.

He had tried to explain this funny aspect of his GULAG experience to Bipin, but Bipin, too compassionate to appreciate the sharp pleasures of irony, could not grasp the sad joke of it. All he ever saw was the omnipresent pain of Villis's ordeal.

"Tell me again how what you did in Camp TTK-6 was funny?" Bipin had said.

"It's not *funny* funny, but *weird* funny, because it was a tragicomical replay of how Man first invented the wheel. And I am an expert in wheels. Get it?"

Bipin had shaken his head.

Villis explained further. "The first wheels made by Neolithic man were felled tree trunks used as rollers beneath things that needed transporting, like they did on Easter Island with the moai. The latest evidence suggests that the wheel was most likely invented by Neolithic peoples of the late Tripolye culture in the lands that until recently were called the Soviet Union – those same lands tormented by our friend Joey Stalin."

"Not *my* friend," Bipin said.

"I'm being sarcastic."

"You're repressing your bitterness."

"In any case, in order to make the tree-trunk rollers roll more easily, those late-Tripolyan men thickened the ends to make them roll straighter; then they sliced off the thickened ends into discs and attached the discs to the ends of a slimmer pole, what we now call the axle. Now, at the camp where I was, the trunks we cut down had to be rolled to the river. But this was a GULAG labour camp, after all, and there were no draught animals to pull the felled trees, so we prisoners

– less than animals to those bastards – had to do the job. With six of us to a tree, we pushed, mile after mile, rolling those goddamned tree trunks in the same way Neolithic man rolled tree trunks on his way to inventing the wheel. Get it? There I was, Mr. Master Degree Villis, Latvian Golden Boy, an expert in the wheel and sundry other arcane bits of useless information, re-enacting a parody of the prehistoric process of the invention of the wheel in those very lands where the wheel most likely originated. Now do you see the irony?"

Bipin had patted his eyes. "I cannot see a thing because my eyes are fuzzy with tears for your suffering."

Villis watched Bipin crumble the last of his sandwich into the creek for the fish. Villis usually followed his friend's example, despite never having seen a single fish eating a single crumb. Still, he liked to think that perhaps someone downstream would later enjoy a soggy feast of his leftover lunch. Perhaps even Frog.

But today Villis had no leftovers. Famished from tracking the asshole, he had devoured his lunch. And, to be honest, he was not in a generous mood, but instead was feeling irritated by Bipin's suggestion that his thoughts had, in some kooky, super-sensible way, summoned the ATV into The Pearl. It wasn't fair, not fair at all, for Bipin to hold him responsible for the manifestation of his own fears.

But then, just at the instant when he was thinking about Bipin's stupid idea, Bipin began talking about that very idea *again*. Villis worried, mightn't *that* be proof of Bipin's thought-attraction theory?

"My friend," Bipin said, nudging his Ray-Bans down so he could peer sympathetically over the rims, "do not fuss and fret. We can use your incomparable thought-flocking capabilities to our advantage."

Villis grunted.

"Simply order your beggar to find the ATV man. Simply button up his trench coat, blow the dust out of his cup and send the beggar out to bring home our asshole."

Villis snorted. Didn't say a word. But in his mind, he saw his beggar pitching the asshole into a black and bottomless abyss.

CHAPTER 5

Earth Against Geezer Bones is the Hardest Kind of Earth

The next morning, when Villis checked his inbox he found an email from Bipin. The subject line read: "NEXUS BRAINSTORM".

Villis clicked his mouse, opening the email, thinking, *Here we go again.* Bipin was always sending emails about breakthroughs, epiphanies, blue-sky thoughts and, Bipin's favourite, brainstorms. In fact, Bipin had such thoughts every day. Whenever Villis complained, saying no one could be *that* creative, Bipin apologized (though he never seemed sorry), saying it was the fault of the World Wise Web.

"It's all those 'good, good, good, good vibrations,'" he said, singing the Beach Boys song. "The Web and myself are syncopated, man. Inspiration is always humming across my synapses."

Villis sighed and read today's message.

Hi Villis. Come to my shed. Pronto this morning. Something is there that will jack up the power of the Resonating Nexus and thereby help us improve our gloomy response to Challenging Question Number Three. Ciao.

This was followed by a string of emoticons, longer than usual and more emphatic, even for Bipin. The emoticons caught Villis's attention.

Something was up. Maybe there really was a power booster in Bipin's shed? Maybe there really was something to the Resonating Nexus? Maybe they could win the contest and go to Easter Island. See the stone statues. Before he kicked the bucket.

Villis deleted the email. As he did so he felt a pang from the force of omnipresent irony. He realized that someday *he* would be deleted. Double-clicked into oblivion.

He wondered – was there an emoticon for "get-me-outta-here"?

Bipin's shed was not really a shed. It was a dilapidated timber garage with a clunky green door that slid sideways on rollers, opening and closing amid rattles and dust. The inside was brown and black, and fingers of sunlight grabbed through cracks in the wooden walls. It was a place Villis always had to dig into, through Bipin's junk and his half-baked projects and the coagulated smell of his leaky oil furnace. The shed, minus the junk, reminded Villis of the barracks at Camp TTK-6. He had never mentioned this to Bipin, but the way the sunlight infiltrated the wooden walls always pushed him back to Perm-36, and a loathing to get out of his bunk in the morning.

It took a moment for his eyes to adjust to the low light. Bipin was standing there, arms akimbo and a tool belt around his hips, making him look like a gunslinger. There was something lurking over Bipin's shoulder, something shrouded by the brown and black – a chunky head thing with eyeless sockets, angular nose and a foreboding expression. It was bigger than Bipin. And bigger, at least for the moment, than Villis's memories from Camp TTK-6.

"Feast your eyes," Bipin announced with obvious pride.

"A moai?"

"Holy cow! You've nailed it."

"Is it real?" Villis reached out his hand. Stepped toward the moai. For a second – no, for much less than a second – he believed that Bipin had somehow acquired an honest-to-goodness stone statue from Easter Island, somehow managed to transport it to his dusty shed in Canada and erect it there, upright, without it toppling. A miracle, even though there were no miracles – *that* was how good this moai looked. Though, on second thought, the light in the shed was poor and any fool could now see that the moai was too small to be authentic.

Bipin poked the side of the moai. "An exact scale replica. Eight feet tall."

Then Bipin explained how he had once worked on a romantic comedy called *Thor Heyerdahl Does Easter Island* (it had been a flop) and had made a half-dozen moai to decorate the set.

"I Facebooked a guy I used to work with and asked him to drive this baby over. It's first-rate. Been in storage in the prop warehouse for a donkey's lifetime."

"I know you have a reason for this," Villis said. "And I know you'll tell me, whether I ask you or not."

"Go ahead. Ask me. Mum's the word until you do."

Villis crossed his arms. "Let me guess."

"Not a snowman's chance in H-E-double-L you can do that."

"You plan to haul this thing, this moai, up to the Resonating Nexus. Set it up there—"

"Who can pull the polyester over your eyes?"

"You think that by doing so, the power of the Resonating Nexus will—"

"INCREASE. INCREASE."

Villis uncrossed his arms. "Precisely."

"So, are you with me? Or 'agin' me?"

"'Agin.'"

"Why forever not? If one has never tried to increase the power of a resonating nexus that has formed inside a circle of butternut trees high atop three Lopsided Ridges in the bush by setting up an Easter Island moai in the near vicinity of said nexus, how does one sincerely know it won't work?" Bipin waggled a finger. "You're skeptical because it's a replica."

"I'm skeptical because it's big. How are we going to get that thing all the way up to the Nexus? Roll it on logs, like they did on Easter Island?"

Bipin patted his pockets. "Where is my blessing book? I've got to write down number 13,998 before I forget ... *Styrofoam*."

"What?"

Bipin pulled a screwdriver from his tool belt and stabbed it into the moai. The screwdriver slid in with a wiggle and squeak. "Styrofoam is a blessing, at least to people who make props. This baby here is 100 percent classic Styrofoam, meticulously spray-painted and airbrushed by an artist of the highest calibre. Myself. As light as puffed rice, it is constructed in four easy-to-take-apart sections: A, B, C and D. Hand me that stool."

Villis did.

Bipin climbed up on the stool, wrapped his arms around the top quarter of the moai and yanked. A section of the moai, roundish like a doughnut and corresponding roughly to the brow and crown of the head, came off. Bipin tossed the section to Villis, who caught it with a grunt of surprise.

"Three more sections to go, my doubting Tom – eyes to chin, chin to chest, chest to the rest. All we have to do is load them one section at a time into my wheelbarrow and, quicker than who's-your-daddy, up we trundle to the Nexus."

"Not a wheelbarrow."

Bipin clapped a hand to his mouth. "Holy cow, I was forgetting my brains. No wheels allowed in The Pearl. What a dummy."

Villis slipped the moai doughnut over his head and rested it across his shoulders like the yoke for an ox. He couldn't see a thing except for the unpainted Styrofoam on the inside of the moai. "If we each carry one section at a time, we can do the job in two trips up the Lopsided Ridges." He shifted the moai piece upward so that it rested across his forehead, wearing it as a two-foot-tall hat. "I'm a beast of burden again, sort of what I was in camp."

Bipin sighed. "If that is more of your irony, I'm still not laughing."

But it was too much to make two trips up and down the Lopsided Ridges in one day; they would have to space the job over two.

When Villis was a younger man, say, in his sixties, this fact – that his body would not always do his bidding – had frustrated him. Back then he was still skirmishing with his limitations, wheeling and dealing with various parts of his body as they showed signs of petering out. Back then he had tried vitamins, omegas and antioxidants, callisthenics, naps, massage, hot packs, cold packs, Aspirin, positive visualization, biofeedback, acupuncture, brickloads of fibre, bucketloads of water, and when all else failed, denial. He had even taken up ballroom dancing.

But gradually, as he'd muddled into his seventies, and then, surprisingly, into his eighties, bits of his body, one after the other, had coughed and fallen to their knees, like cowboys shot at high noon. Eyes, easily tired now; knees, aching; colon ... well, that was a long, operatic lament every morning echoing off the porcelain of his toilet bowl.

And so he had cultivated an air of detachment, picturing himself waving like the Queen as his collapsing body parts paraded past.

Therefore, two trips up the Lopsided Ridges it had to be. Day One. Day Two.

On Day One of Operation Moai Moving, as Bipin had dubbed it, after taking forty-five minutes to climb the ridges, setting down the moai pieces whenever Villis needed a rest, they reached the Nexus without fuss and unloaded the bottom two sections of the moai in the centre of the butternut tree circle. Then they covered the moai with a khaki tarp they had brought along. Just in case. Though they both agreed it was unlikely anybody would happen by. Even ATV man wasn't expected to find the Nexus, simply because the trail up was too steep for a machine. And, as Villis remarked with the confidence of a man certain of his enemy, ATV asshole was likely too much of a sissy to walk. And too fat, probably, though Villis didn't say so out loud.

On Day Two, after resting from the climb and invigorating themselves with power bars, Bipin and Villis set to assembling the four pieces of the moai.

"Gather rocks," Bipin instructed. "They are for weighing down the bottom section." He tilted the "A" piece up and pointed to support bars that criss-crossed the bottom of the doughnut hole. "We pile the rocks inside, on top of the crossbars, before putting on the second section. And behold these dowels sticking straight down from the bottom? Those we shove into the ground, like skinny yet sturdy legs, ho ho, just like mine" – he flexed his legs, grinning – "to prevent torquing."

There were more dowels, poking out the bottom of each section, that fit into the top of the corresponding section below – pegs in holes designed to hold the four moai pieces as one.

After they had put together A, B and C, Villis gave the moai a test shove. "Well-made. Doesn't fall over. Might even withstand a good wind."

Bipin accepted the compliment with a grateful nod. "One always has to account for clumsy actors crashing into one's props."

Villis lifted the top section and stretched up to set it in place. "I can't reach it. It's too high. I can't get the dowels into the holes."

"Not to worry, my friend." Bipin put a hand on his belly below his navel and closed his eyes.

"What are you doing?"

"Getting in tune with my *hara*."

Villis nodded. Of course.

After a moment, Bipin opened his eyes and, without saying a word, lowered himself gracefully to his hands and knees. Like a cat, he crawled to the base of the moai and then waited there, looking calmly at Villis.

"Uh-uh. I'm not standing on you."

Bipin lifted one paw and patted his *hara*. "Mind over matter. This isn't a back. It's a bench."

"I'll fall."

"Brace yourself on the moai."

"For crying out loud."

"And take off your shoes."

Villis ripped the Velcro on his runners and kicked them off. He picked up the D section of the moai and rested it on his head and shoulders. Then he placed first one foot, then the other, on Bipin's back, resting a hand against the moai until he was sure of his balance. For a moment – no, for less than a moment – he was an acrobat in the Cirque du Soleil, iridescent tights poised in a dangerous high place. *Who would have thunk it?* he thought. *Look at me, look at me,* he wanted to shout, as he had shouted as a boy climbing trees.

Then he plunked the top section of the moai into place.

Then he fell.

Earth against geezer bones is the hardest kind of earth. Villis had that thought just as he felt the triple jolt of ground against tailbone, shoulder blades, skull. When he opened his eyes he saw above him blue sky in rags, tattered green of leaves and Bipin's grim lips.

"Can you budge?"

Villis tried. "Crapola."

"Is that yes, you can budge, or no, you cannot?"

"Ugh. Here, give me a hand."

When Villis was on his feet again, Bipin stood there, clucking at him. "No way you can perambulate, my friend."

"Says who?" Villis took a couple of steps. A spear, perhaps one with a bifacial tip, pierced the very lowest part of his back. He winced.

"Pain and suffering?" Bipin said solemnly.

"Tailbone."

"Coccyx. When injured, described in the literature as *coccydynia*. No Lopsided Ridges for you, my friend. I'll dash home, fetch the wheelbarrow. Return post-haste for you. Wheel you to a safe haven."

"Not the wheelbarrow." Villis tried to sit down on a log. "Crapola!"

"I'll bring some cushions. *Coccydynia* cannot abide pressure on the butt." Bipin picked up the tarp and spread it on the ground at the foot of the moai. "Lie down on this until my return. Meditate on a calm coccyx. And keep your asshole aiming up."

CHAPTER 6

How to Track Your Enemy

Settling himself on the tarp, stomach down, head resting on his arms, ground-level view, Villis watched Bipin's feet, then calves, disappear over the lip of the first ridge. How long might it take an eighty-eight-year-old Indian man, even one as fit as Bipin, to hike the distance from Nexus to shed, to his house for butt pillows, then back to the Nexus again? This question preoccupied Villis for ten minutes while he walked the route in his mind, taking into account Bipin's inevitable increasing fatigue and the fact that he often stopped to stare at things. An hour and a half, maybe. No, more like two. He should have had Bipin activate the homing signal on the GPS so he could have tracked his progress through The Pearl.

Villis peered around. A limited view. Nearby, dead leaves, twigs, and a frontier of tree roots and low-flying moths. Now was as good a time as any to look for arrowheads and mammoth bones. Maybe from this vantage, call it perhaps the artifact's point of view (he thought this funny, hoped he could remember to tell Bipin), he might spot something.

But what if the asshole came along?

God, how embarrassing. To confront his enemy finally, in this position. Surely a position of weakness.

And what if the asshole offered to help him? What if he hauled him home on his ATV?

Irony.

Villis snorted.

He had suffered worse. There were no sufferings greater than those of Camp TTK-6. Villis had a list of them that was really a litany: Cold. Hunger. Boredom. Constantly wet feet. Bowels – either too loose or too tight. The way you were always watched. But worst of all was how imprisonment subverted time, turning a fellow's pleasant memories of the past into pains, making the present endless and the future dead before it happened. He supposed, if Bipin were here with his damned blessing notebook, he would insist on converting all *that* into a blessing. He could hear Bipin's singsong Indian accent – "My friend, your sufferings in Camp TTK-6 are a blessing because forever and ever after nothing you experience will ever be as bad as that."

Villis reached out one hand and rummaged through a mat of nearby dead leaves, because you never knew. Verte*BRAE*, scapu*LAE*, ribs *AND* fe-murs. And what else was there to do, ditched here, face down? Coccyx burning. Sore knee crammed against the earth. Maybe he should root through the soil and search for nematodes.

After a while, he remembered his manhunting pages. He had folded them into his jacket pocket before setting out that morning. He had planned to read paragraphs out loud to Bipin while they were eating their lunch in the Nexus, and before they had gotten started on their discussion of Challenging Question Number Three: Why do people shop? He had downloaded the pages from a website on Combat Tracking Techniques, entitled *How to Track Your Enemy,* by Captain John Early. He was hoping for decent tips on locating the asshole.

He couldn't remember where he had tucked the pages. Left pocket? Right? He rolled to one side, holding his breath against the pain in his tailbone, and patted the pocket there. Crapola – Villis said this to himself, and then, remembering he was alone, chuckled darkly and said, out loud, "Shit."

He rolled to the other side, gasped while his tailbone pulsed, found the manhunting pages, pulled them out.

Propping himself on his elbows, he read: "Sweat stings tired, dust-filled eyes. Adrenaline throbs like an electric river through your body as you search the nearby bush."

Villis read that again, enjoying the dramatic image suggested by the words. Throbbing electric river. Yup, in his tailbone. He couldn't have said it better himself. How was it that the writer of this long-ago article (from 1979) was able so vividly to describe Villis's current situation? He felt an odd super-temporal connection with Captain John Early. It was as if he was meant to read the Captain's words at precisely this moment. Was it possible to attribute this to a manifestation of Bipin's World Wise Web? Everything is connected, Bipin was always going on. There are no coincidences. And what did Bipin's fit, blonde woman say? Time *isn't*.

But then, Villis knew, pain and abandonment did funny things to a person's point of view.

He read on.

"Every nerve feels for the enemy you know is there. Somewhere."

By God! Villis put down the pages and waited for his nerves to scope out the locale. It was tricky, given that his nerves were mostly preoccupied with his coccyx. He gave it his best effort. Where *was* the bastard?

There were further remarks from Early. "Your first concern is the terrain. You can't track in it if you don't have a rudimentary knowledge of the lay of the land."

This was heartening. He certainly had a rudimentary knowledge. Fact: he was an expert on how this particular land lay. Check, Villis thought.

"First: psychologically and physically prepare for the hunt."

Villis picked up a nearby stone, thinking he might use it as a weapon. Check.

"You should be in good physical condition with excellent reserves of stamina, alert, reasonably well-fed–"

Where were the power bars? In Bipin's fanny pack. Phooey. He couldn't confirm to John Early that he was well-fed. Come to think of it, he was hungry. And where *was* Bipin? How long had he been gone? An hour? More?

And what about the question of stamina? Did he have it? Stamina stamina stamina. A queer word, he thought, saying it out loud.

"Much of tracking means noting what is out of context in nature."

Villis nodded. Check. *That* he was good at. He should invite Early to do the rounds of the road with him. Notice, Captain – not even the tiniest plastic ring from a water bottle snagged on the petals of a cornflower could escape his formidable powers of observation. Early would be impressed.

"Move from sign to sign," Early advised. "There are, of course, the obvious: footprints in the mud near streams ... if the enemy has passed through after sunrise the dew will be disturbed and a faint darkened area will reveal his trail; watch for broken webs ... leaves on plants that have been turned over so that the light underside contrasts with the surroundings–"

Villis peered at leaves on bushes close by. He thought he spotted one or two exposed undersides, like pale bums. Maybe. Maybe not.

"–scuffed tree bark; mud scraped from passing boots and the impression of rifle butts used as crutches up steep slopes."

Rifle butts? This was something Villis hadn't thought of. What if ATV man was a hunter? Made sense, Villis thought, since hunters were frequently assholes.

Early continued – "of course, there is the old favorite, blood on the vegetation and trail."

Blood on the trail? Villis imagined situations that might cause ATV man to bleed. A stabbing onslaught of mosquitoes. A slash across the face from the cloven hoof of a doe; and for large quantities of blood, the canine teeth of coyotes. What else? Scratches from angry saplings, perhaps sisters to those ATV man had run over with his machine. And if all the nematodes living in the soil, angry over ATV man's chewing up of the trail, arose and started chewing him ... did nematodes chew?

He was tired. Nodding off. How easy would it be to fall asleep in The Pearl?

But what if something happened to Bipin? What if he never came back with the wheelbarrow?

Villis sighed. Nothing ever happened to Bipin. Bipin happened to himself.

Villis slid the manhunting pages under his face and turned his head to look at the moai – at least, the base of it.

This wasn't so bad, he thought. He might just fall asleep. Safe in The Pearl; he could feel it cupping him as if he were a bead of dew on a leaf, resting undisturbed by passing enemies. He might try to meditate on a calm coccyx. Calm ... He blinked. His eyes were going funny. A relief ... to close them.

He didn't think he had fallen asleep, but he must have. MUST have.

Because there were suddenly two bare feet just behind the moai. Close. He could've touched them. He supposed he should have. But. Tired. Really, too tired to lift his arm.

Still ...

If he touched the feet, he might confirm if they were real or not. Prove they were a dream.

But ...

Why bother? Who cares. Real? Not real? Because?

Because those two feet were interesting. They seemed to glow green. Quite interesting.

Dirty. Wide spaces between the toes. Almost no nails. Hairy on the toe knuckles. Is *that* what they were called – toe knuckles?

Villis lay there, staring at the feet, which unexpectedly moved. What? Knees, now squatting knees, and then hands, arms, a face, coming down, close, a stranger scrutinizing him, but who cares, the face, also glowing green, was remarkable. Rough. Deep eyes. Heavy brow. Crazy hair, and smiling, a smiling face. A smile of radiant tenderness, of love, it certainly was that, a smile of the most immeasurable love, and then, above the love, dark eyes filling with tears.

Palaeolithic man, Villis thought. Had to be.

Shit.

The man cocked his head, still the tender smile, his eyes digging into Villis. Villis knew – he was certain of it, even though Palaeolithic man was silent – that he was trying to tell him something. Peculiar, but an image was suddenly in the middle of his mind as if someone had slipped in one of those old-time slides; an image of the Earth from outer space, at night, darkness wrapping the planet, except for where city lights seeped through the black like patches that glowed. Then, all at once, all together, all the lights went out. Every city, extinguished. A warning? A truth? Both? Yes, both. A truth *and* a warning.

But what exactly did it mean?

"What?" Villis said this out loud to Palaeolithic man – at least, he assumed he said it out loud.

Palaeolithic man turned his palms up. His smile dissolved. Then he disappeared. Gone. Like the lights from the dark Earth. But gone to where? The air? And Villis hadn't thought to ask where he might find an arrowhead or mammoth bone.

My eyes were closed, Villis reminded himself. So, how was it he had been able to see what he had just seen?

And now what?

A sound. Droning, humming, mechanical, distant, yet coming, coming closer, slamming against the soft hills, against trunks of trees, against baby blanket of sky, slamming with the damning mania of a pinball.

It was coming from below the ridge. Not Bipin.

Villis listened. Suddenly, the droning stopped. But what was that? Some other noise. Singing?

Did Palaeolithic man sing?

"*I said shake, rattle and roll.*"

Not Palaeolithic man.

"*I said shake, rattle and roll.*"

Villis tucked his knees in, aimed his bottom higher still, winced as his tailbone stabbed, and somehow bumbled to his feet. What would Captain Early do in this situation? Surely, Early, in these circumstances – rifle-less, sore butt and ninety years old – would advise camouflage. Villis grabbed up the khaki tarp and wrapped himself in it. Shrouded like a mummy, he shambled toward the edge of the ridge. The singing was drowned out by the rustling of his camouflage, which meant he had to pause every now and then to listen.

"*I said shake, rattle and roll. Well you won't do right to save your doggone soul–*"

A few feet from the top of the ridge, he crouched, whimpering in whispers, then dropped to hands and feet, like Bipin's cat, and from there to his tummy. Rolling himself in the tarp, a nematode in fatigues, he wriggled and crawled, listening to the enemy's voice shake-rattle-rolling, until he was at the edge of the ridge, looking down at the bottom of the ravine.

ATV man! Had to be.

Shit.

Singing?

It was the ravine, he realized, that was lifting the song upwards to his ears. Without the help of the ravine, ATV man's voice would have been too insignificant to be heard. Villis snorted. The asshole didn't look so big down there: a fake colour snagged in the leafy dell like the plastic ring from a water bottle.

ATV man was sitting on his machine, astride it like a boy on his horsey-back, shopping-mall ride. Put in another loonie, Villis thought, and get lost.

But he had been wrong about one thing. The asshole was not fat. Fact: he looked almost handsome, though who could be certain? Still, he seemed to have celebrity hair, black and wavy; long, strong legs; an aloof slope to his shoulders. Not a bad voice, either, though those sorts of things didn't impress Villis. Still, it sounded familiar, though he couldn't say why.

"I believe you're doing me wrong and now I know."

Villis pulled the tarp overtop of his head. If ATV man happened to glance up he would never detect that someone was watching him. I can wait here all day if need be, Villis thought. He could outlast the asshole. Didn't all young people have attention deficit whatever? Weren't their brains tuned to sound bites and didn't they have thoughts no bigger than tweets?

And, truth to tell, given the pain from his *coccydynia*, he couldn't really get away.

Still, if only he had a power bar.

Just as he was longing for a power bar, thinking about Bipin and his fanny pack full of them, just at that moment, he looked down the length of the dell and saw Bipin pushing the wheelbarrow, piled, it seemed, with pillows.

Villis wondered – had his thought-beggar done *that*? Had he, Villis, buttoned up the trench coat, blown the dust out of the empty cup and sent his beggar out for power bars?

Go back, he commanded the beggar, and tell Bipin to turn around.

But, of course, Bipin wouldn't.

Fact: Bipin loved experiences, no matter how dicey. Everything that happened, Bipin was apt to say, was a ping from the World Wise Web.

Villis clenched his teeth. Bipin was bearing down on the asshole, smiling and trundling. Ping, Villis thought. Then pong.

"Greetings, my friend," Villis heard Bipin shout, resting the wheelbarrow and waving at ATV man as he did so. "Beautiful day for a *walk* in the woods."

ATV man stopped singing mid-rattle and turned to face Bipin. Then he lit a cigarette and crumpled the package in one hand. Villis could tell, even from where he was – the asshole was not pleased.

"Whatever," the asshole said, tentatively, as if that single word took too much effort to speak. As expected, Villis thought, the asshole had the vocabulary of a Neanderthal. Then he caught himself, feeling guilty for insulting Neanderthals.

Bipin did one of his head-bowing "*Namaste*"s.

ATV man's eyes widened. "So, like, Buddy, where's your turban?"

Bipin patted his head thoughtfully. "In western culture the turban is uncommon, though it *was* fashionable in the 1940s and 50s for chic ladies, such as Carmen Miranda, to wear them piled high with fake fruits; otherwise, if you hanker to see turbans you need to locate some Pashtuns, or some Sikhs, but keep away from those Taliban guys who wear the big, sloppy, twisted black ones; moreover, you might wish to seek out various sheikhs, imams and hajji – you can tell the hajii because they favour green ones – also, if you happen to find yourself holidaying in certain regions of Africa, then give my regards to the gentlemen from the Tuareg, Berber, Songhai, Wodaabe, Fulani and Hausa tribes, all of whom fancy the turban style of headgear; in addition, closer to home, on the faded jewel that is Jamaica, certain hipster Rastafarians use turbans to compress their dreads. As for mine, it's at the cleaner's."

"Whatever."

Bipin pointed at the all-terrain vehicle. "I am so sorry to inform you, but wheeled vehicles are prohibited in The Pearl."

ATV man frowned. "What? The Pearl?"

"Wheeled vehicles are not permitted in these forested domains."

"I don't get it."

"You can't drive that contraption in here."

ATV man brightened.

Finally, Villis thought, watching, riveted, from beneath the tarp – the light turns on.

"Says who?"

"Say I."

"Say I?"

Bipin sighed. "Says *me*."

"Who's *me*?"

"Call me Bipin."

ATV man laughed. "Bipin Bipin bo-Bipin, fee-fi-fo-fipin. What kind of a name is that? Bipin? You some kind of tall Hobbit? Where's your friend Bilbo?"

Up here, Villis thought, seething, wishing he were young, that he were Captain John Early with a rifle that he might use as a crutch. Or worse.

ATV man laughed again, tossed his cigarette package on the ground and switched on the all-terrain vehicle. The sound of it scratched against the forest like nails on a chalkboard. Then he revved his machine with one foot, adjusted his crotch.

Bipin dropped to the ground immediately in front of the ATV and folded himself into Full Lotus position, blocking the vehicle from moving forward. He closed his eyes and began moving his lips.

The ATV was too loud for Villis to make out what Bipin was saying, but he knew – Bipin was surely chanting some favourable mantra. It was his Gandhi days all over again. Villis could see this instantly. The noble practice of peaceful protest. He was swept with pride for his friend. What grace. What discipline. What high humanity.

The asshole was clearly taken aback, slouching more than before.

We've got him, Villis wanted to shout. I'm coming, my friend, I'm coming.

But before Villis could disentangle himself from the tarp, the asshole revved his machine louder still and slammed it into reverse. As the wheels of the ATV spun, the discarded cigarette package was caught up in the wheels' momentum and flung like a projectile through the air, straight for Bipin, hitting him with a slap across the cheek.

The ATV man paused in his reversing, no doubt waiting to see how Bipin would respond. But Bipin did not open his eyes. Nor did he flinch. Instead, he continued to chant – the mantra, of course, though Villis still couldn't make it out. Bipin was all right, Villis knew this. When Bipin was meditating nothing could knock him off his bliss. But damn it! The arrogance. And ignorance! If only the asshole knew how great a man that scrawny little Indian guy was.

The asshole shook his head (who knows what nitwit thoughts he was thinking?), pulled a small notebook from his back pocket and a pencil from behind his ear. He scribbled in the notebook, then slipped the notebook back in his pocket, the pencil behind his ear. After that, he turned his machine and lurched away, his wheels pummelling circles into The Pearl.

It was the pencil behind the ear that must have jumped the old scene forward. After all these years, Villis thought, after sixty-some-odd years, how could that be? Such a run-of-the-mill thing, a pencil behind an ear, and the past floods in?

It was the day of his arrival in Camp TTK-6. He had stood, then, stripped naked, in an office along with the other captives, men and women together, sick and cold, while an official sitting at a desk thumbed pages of a ledger. The official had looked the captives over, a measured and methodical look. He must have seen their nakedness, their shame (how could he have not?), and yet all he did was pull a pencil from behind his ear and write in his ledger and put the pencil back behind his ear.

Now isn't then, Villis told himself, watching the asshole disappear. It wasn't the same thing at all. Camp TTK-6 had been the unjust destruction of the innocently living by men with dead eyes. Wasn't this just a young idiot tearing up a few trails?

Still hiding beneath his tarp, still lying on his stomach, Villis watched his friend, waiting for the sound of the ATV to fade and Bipin's chant to sail up the sides of the ravine. He listened. He knew that he had only to wait a moment for the young leaves of forest trees to swaddle the clatter of the disappearing ATV in their yellow-green velvet, while between them, the hills and ravines relayed the noise up and down, up and down, passing the racket to the edge of The Pearl, like a thing unwanted, and then passing the racket out. Villis kept his eyes on Bipin. Bipin's lips were still moving, but finally Villis could make out his words.

Bipin was not chanting. He was singing. In his cute Indian accent, Bipin was quietly crooning, *"I said shake, rattle and roll."*

Bipin stopped singing and turned toward Villis, waving up at him and shouting cheerfully, "My friend, that went well, don't you think?"

CHAPTER 7

A Visit From Frog and an Elvis Look-alike

Frog's dark eyes were staring at him. Villis squinted. For a second, Frog's eyes reminded him of the eyes of Palaeolithic man, just at the moment when they had begun to tear up.

Villis was lying on his stomach on the warm wooden planks of the First/Third Bridge, nursing his tailbone, waiting for Bipin to return from doing the garbage rounds on the road. He stared back at Frog, trying to read his mind. What interested frogs? Sunbathing? The daily habits of bugs? Abandoning themselves body and soul to the ebbing of the creek?

Two weeks had passed since they had sighted the asshole at the base of the Lopsided Ridges. Between then and now there had been plenty more signs of his forbidden activities in The Pearl. Two weeks of increasing destruction, reported to Villis by Bipin, who was conducting the manhunt on his own while Villis was sidelined by his tailbone. So far Bipin had discovered: an arching swath of Calypso orchids, like a fluttering scarf, torn up; a rounded congregation of brown-capped mushrooms, bald like monks, pulverized; and a fanning of Cinnamon ferns, snapped at their bases by the hundreds. Added to these were many gouges in the trails. Then rain

had come, and on the hilly places the gouges had widened and deep-
ened and rainwater had washed away the spongy protection of soil,
exposing the roots of a family of pawpaw trees, leaving them
vulnerable. There had even been a mini-mudslide down one slope
(caused by the repeated agitation of the earth by the wheels of the
ATV) that had uprooted walnut saplings and suffocated all life –
plant, reptile, insect – in its path.

And, of course, Bipin had found garbage: cigarette packages and
wafer wrappers that ATV man had dribbled onto the living palette of
The Pearl like drops of acid onto a masterpiece.

"As soon as I'm better," Villis said to Frog, "we have to do something to get rid of that guy."

But what could he do?

So far, he had two rough ideas: (1) Revenge in the Woods, and (2)
GULAG-AGAIN.

In Revenge in the Woods, he would order ATV man, at the business
end of Captain Early's rifle, to park his vehicle in the middle of the road,
and then wait, watching from the cover of the shrubbery, as the ATV was
flattened like a bug beneath a gravel truck. Then, still under the power
of the gun, he would march ATV man into a gnarly part of The Pearl
– that boggy lowland upstream of the Third/First Bridge where there
were splodges of mud like the tar pits that sucked down dinosaurs in Los
Angeles – and he would leave him there, chained to an ancient willow,
a target for mosquitoes and frantic bats and whatever else was blood-
hungry and swarmed in the woods at night.

In GULAG-AGAIN, ATV man would be a prisoner. A light would
break into his eyes at night while he was huddled, almost frozen, on
his bunk, rags wrapped around his body, though it would be impossible
to protect himself from the cold. This light would mean that a guard
wanted him up. *Now!* He would stumble. *Durak!* Dumb asshole!
There were the other prisoners. He would know them, of course, but
would not feel their suffering since his compassion had thinned into
nothing, along with the flesh from his bones. It would be another
midnight strip search. What could he have, what could any of them
have, that would interest these men with boots and guns? Prisoners

– they have nothing to give, except suffering. Which is exactly what the guards are after: the pleasure of torment; the scratching of their itches for power. *Clothes off.* He unties pant strings and his rags fall. The other prisoners, naked too, are scarcely men – pelvis, ribs and collarbones like bent hangers.

Line up. He does. *Against the wall.* Oh, that wall again. *Raise arms. Raise them!* Arms shake, but up they go. *Spread legs.* How wide? Wider still? He thinks of dying. This is always the first thought. Then he thinks of breakfast – always the second thought. He thinks of a bit of potato bobbing in the white water of his soup, or perhaps a curl of onion, no bigger than a wood shaving, or a dull disc of carrot. Such a breakfast, miserable as all that, might still raise a shaking fist against the psychopathic hunger that strangles his body, his breath, each thought.

After the bastards are done, his rags repositioned, he returns to the barracks for two more hours of pitching upon the uneven planks of his bunk that press devil fingers into his tender bruises, his thinning skin, into his bones that hurt everywhere. Does he sleep in this place where no one dreams, where the part of the mind that imagines has long since collapsed?

Then morning. The very worst time of day. It comes a cold fog, promising nothing. At breakfast he searches his soup with panicky focus. Blob of potato? Curl of onion? Disc of carrot? No. There is only white water, barely warm. He cannot stop it – he cries like a baby while the psychopathic hunger surveys the scene. Then a man with boots bashes him in the ribs, slamming against thinning skin and bones. *Zatknis, govniuk.* Shut up, shithead.

Villis sighed. Shook it off. "Well, Frog, do we wish that on anybody, even the ATV asshole?"

Frog shifted in his basket, lifted one haunch, settled it down again.

No, he supposed not. Except – maybe just the part about finding no carrot.

He was debating whether or not to tell Bipin about what had happened at the moai when he had seen his vision (he didn't know what else to call it) of Palaeolithic man. He wanted to know what Bipin thought Palaeolithic man had been warning him about. And Bipin would enjoy hearing about such details as the hairs on Palaeolithic man's toe knuckles. But he would definitely not tell Bipin about the picture that had arisen in his mind – the one in which all the lights had gone out on Earth.

Was this because it was a disturbing apocalyptic image and he was sparing Bipin's soul? To be honest, the answer had to be no. He did not regard the darkening of the Earth as apocalyptic. Truth was, the idea of lights going down on Earth did not disturb him. He couldn't help it – he cherished the darkness of night. Electric lights were agitators, tripping up circadian rhythms like marbles flung beneath the feet of dancers. Without electric lights, people wouldn't stay up late watching TV, scaring themselves silly with cop dramas. They would go to bed; get enough rest; and upon wakening, wonder what surprises might dart across their paths like hummingbirds sipping sweetness from the coming day.

Still, he supposed he owed it to his friend to share the vision with him. Bipin had been so helpful with respect to his *coccydynia*. Hadn't Bipin trundled him home in the wheelbarrow, adjusting the cushions whenever necessary so as to soften the blows to his coccyx? And who but Bipin had bought him the gift of a rubber haemorrhoid pillow so that he could sit without too much pain? And only today, hadn't Bipin's tender considerations led him to bring Frog for a visit?

Frog hadn't minded Bipin carrying him from his bend in the creek, upstream and about ten minutes' walk, to the First/Third Bridge. Bipin had transported him in a wicker basket lined with moss. According to Bipin, Frog had enjoyed the passing scenery, placid in the centre of the basket like a ripened Buddha.

Villis stroked the top of Frog's head. He had been telling him about the incident with ATV man. "The guy was singing. *Shake, rattle and roll*. Dumb." Frog blinked. Villis continued, "*If* you ever hear that song, get out of the way. Ditto, of course, if you hear the ATV."

Villis lifted his head and looked around. There was Bipin coming along the trail toward the bridge, carrying a shoe. He waved the shoe as he approached, calling cheerfully, "Look, my flattened friend, what the World Wise Web has given us."

Villis propped himself on his elbows. "More garbage?"

"This first-rate blue shoe. Leather. Barely worn." He bent the shoe for Villis and showed him the insole. "Super-duper spotless. Have a sniff. No foot odour whatsoever."

Villis waved the shoe away. "I'll take your word."

"Notice, this shoe fits my foot." Bipin demonstrated, slipping the shoe on, then toe-tapping against the planks of the bridge. *"I said shake, rattle and roll."*

"Argh."

"Won't do right to save your doggone soul." Now he was snapping.

"One shoe is one shoe too few."

"I may find the other one the next time I do the rounds. Or I may lose a foot. Either way."

"Either way?"

"I'm keeping it."

"Don't sing that stupid song."

"I'm only doing it to lure the asshole. Like attracts like. Birds of a feather, etcetera. Although I must confess, I don't know which version to sing – Big Joe Turner's original composition or Elvis's cover."

"There's a difference?"

"Absolutely."

Bipin bent over Villis and hovered one hand, palm down, inches above Villis's tailbone. "It's Reiki time, my friend."

Villis sighed. Reiki time. There seemed to be something to it – perhaps it was the well-documented placebo effect? – though Villis was nobody's fool. Nevertheless, over the past two weeks, since Bipin had begun conducting Reiki over his bum, his *coccydynia* had improved.

"On second thought," Bipin said, "I think I'll opt for the Elvis version. *Well I said shake, rattle and roll.* Can you guess why, my friend?"

Villis grunted.

"Because the asshole was the spitting image of Elvis. Did you not notice? Blue-black slick of hair, those loose hips, crooked grin."

"Elvis? Hmm. But don't sing any version, Elvis's or Big Joe's, when you're around me."

Bipin clucked sympathetically. Villis couldn't see what Bipin was doing with his Reiki hands, but a buzzing warmth was mushrooming across his backside.

"You are having first chakra hitches, my friend, which is most surely why you whacked your tailbone. Your root issues are calling for awareness. There are struggles in the dark soil of your soul."

"Struggles in The Pearl, you mean. That idiot mucking up the land with his stupid wheels."

"A chakra moves like a wheel."

"So does a toilet vortex."

"There is the wheeling of the Earth around the sun."

"And the destruction of a wheeling tornado."

"The Wheel of Fortune – not the TV show, but the cosmic one."

"The Wheel of Poverty."

"The Wheel of Life."

"In which we suckers are just one cog in a grinding gear."

Bipin sighed, rubbed his hands and repositioned them above the back of Villis's head. "Your brain is frying, my friend. Try to relax."

"What's for lunch today?" Villis asked this a little impatiently but he couldn't help it. Ever since Camp TTK-6 he had been hopeless at controlling his hunger once he had the idea of eating.

"Wild leeks and garlic, picked from our favourite patch just past Killer Hill. And fiddleheads from behind my house."

"Excellent," Villis said. A familiar relief stirred the depths of his gut. Could this be his root chakra beginning to spin?

After lunch, Bipin insisted that they work on their answer to Question Number Three for the *So You Think You Can Think* contest: Why do people shop?

"The deadline swiftly approaches. I must submit our application."

Villis worked a piece of wild leek from between his teeth. "Why do people shop? It's too taxing a question for my fried brain."

"Holy cow! That's it, my friend. You've nailed the hammer against the head. Too taxing! I'm just at this moment flooded with inspiration. People shop to pay taxes."

"No one shops to pay taxes."

"I didn't say they *want* to pay taxes, just that they do. Shopping is a surefire way to pay taxes, you must allow me that."

"Go on."

"So – where do the taxes go, after they leave the debit cards, and the MasterCards and the penny-purses of old ladies?"

"To pay for services, I guess."

"Such as?"

"Schools?"

Bipin slapped his forehead. "You've nailed the hammer against the head AGAIN. My friend, you have wellsprings of genius. Taxes for schools, exactly right, but to what purpose?"

"To pay for knowledge. Enlightenment."

"Ho ho, good one! But, as everyone knows, schools are the *worst* places for knowledge and enlightenment. No, the primary function of schools is to train children to wake up at the same time each day, which is *the* most essential skill required for keeping a job. And why is it important to keep a job? Of course it's obvious, my friend, so I will take the liberty of answering for you – jobs are for getting money, legally, at least. And what is money for?"

"Shopping?"

"Precisely! Jobs for money, money to shop, and, more importantly, to keep on shopping. Why, this is a perfect example of Perpetual Motion! And Perpetual Motion is the illusion of progress, which is *the* great delusion of the capitalist consumer culture. Tweetly put – people shop because they think it is Progress. *'Cause the harder I work the faster my money goes.*"

"Don't sing that song."

Bipin nodded. "I'll try my best to subdue it." Then he shrugged, which Villis knew was his way of saying: Don't bet the farm.

The next day, Villis began to walk the trails of The Pearl again, making it all the way to the Third/First Bridge. A week after that he was ready to return to the Nexus.

Bipin still hadn't submitted the application for the *So You Think You Can Think* contest.

"We have only three more days, my friend," Bipin warned. "And we must get back to the Nexus to take a photo."

"Of what?"

"Of you and me, of course, posing smack dab in front of the Easter Island moai. A photo is the final requirement of the application process."

"In front of a moai?"

"The application does not specify that one take a picture in front of a moai. Holy cow, who on earth has a moai? Except for us, which is why taking the picture there will be indisputably awe-inspiring. What reality TV show producer could resist such a compelling hook?"

"I'm not doing it."

"Such a photo will put us in like Finn."

"Flynn."

"Come come, it's just one snapshot. What possible trouble could arise from that?"

Possible trouble? Where Bipin was concerned, trouble was always possible. Still. Bipin *had* bought him that rubber haemorrhoid pillow. And Reikied his sore butt.

"Okay. But just one."

CHAPTER 8

The Asshole Asks a Question

They were nearly at the Resonating Nexus. Other than a quick pause along the way to say hello to Frog, they had managed the entire walk to the Lopsided Ridges without stopping. Villis was pleased with how well he was doing. The three ridges were no piece of cake, especially when almost every step brought with it a twinge of heat from his tailbone, but, all things considered, he was fine. Now that he had agreed to have his picture taken for the application form he didn't want his face to look hot and sweaty.

About to climb the final ridge, nearly at the flat spot where they had left the moai three weeks ago, Villis thought he saw something bright red snagged in the twisting branches of a dogwood.

What was it Captain Early had said? – "*... and, of course, there is the old favourite, blood on the trail.*" But, of course, this wasn't blood. Villis went over to investigate.

"Aha! Another sign. From ATV asshole. A cigarette pack." Villis unhooked the packet from the dogwood and held it up for Bipin to see. "*Move from sign to sign,*" Villis went on, still remembering his Captain Early. "From sign to sign." He scanned the area, his eyes keen for more evidence.

Bipin obligingly bent his head and snooped alongside. "What sort of signs, my friend?"

"Broken webs. Disturbed dew. Rifle butt imprints in mud."

"Or this?" Bipin was at the top of the ridge, pointing.

Villis hurried up – at least, as hurrying as his tailbone allowed.

Bipin held up one hand like a crossing guard. "Count to three, my friend."

Villis crested the ridge and looked where Bipin was pointing. There was the moai, just as they had left it, but everywhere else, signs of the enemy. In fact, they were standing at the edge of the enemy's lair. So much damage done in only three weeks. Count to three? No man could.

What once had been the prettiest haven in all of The Pearl was now a cluttered encampment of man-made ugliness: garbage scattered; a vinyl lawn chair in front of the moai, and behind it a two-panelled screen constructed out of the chopped trunks of saplings, bound with rope and standing like a room divider; a camp stove, the kind with a propane tank attached; a blue plastic cooler with a plastic bag labelled GLACIER ICE, limp on the ground beside it; a card table with one leg bandaged by duct tape; a dartboard nailed to a maple; and beer bottles, twenty or thirty of them, strung up by their necks with string and dangling from the branches of the encircling butternut trees like hanged prisoners.

Villis slumped down onto a tree stump. In a disconcerting way, this camp in the woods reminded him of his old camp with the Forest Brothers in Dundega. But surely this wasn't the same thing at all. Back in 1945 the Brothers had been hunted. The woods were their sanctuary. The woods kept the Brothers alive. Sitting on the tree stump, taking in ATV man's camp, Villis could suddenly see his fellow partisans – the twins, Juozas and Janis, and beside them Gregori and Endres – strong young men, the best, bundled in plump white coats against the winter, German machine guns balanced across their knees, leaning into the campfire, sipping hot tea from tin mugs, steam rising in the freezing air along with their brave hopes for Latvia. They had been captured together in their camp, all five of them packed into railcars and shipped to Perm-36. Juozas, Janis, Gregori, Endres: strong young men now goners in Camp TTK-6 – all dead before the age of thirty. He would cry. He would cry, but he would not. Villis knew how to stop tears. He had learned that lesson from the boots of his guards.

Bipin laid a hand on his shoulder. "We'll get the wheelbarrow. We'll clean up this mess. Look, I'm starting now." Bipin went over to the vinyl lawn chair and collapsed it. Then he nipped behind the moai and gave a strong side kick to the screen made of saplings. It wobbled. Bipin wound up and kicked a second time. It fell backwards with a soft *thwunk* into leaves.

Villis waved a hand. "Look at all the trees that idiot has cut down. How many? One, two, three, four, there's five, six. How are we going to fix that?"

Bipin didn't answer. Villis didn't expect him to.

"When I was with the Forest Brothers we respected the woods. We only cut up dead wood for our fires. Never a living tree. And never saplings. Youngsters. Who kills the young ones? And we *had* to do what we did. Secret police were everywhere, crawling in the towns and villages. What's with this guy? He comes in here on his machine, with his stuff, his garbage, his beer. Why? Why does he come into the woods and do this?"

"Are they with you again? Your young friends?"

Villis felt Bipin's hand press his shoulder, this hand of his old friend who understood how it was with the past.

"Yes."

Bipin unzipped his fanny pack and pulled out his camera. "Come over to the moai, my friend. We'll do what we intended to do. We won't allow the actions of the asshole to deter us from our purpose. We'll shoot the digital photo. Appear on Reality TV. Win the cash. Vacation on Easter Island. Come now."

"Not interested."

Bipin fiddled with a knob on the camera. "I'm setting it to auto-shoot." He peered through the lens at the moai. "Ho! What's that? A note of some sort?"

Villis looked up. There was a piece of paper stuck onto the moai with a nail. Bipin headed over, pulled off the note, read.

"From the asshole," Villis said – a statement rather than a question. Bipin nodded. "There's no signature, but one may so assume."

"What's he say?"

"The asshole asks a question."

Villis fumed – another stupid question. Why do people have their pictures taken with celebrities? Why do people tan? Why do people shop? Why do people destroy?

"So what?"

"The asshole wants to know, is this a time portal?"

"Your old Styrofoam stage prop? *A time portal?*" Villis scrunched his face, thinking: wasn't he a survivor of the GULAG, hero of the Forest Brothers, and, best of all, an old man with three-times-thirty years of living – three times the lives of Juozas, Janis, Gregori and Endres? So how could this happen, something that he had never, in all his imaginings, expected – that some idiot might think there was a time portal in The Pearl?

"Come, my friend. Bring you and your somewhat sore bottom over here and we'll auto-shoot ourselves for the Reality TV show. If this *is* a time portal, then perhaps we can nip into the future and find out what the answers are to the three most challenging questions."

Villis struggled up and went over to have his picture taken. Bipin lazed his arm across his shoulder. "Now at the count of three, say 'sexy cheese.'"

One. Two. Three. *Click.*

But Villis didn't say "sexy cheese". Instead, he said the one Russian word that he had dared whisper under his breath at his guards and their boots. *Govniuk.* Shithead.

"I will write the asshole an answer to his question." Bipin said this, withdrawing his blessing notebook from his fanny pack. "Which reminds me." He flipped it open. "Blessing Number 14,021 – *Thank you for memories down which we slide into yesterday to sit once again in the camp of our companions.*"

"That's your answer to 'Is this a time portal?'"

Bipin bobbed his head, looking thoughtful. "Holy cow, in an accidental way it seems so. What better time portal into the past is there than memory? And if one desires a portal into the future, why, all one need do is dream. But of course the asshole will never grasp such a subtle concept, so in sympathy with his nursery school sensibilities I will put it simply: 'This is NOT a time portal.' Then tack my note I most definitely will, back onto the moai where we found the other one."

Villis walked over to the empty ice bag and snapped it up, then a cookie package loitering nearby, then a comic book on a rock. "Not good enough," he said, flipping through the comic book, thinking here was proof positive, if ever there was, that the asshole was a simpleton. "You need to spell things out for that kid. You need to say, 'The woods are not your hangout. You cannot come here. Your ATV is not allowed. Go away. Do not come back. AND ... no, this is NOT a time portal.'"

"Hold it, hold it. I'm taking it down. Repeat, repeat."

"And finish off with 'OR ELSE'. In capitals."

"Shouldn't we make our threat more specific? Or else, we will call the cops–"

"No police!"

"Right, right. How about this? 'Or else we'll paint-bomb your ATV, or else we'll rip your comic books, or else, or else ...' I confess I am having trouble developing suitable threats."

"Or else it will be the end of you."

"But it won't."

"Write it anyway. It's a bluff. Hopefully this will be enough to frighten him away."

"Like putting up a scarecrow. Good, good." Bipin nodded, scribbled and then stuck the note onto the moai.

They decided to return to the Resonating Nexus the next day and dismantle the asshole's encampment. To do the job they agreed to bend the no-wheels-in-The-Pearl policy, though only in order to use the wheelbarrow to cart away ATV man's junk.

In the morning they loaded their equipment in the wheelbarrow: Villis's old Forest Brothers knife for cutting down the beer bottles;

a box of biodegradable garbage bags; a saw that had been aging in Bipin's shed for so long it had rust in its teeth; and Villis's chopsticks. The chopsticks were, in Villis's opinion, an inspired idea that had come to him during the night. Unable to sleep, worrying about the likelihood of condoms or, worse, diseased drug needles discarded in the Nexus by you-know-who, the idea had hit him at dawn like a bash to his brain when the birds outside his open window had barely begun to cheep – only his chopsticks would do for slackened rubbers and druggie paraphernalia. After that, he had fallen asleep.

They made good time on the walk back up to the Nexus, with both of them cresting the final ridge on the same intake of breath and at the same moment exhaling and taking in the scene. The crisis in the Nexus had escalated. The two-panelled screen made of saplings that Bipin had kicked over the day before was upright again, the lawn chair unfolded and repositioned, and beside it two more identical lawn chairs, lined up as if expecting guests for a garage party. Yellow caution tape now encircled the butternut trees, giving the Nexus the appearance of a crime scene. There was a note stuck on the moai that Villis could tell, even from where he stood, was not the same one they had left there the day before.

"I'm getting the note," Villis said. He grabbed his Forest Brothers knife from the wheelbarrow and sliced through the line of caution tape. It felt good (funny good) to have that knife in his hand again after all these years. A few steps and he was at the moai, plucking at the note.

"Take care not to rip it, my friend," Bipin called.

"Why not? Throw it away without reading it, that's what we should do. Why do we care what that idiot has to say?"

"Because we have a sick fascination with him that cannot be denied."

Villis frowned at Bipin, but nonetheless removed the paper, unfolding it with exaggerated carefulness.

He read out loud, "'You don't scare me, you old dumb-asses. Don't touch my stuff. OR ELSE ... P.S. I know this is a time portal.'"

"P.S.?" Bipin said. "Who would've thought the asshole knew Latin?

But what does he mean, 'OR ELSE'?"

Villis crammed the note into his pocket. Though he told himself it was nothing more than crumpled paper, it lay in his pocket as if it were decomposing there. He wanted to pitch it, but not in The Pearl.

"That guy!" he said, pressing the lump of the note through the fabric of his pants. "What a rinky-dink, stupid stupid who knows zippity-doo-dah about the world. Did he march with Gandhi at the age of eight to throw off the oppression of the British? I bet he doesn't even know who Gandhi is. Has he fought for anything? Does he care? Me myself and I, that's what. I bet he never watched his friends, little by little, turn into skeletons-with-eyes and then up and die and leave him the last one alive in charge of remembering. What a pig. Junk food junkie, wrappers far and wide. We would have licked those wrappers if we'd had wrappers to lick."

"*Durak?*" Bipin said.

"*Govniuk!*"

"I say we touch his stuff."

They spent the morning tidying up for the second time. They piled the lawn chairs in the wheelbarrow, with the cooler next, the beer bottles inside the cooler and the dartboard on top of the whole lot. They bent and scooped the garbage, wound the caution tape, dismantled the screen and sawed the saplings into smaller pieces, which they stacked in a hidden spot for later retrieval. There was no room in the wheelbarrow for the camp stove, so they hid that with the saplings.

Then they left another note on the moai:

This is a moai, NOT a time portal. We are selling your stuff on eBay and depositing the cash in our travel fund. After you read this note, turn around and leave this forest domain. Do not return. OR ELSE we will find a way to get you once and for all. Don't kid yourself. We may be old but we are NOT dumb-asses.

But ATV man did return, several times, each time with more stuff. He brought a new cooler, a set of lawn darts, more caution tape, wrapping the entire site in a yellow plastic perimeter. He was up to five lawn chairs positioned neatly. He had found the camp stove and the stack of cut saplings. He had constructed a firepit out of the cut half of an oil drum, and tried (but failed) to burn the saplings. Too green to catch fire – Villis had snorted, toeing the barely charred pieces, smugly pleased by this added proof of the asshole's lack of woodsman skills.

Each time, the asshole left another note on the moai.

I KNOW this is a time portal so don't go and try to tell me it is not ONE.

Bipin wrote back:

How do you KNOW?

Villis had been opposed to asking that. "It'll encourage him," he had said. But Bipin was insistent. If they understood the asshole's logic, perhaps they could do something to upset it.

ATV man had answered:

BECAUSE this is one of those Easter Island monolifts, and THEY are known in the world of Super-arcane Mysteries to be time portals.

Then, in brackets,

(Google it, dude!)

Bipin was impressed that the asshole had known to use brackets. Villis felt that they were at war. Strangely, this thought invigorated him. Not that he welcomed war, and not because the asshole wasn't driving him crazy, but there was something about this campaign to protect The Pearl that he found oddly energizing.

When he mentioned this to Bipin, Bipin shrugged as if he had expected as much. "It's simply and only your root chakra, finally spinning at a decent rate. But how untoward that it has taken conflict to kick-start it. Better for your individual evolution if it had started gyrating for love."

"But I love The Pearl," Villis said.

CHAPTER 9

Thank You For Fools Who Blow By Us

Two weeks passed. The war against the asshole continued, tit for tat. Villis couldn't have said who was winning, though the asshole was proving to be more energetic than Villis had given him credit for. And ATV man was younger, which meant the odds of victory based solely on lifespan significantly favoured the asshole. The very best that Villis could say was that they were at an impasse. The asshole carted stuff up, they carted stuff down, both sides straddling a non-stop see-saw teetering atop the Lopsided Ridges.

But where did the asshole get his junk? It must have been costing him a fortune to replace it.

"It's obvious," Bipin was saying. "Walmart. Cheap plastic goods in incessant supply."

"A nightmare," Villis said.

"A tragedy. Our beloved Mother Earth is morphing into a Barbie doll."

They were on their way to the First/Third Bridge for an afternoon break. Bipin had stopped along the trail, as usual, so that he could prepare his "greens" concoction in the water bottle that was hanging from a carabiner attached to his fanny pack. Before leaving home, he had filled the bottle with reverse-osmosis water from his whole-house purification system; now all he needed to do was add two scoops of "greens" powder. Bipin always shared his greens drink with Villis. Though Villis never said so, he preferred his usual malt chocolate beads mixed with milk.

While Bipin measured out the greens powder (it looked like desiccated seaweed), Villis took in the woods. In the days before ATV man, when he had done this taking in of the woods, his senses extending, widening, waiting for the woods to settle on his skin like dew, he had noticed lovely things: a blue billowing of forget-me-nots across a sunny patch; those Turk's cap lilies that seemed too dreamy for a Canadian woods, and yet there they were; and leaves in the breeze brushing the sky until the blue shone. But now, because of the asshole, he scanned suspiciously, checking for Captain Early's tracking signs. Checking for signs of invasion.

When Bipin was done with his powder, he tightened the lid on the bottle and they set off again for the bridge. The bottle jostled as Bipin walked, mixing the green powder with the RO water, ensuring it would reach the ideal gloopy consistency for consumption.

At the bridge, Villis pulled his haemorrhoid pillow out of his backpack, blew it up – careful not to hyperventilate as he had done just the other day, nearly fainting – and then settled into it like a hen with no tail feathers.

Bipin handed him a cupful of greens drink. "You are sitting down with rather more gracefulness than you did only last week."

Villis stared into the greens, a swamp in his cup. "Thanks."

"Antioxidants, essential for healing. Efficacious for *coccydynia*."

If he downed it quickly, he could get it over with. "Be careful what you wish for," he said, and then emptied the swamp down his throat.

Bipin, looking pleased, held out the bottle. "More?"

Villis wiped the green slime from his lips. "No sign of you-know-who. Not here, at least."

"Maybe he's tumbled ass over teakettle into the time portal." Bipin screwed the lid back on the water bottle. "I'll save this for you."

"Gone somewhere back in time – to before the invention of greens drinks."

"Terrible to think of."

"*If* there were such a thing as a time portal, I'd go back to see The Pearl the way it was when mammoths and Palaeolithic peoples were here."

"One absolutely cannot time-travel with one's body. That's the Hollywood Sci-fi Fantasy view of the thing. Time travel is simple, but you need to leave your body behind to do it. The only piece of you that can time-travel is your consciousness. When time-travelling, no bodies allowed. Physical bodies mucking around in the past would interfere with the order of all things, and so it is positively prohibited by the laws of science and nature. You may be a witness to the past, but never, never a participant. Only your inner eye may travel backwards so that you can observe to your heart's content all the scintillating shenanigans of days gone by; however, I must say, based on what I've seen, not a lot has changed over the eons, though it is nice to see the different styles of clothes." Bipin lay on his back, stretching his length across the width of the bridge. "Let's do Corpse pose. It will align your coccyx with the rest of your spine."

"Later." Villis wanted to stay on guard for the asshole. "You go ahead, though. Relax."

Bipin sighed. "How can a fellow relax with you focusing on the imminent attacking of Elvis on his ATV?"

"I didn't say anything about an attack."

"You don't have to say so. You are hunching like a turkey vulture scoping for its prey."

"Did I ever tell you about Palaeolithic man?"

"You talk about him all the time. Hairy toe knuckles. Eyes brimming with tenderness. Weeping, weeping. Vision of the Earth with the lights gone out. Etcetera." Bipin sat up, held out the water bottle. "Here. Have another shot. Antioxidants are good for memory."

"He was green. Well, not really, but he seemed green. It may have been one of your dumb aura things."

Bipin looked surprised. "You saw an aura."

"What does it mean? A green one?"

"Green is the heart chakra, in full-out force. It's good. Very good."

"Love?" Villis was remembering Palaeolithic man's smile.

Bipin nodded.

"I'll have some more." Villis pointed at the water bottle.

Bipin beamed. "I concoct it especially for you, my friend."

Villis reached for the bottle, unscrewed the lid, poured himself a cupful. But what was that? He paused, the beverage halfway to his lips. Glanced at Bipin. Frowned a question at him.

Bipin jumped up. "I hear it, I hear it."

They looked at each other, expecting trouble. Then, at the same time, though not in the same way (Villis disgusted, Bipin resigned), they said, "ATV man."

It was. ATV man in full-out force, a spinning mechanical chakra of black tires, yellow paint job garish and out of place, butt raised like a jockey only bigger, bombing down the trail toward the First/Third Bridge.

"Don't let him cross!" Villis said, struggling to his feet, seizing the haemorrhoid pillow like a shield.

"Holy cow!" Bipin windmilled his arms.

ATV man geared down, driving onto the bridge, settling his machine and his jockey butt in one effortless move. Villis couldn't help envying him the fluidity of his tailbone.

"Yo, it's you again, Turban Man." ATV man jerked his chin at Villis. "Who's this? Another geezer for your geezer convention?"

Bipin put a hand on Villis's arm. Villis scowled, then blushed, realizing he was still defending himself with the haemorrhoid pillow. He let it fall to the bridge behind his back.

ATV man noted the pillow, raising an eyebrow in a way that suggested he understood he was in the presence of mental defectives. Then he reached into a saddlebag snugged against the side of the ATV and withdrew a plastic red thing, the size of a calculator only not a calculator, with rows of buttons. He considered for a moment, then pressed a button.

A shotgun went off – at least, as Villis quickly realized, the sound of a gun, in miniature, shooting from the plastic red thing.

ATV man indicated the red thing. "Sound Machine. Twenty

bucks plus tax. Get it? Bang-bang." He started to sing in an Elvis voice. *"Goin' to the ti-ime por-tal and I'm"* – (snap, snap) – *"gonna get ma-a-arried–"*

"It's not a time portal, you idiot," Villis said. "And no machines allowed on this bridge."

"I don't believe Presley covered *Chapel of Love,*" Bipin said, "though, as the King of Rock 'n' Roll, he certainly should have."

ATV man pointed at the haemorrhoid pillow. "That thing float?"

Bipin lay down in Corpse pose in front of the ATV, blocking it from going forward on the bridge. He inhaled, purring from the back of his throat, and shut his eyes.

"Because if it does I suggest you hop aboard and float your scrawny old asses downstream, before–"

Bipin peeked up at the asshole. "The definitive version was record-ed in 1964 by The Dixie Cups, though it had previously been recorded by The Ronettes and The Blossoms. It doesn't float." Then he closed his eyes again, and resumed purring.

The ATV man reactivated the Sound Machine, shooting bang-bangs. "Move it, Old Man. Like, I mean, get the F out of here."

Bipin, eyes still closed, said, "Does brandishing it about improve its functionality?"

Villis picked up the haemorrhoid pillow and flapped it at the asshole. Moronic gesture, he realized, but no more so than shooting people with sound effects. "Get the F lost!" Villis said.

ATV man whinnied his lips. For a split second Villis thought there must be a button on the Sound Machine for horse noises, but on second thought, obviously, the sound was originating directly from the asshole. What could he mean by whinnying? Disgust? Disdain? A desire for oats?

Bipin must have been wondering too, because he opened his eyes. "Sometimes that which you don't understand is drawn to you so that you will understand it."

The asshole revved his ATV, re-snugged the Sound Machine in his saddlebag. "Like they say, I'm gonna count to three." He drove the ATV backwards off the bridge and then reversed one hundred feet up the trail. "One ..." he shouted from where he was.

Villis nudged Bipin with his toe. What he thought he should do was bend down, grab his friend's arm and drag him off the bridge, but his coccyx wasn't up to it.

"Up up up!" He said this under his breath so that the asshole couldn't hear. Then he nudged Bipin harder.

"Two ..."

"He means business." But Bipin, still stretched in Corpse across the entire width of the bridge, had closed his eyes again and was breathing so deeply he appeared peacefully deceased.

"Two and a half ..."

"He'll squash you." Villis bent and, despite the pain that stabbed at the base of his spine, grabbed Bipin's arm and tugged. A corpse, he realized, even a living one, was a dead weight – Bipin didn't budge.

"Three!"

"Don't you dare!" Villis shouted.

Like a dog, ATV man lowered his head and lurched his machine toward them. When the wheels grumbled over the planks of the bridge, the entire wooden structure shuddered beneath Villis's feet.

"He's coming!" Villis tugged again on Bipin. Bipin remained still and blissful.

The ATV picked up speed. It was a long bridge, forty feet at least, but moving as he was, with quickness and canine focus, the wheels clamouring closer and closer, ATV man was upon them in a few fast seconds.

"Watch out!" Villis stepped back, nearly falling backwards off the bridge. Out of the corner of his eye he caught Bipin going into action with a motion so smooth, so singular in its grace and unexpected power, that both he and ATV man paused to watch.

Bipin, eyes now wide open, raised his legs like levers, rolled up his spine as neat as a Kashmir carpet, raised aloft his buttocks like two tight balloons and then, in a flash almost too fast to take note of, propelled his legs straight up until he was balancing in full shoulder-stand position, elbows angled like Christmas tree stands, toes hooked into the blue sky above. His old body, so surprisingly nimble, had arranged itself in an instant of peril into a human flagpole resting on shoulders, with two lean feet easy in the breeze. Villis thought, surely this display of exceptional agility would awe the asshole into submission.

But the asshole didn't appear to be impressed. In fact, if Villis had had to put a word to the expression on the asshole's face – rounded eyes, tight lips, a flare to the nostrils that suggested a stench – that word would have been *alarm*. The asshole was clearly unnerved – nonplussed, it would seem, by the vision of a scrawny old Indian man using his shoulders for feet and his feet for flags. ATV man sped past them, the roll of his wheels barely missing Bipin and then barely missing Villis. His machine crunched over the water bottle, sending splatters of greens drink flying.

"You're wrecking The Pearl!" Villis shook his fist as ATV man sped off the bridge and up the path. There were green drops all over his arm.

Bipin was still in shoulder-stand position.

"Come out of that," Villis snapped. He watched the ATV disappear in the woods, the scratch of its engine fading too. "He's not coming back. Bastard."

"I cannot. It's been so long, I've forgotten how. But in any case, I am rather liking this position. This view of my feet is unprecedented."

Villis sidled up to Bipin, afraid to touch him in case he caused a collapse. "You can't stay like that."

"Ho-hum."

"That goddamned bastard idiot *govniuk* asshole!"

"You forgot *durak*."

"He's trespassing."

"We could call the cops." Bipin sounded snuffly, his throat constricted by the pressures of shoulder-stand position on his vocal cords. "Have him arrested and toted off to prison, lickety-split."

"No police!"

"Okay okay. No bringing the heat." Bipin frowned, then grinned. "Holy cow, I *do* remember how to get out of this. There's a rhyme for it: knees to ears, roll down spine, one vert-e-bra at a time."

"Do it."

"Done." Bipin bent his legs, clamped knees over ears on either side of his head and then rolled his back flat upon the bridge. "Rob's your uncle!"

"BOB. Not Rob. Bob Bob Bob Bob Bob."

"Bob who?"

"Your uncle!"

"If we are descending into nitpickiness, then it's *your* Uncle Bob. Not mine. Bob's *your* uncle."

"He could have killed you!" Villis pointed at the place where ATV man had disappeared.

Bipin nodded. "A vivid fashion in which to cross over to the disembodied beyond."

"Look – green blood." Villis showed Bipin the splatters of drink on his arms.

"Deeply symbolic."

"What do we do now? I want to get that guy. Get him good."

"We tally our blessings."

"Why don't you admit it, just this once – there isn't always a silver lining."

Bipin unzipped his fanny pack, found his red notebook. "Blessing Number 14,022 – *Thank you for the fools who blow by us; for in the wind of their passing the curtain of our courage may gust open, revealing strengths we had forgotten we possessed.*"

"Like the ability to still do shoulder-stands?" Villis said.

"Like the ability to see silver linings."

CHAPTER 10

Premonitions and Regrets

The next day, Villis saw a sign that even Captain John Early couldn't have anticipated. It was a blameless July morning in The Pearl, the new day pealing like bells as sunbeams yawned through leaf tops; the time of day when it pleased Villis to walk barefoot, the calloused soles of his feet savouring the night before, which still lingered coolly in the earth.

The sign he saw was not blood on the trail, nor a rifle butt in the mud, nor even something as understated as disturbed dew. It did not signify politics, nor the transfer of troops, nor even something as banal as boys being boys. Anyone else would have passed over the sign, not noticing, but to Villis it was *the* single burdensome straw added to the camel's back.

It was on the Second Bridge – the bridge of balance, the place that Bipin, coming from his property to the east, and Villis, from the west, called "halfway". The sign was gouges in the planks of the bridge – like the teethmarks of chains, chewing.

When Villis saw the gouges he froze and stared and fumed.

"See what he's done? He's revved his machine on purpose! He's spun his wheels, and now see what he's done to the bridge."

Bipin came over to inspect. "It's the asshole's way of flipping us the bird."

"We have to do something."

"We could pray."

"If we don't take pre-emptive action he'll just keep on doing as he pleases."

"We could resist."

"Yes! Resistance."

"I meant the passive type. The kind I learned from Gandhiji."

"Passive won't get this guy out of The Pearl."

"It got the British out of India."

Villis remembered something he had read in the tracking article from Captain Early – on the construction of mantraps. "I say we dig a pit, cover it with branches, and as sure as Bob's your uncle, we wait for the asshole to fall in."

Bipin considered. "That does have elements of passivity to it, certainly the part where we wait for the asshole to fall. But what if we ensnare some unsuspecting creature? Why should a Jefferson salamander minding its own business have to endure suffering on account of the asshole's misbehaviour?"

"It's a chance we'll have to take."

"What if we dig the pit and the asshole tumbles in and maims himself? Most undoubtedly I wouldn't want harm to befall the fellow."

Villis thought, harm the asshole? Yes, that was just what he wanted to do. Hurt him, dishevel his Elvis Presley hairstyle, smack his smirk into submission.

"Didn't you want to get at that crazy guy who shot Gandhi?" he said to Bipin. "Just for argument's sake, if you'd been there at the time and there had been a clear path between your fist and that lunatic's face, wouldn't you have bashed the bejesus out of him?"

"There was."

"Was what?"

"A clear path."

Villis frowned, not understanding.

"I *was* there," Bipin said, plainly, forlornly.

"You were there? At Gandhi's actual assassination? You've never told me this."

"It is the anguish of my life."

Villis put his hand on Bipin's shoulder. "I told you about the GULAG. And about the ... you know. About those bastards I had to shoot."

"You are stronger than I am, my friend."

Villis considered this. What was strength? When Villis was a very young man, he'd been certain that strength was muscle power and the might of the gun. During his years in the GULAG he had updated his opinion, deciding that strength was resilience against adversity. After his release from the camp, and for most of his life, he'd behaved as if strength came from the controlling of situations. But now, after years of watching Bipin's ancient body flex with the easy grace of youth, Villis had come to the conclusion that strength came from suppleness. And though he could concede some positive attributes about himself, "supple" was not one of them.

"I don't see it. Me, stronger than you."

"I knew about the assassination before it happened. I had a dream. I didn't warn Bapu. My courage failed. I thought, surely this dream is a fantasy from my foolish brain, because who am I to have such a momentous dream about Gandhiji? I doubted myself, and Gandhi died."

"I don't dream," Villis said, hoping to change the subject. He didn't want to stir it up in Bipin – the anguish of his life. Perhaps it was better left untold. "So maybe *that's* why I'm stronger." He said this with one of his dark chuckles, meaning it ironically, forgetting for the moment that Bipin didn't pick up on irony.

Bipin went on, "I *did* want to kill that guy who killed Gandhi. I was so ashamed."

"It's a natural reaction."

"If I am to die by the bullet of a madman, I must do so smiling. There must be no anger within me. God must be in my heart and on my lips."

"If I am to die under the wheels of an asshole, I must do so cursing, ha ha."

"Those are not *my* words, my friend. Dearest Gandhiji uttered them forty-eight hours before he was actually shot to death by the madman."

"Oh!" Villis wished he hadn't made the crack about dying beneath the wheels of an asshole. And he wished Bipin hadn't told him about witnessing the murder. What could he possibly say to comfort his old friend? Words of wisdom, if he had any, were on the other side of a black wall, the one he came nose to nose with whenever he thought about killing. He could not, dared not, never would look over that wall.

Finally, he said, "It seems that Gandhi himself had a premonition about his own death and did nothing to protect himself, so you don't have to feel badly about not–" Villis stopped. There was an expression on Bipin's face that he had never seen in their forty years of friendship – in his eyes, a drawing-in of light as if Bipin were stepping backwards in a tunnel.

"I am ashamed of my craving to kill the madman. If Gandhiji himself planned to die smiling, how could I, who did not suffer the outrage of a steely bullet shredding the tender tissues of my body, how could I be so corruptible as to feel anger? In all my years of learning at the blessed feet of Bapu, at the moment of trial, I failed."

"Anger is only human."

"Which is problematic if one is trying for the Godhead." Bipin bent down to the bridge and traced with his fingers the gouges in the bridge. "These are scars across the cheek of my child."

"I say we get that guy."

Bipin straightened. "A slice of my mind agrees with you."

Villis clapped him on the shoulder. "Not yet gods, the two of us, eh?"

"And a slice of my mind doesn't. Let me meditate on it." Then Bipin stepped off the bridge and continued up the trail.

As they walked along, summer swirling the forest, the coming-and-going breeze stirring the colours – blue sky, green leaves, gold blaze of sun – like reflections in water, Villis wondered what it would take to convince Bipin to retaliate against the asshole. He also wondered about good and evil, miffed that anyone could be so gullible as to imagine that evil could be beaten without anger. Wasn't it anger that had fed his survival in the GULAG? Wasn't it anger that had blown out the top of his head, keeping him upright, keeping him from succumbing in the muddy road of despair?

"Stop, my friend!" Bipin called from just ahead on the trail. He was squatting, cupping both hands over something on the ground. There was a mean tire mark in the trail leading to Bipin's hands.

Villis didn't stop but instead sped up. "What now?" He didn't like the look on Bipin's face – in such a short time, again, that same expression in Bipin's eyes, the drawing-in of light. What had the asshole and his damned wheels done now?

Bipin pivoted, blocking from Villis's view whatever it was that lay beneath his hands. All Villis could see was the mean tire mark, a little shiny, he now noticed, from dampness. "Hand me your shirt," Bipin said, in the same forlorn way he had only minutes ago spoken about Gandhi's assassination.

"Why?"

Bipin only shook his head.

Villis pulled off his T-shirt, clumped it into a ball, lined it up with the tire mark – clear-cut, as he now noticed, the imprints of the tread like the boot print of a monster – and pitched the shirt. It landed with a *whumph* on the trail beside Bipin.

"*Om namo narayana,*" Bipin whispered, taking up the T-shirt and spreading it across the spot on the path. "*Om namo narayana.* Rest in peace, my beloved." Then he turned to Villis, teary-eyed. "It's Frog."

CHAPTER 11

A Half-baked Plan

Bipin lifted Frog's remains with a gentle scrunching of the T-shirt, folding it around the body to form a tiny shroud. "We need to dig a grave."

"Don't let me see anything," Villis said. Who was the strong one now? He hadn't even the courage to bear witness to the injustice that had been brought down upon poor innocent Frog by the killing machine of the asshole.

"I have looked for the both of us," Bipin said. "He's not too too bad. Still looks like Frog."

Villis was relieved to hear this. He had been imagining terrible things.

Bipin continued. "Think of him sunbathing in his pretty bend in the creek. Remember how he loved to rest one leg upon the sunken log – a pose of such self-satisfied relaxation."

"Fucking bastard."

"Yes."

They decided to bury Frog near his bend in the creek. Not too far, and yet, as Bipin gently carried their shrouded friend flat upon his palm, Villis wondered – why had Frog wandered from home? If only he had stayed nearer the log.

The soil near Frog's Bend was rich, like chocolate crumbs. Villis scooped some up, sniffed. It was made of all that Frog must have loved: leaves, dry and spicy, fallen from trees that had protected his skin from the sun; tiny twigs against which he must have braced himself before stretching his legs to jump; and moss that was so soft it must have been a pleasure to rest his white, tender belly upon it.

Villis dug a small hole with his hands, extra deep, taking care to round and pack the sides with earth. "Fucking bastard. I can't do this."

The last time he had dug a grave it had been for his friend, Juozas. How many men could even say that – that they had dug a grave? How many could say that they had dug a grave for their friend under the watch of guards who were arguing over the heel of the rye bread? How many men could say that they had dug a grave for the unshrouded body of their boyhood pal, the pal they had perched beside on the hillside overlooking the lake, sharing salty goat cheese with; and who could say that, because the guards were impatient with their own hunger (the heel of the rye bread was small), the grave dug was no deeper than a drainage ditch, with no protection for what remained of your boyhood-pal-from-those-hillside-goat-cheese-times; no protection for his body against dogs and waterlogging rains; and that while digging that grave that was no better than an after-thought you were relieved-yet-ashamed-to-be-relieved that the body had finally died, since it was so emaciated from hunger and hard labour that it had for several months been no better than a walking skeleton?

"I'll do it for the both of us," Bipin said, lowering Frog into the hole. He recited something in Hindi, a prayer for the dead, Villis thought. Then, with a few sweeps of his hand, Bipin filled the hole with earth.

"Do you want to say a few words?" Bipin asked.

Say a few words? Just one. Sorry sorry sorry sorry sorry.

But Villis only shook his head. It was too much anguish to tell.

The next morning, Villis couldn't bring himself to do the rounds of the road. What was the point? Garbage picked up today would only make room for garbage pitched tomorrow. And how trivial did a few flattened coffee cups now seem when compared to the death of Frog?

Villis was on his way to Bipin's shed, hoping to find materials amid the clutter there that they could use to really get the asshole. Once and for all, you asshole! OUT OF THE PEARL.

He would not stop at Frog's Bend in the creek. He steeled himself for this part of the trail, resolving to walk briskly past with his face turned away. But, of course, he thought: Such a namby-pamby baby. Such a fuss over a frog.

He sat down on a rock at Frog's Bend, staring at the sunken log. Waiting. He believed he ought to cry.

Fact: anthropologists are incapable of crying.

No. Fact: survivors of GULAG camps were incapable of crying. Why was that? Didn't make sense. All that pain (more than one's fair share) and you'd think a person might weep once in a while.

Bipin could cry at the drop of a hat. Bipin could cry when he was sad, when someone else was sad, when something happy happened to himself or to someone else. Villis had even seen those good brown eyes of Bipin's tear up while gazing at the perfect blue of a robin's egg.

So many things to be ashamed of, Villis thought, including the inability to cry over the death – correction, murder – of a friend.

And to top it off, Palaeolithic man had cried, which meant that right from the beginning crying was a human trait. Perhaps, Villis thought, it was *the* singular trait that set humans apart from all other species?

He sighed. He did not wish to be set apart from other species. He much preferred the company of creatures to that of human beings.

Except for Bipin.

Bipin was waiting for him in the shed, pulling nails out of a two-by-six plank.

"The slice of my mind that agrees with you has told me this might work," Bipin said.

"You changed your mind because of Frog?"

"Though I am profoundly committed to the notion of no harm coming to the asshole, I feel no such moral compunctions about compromising his all-terrain vehicle."

"Captain Early salutes you."

"This is for a ramp. You know how the asshole delights in bombing down Killer Hill?"

Villis nodded. Indeed he did. The asshole had torn the forest floor up so badly there, bombing down and circling back in order to bomb down again, that he had carved a traffic roundabout in the woods.

"You know how the land slopes and curves at the bottom of Killer Hill, just at that place where Mother Earth is shrugging her shoulder? That's where we will assemble our ramp, this sturdy Canadian pine plank here, camouflaged with dead leaves and branches and the like, supported to a tilting position by Mother Earth's shrugging shoulder and a few well placed rocks, and–"

"Rob's your uncle, asshole hits the ramp at top speed, causing the ATV to flip over, sideways."

"I thought you said it was Bob."

"How will we make sure the ATV gets 'compromised', as you put it? A single sideways topple won't necessarily do the trick."

Bipin grinned. "Despite your concerns, it will not take too much. With even the slightest topsy-turvy mishap a few scratches to the paint job are bound to ensue, guaranteed to infuriate the asshole. Moreover, he will constantly agonize: when will those crazy geezer guys booby-trap me again? Forever after he will be obliged to be looking over his shoulder, his anxieties quite naturally mounting as we booby-trap the trails each and every day, always at different locales, freaking him out so that in due course he renounces The Pearl."

Villis took the two-by-six from Bipin and slung it over his shoulder. "I'll carry this. For once, something I can do that doesn't test my tailbone."

"What shall my burden be, my friend?" Bipin asked.

"Just your faith that this half-baked plan might actually work."

Actually, Villis did think the half-baked plan might work. In fact, he was imagining more than scratches on paint; in his version of the plan, ATV man would fly off his machine like a pair of dirty socks and land with a whump and a crack to the noggin. Enough to muss his hair; maybe KO him, if only briefly. Surely, Villis thought, a mild concussion ought to be sufficient to make the point: KEEP OUT OF THE PEARL. OR ELSE.

The path to Killer Hill took them past Frog's Bend. This time Villis managed not to look at the sunken log, but in not looking he was filled with other thoughts – unsettling ones, as it turned out. He remembered – hadn't he only a few days ago made a smart remark about dying under the wheels of the asshole? Hadn't he not long ago chastised Bipin for wanting to name Frog Mahatma, in honour of Gandhi? Now, see what had happened! Frog was murdered (as was Mahatma Gandhi), most specifically flattened under the wheels of the asshole. Coincidence? Or the manifestations of his own thought-flocking powers?

Villis shook his head. He had better not think any more. Was that why old men lost their minds? Was the dementia of old age a blessing in disguise? No more thoughts. No more damage inflicted. No more memories of damage survived.

At the bottom of Killer Hill the damage caused by the asshole's ATV was extensive. In the roundabout ruts dug by his wheels water was trapped, rendering the once chocolaty loam of the forest a muddy mess that drowned plants and small creatures.

Villis gritted his teeth, trying to clear his mind of thoughts, as Bipin had taught him, trying to remember the mantra Bipin had given him years ago during a lesson on meditation. What was it? IMA? OMA? RAMA? BLAM? Did it matter? Surely any nonsensical sound would do. How about PHOOEY? Villis tried it, repeating – *Phooey Phooey Phooey* – as he picked his way over the ruts. What was his mind doing now? Thinking: Get that guy out of here, out of here, out of here.

"Here is the spot where Mother Earth shrugs," Bipin was saying. "The ramp goes like so." He took the two-by-six from Villis and laid it flat against the tilted spot on the trail. "Now you fetch a few rocks to prop it up on one side, and I'll gather the camouflage."

They fussed with the ramp for half an hour, mostly fiddling with fans of pine and a few fern fronds cleverly placed to hide their handi-work. When they were finished, Bipin walked around the ramp, checking for breaches in the camouflage.

"Even your exacting Captain Early could not detect our deed," Bipin said.

Villis checked the time on his GPS. "Oh-nine-hundred hours. The asshole's never out and about this early. I say we return to base, rendezvous back here after lunch."

Bipin chuckled. "Always thinking of your stomach, my friend."

After lunch, Villis was trotting ahead of Bipin on the trail, for once moving faster than the old Indian, for once the burning in his knees not burning. Perhaps it had been the smoothie Bipin had given him for lunch, made with super-food maca powder supposed to be good for everything.

They were almost back at the base of Killer Hill. Villis saw something ahead on the trail – a flash of primary yellow, too monochromatic to belong to the forest. The ATV, he realized, tipped over.

"Yes!" He pumped his fist. The ramp had worked – better than they had hoped. Here was the despised all-terrain vehicle, downed like a motorized bull, no longer swinging its manly mechanical balls.

Villis reached the ATV first. It was lying on its side, its underbelly exposed – four fat wheels motionless, one wheel clearly bent. Had he dared hope for a bent wheel? A dream come true! Villis advanced, his nose picking up the sick tickle of spilt oil. Bipin was close behind him, clucking. Then Villis saw something that shouldn't have been there, poking up from a mess of leaves beneath the tipped-over ATV. He put out his arm to stop Bipin.

"What is it, my friend?"

"A shoe."

"What kind of a shoe?"

"The kind with a foot in it."

CHAPTER 12

What to do About Incriminating Evidence

The asshole was dead. No doubt about it. Broken neck, though they couldn't be certain. There was an odd twist to the head, Villis noticed this right away, which meant the asshole must have landed funny when he flipped off the ATV. A fluke.

"This was an accident," Villis said. "Do you have something to cover his face?"

Bipin was kneeling beside the asshole, hands folded in a prayer. "*Om namo narayana.*"

"How could he have been so stupid?"

"Rest in peace, poor young man, needlessly deadened in the glowing of your youth. This is so tragic, I can barely speak." Bipin began to cry.

"Prayers. Waste of time. And he was hardly glowing."

"My friend, it was our hands, yours and mine, that positioned the plank," Bipin said sternly, through sniffles.

"Any idiot should have been able to drive over that ramp and not end up like that."

"You mean passed away? The sadness is clamming in the back of my throat. Never again will the asshole know the pleasure of a revved engine, or delight in the sharp curl of gasoline at the outer edges of his nostrils."

"Stop being so goddamned melodramatic." Villis was feeling irritated. He had seen many dead bodies in his GULAG days, though none of them had looked as healthy as this one. Nevertheless, there was no mistaking the motionlessness of death.

Bipin, still kneeling, cocked his head as if trying to work out the awkward angle of the asshole's neck. Villis handed him a fern frond. "Use this on the face."

Bipin sighed, but covered the face with the fern. "Pass me one more. His nose is sticking out."

"That's not his nose," Villis said, handing Bipin another frond.

"This is a matter for the heat."

"No cops!"

"It's a murder scene."

"An accident!"

Bipin stood up, started to pace. "I must insist! NOT an accident. Most assuredly a function of cause and effect. We, the two of us, have caused the cause." He pointed dramatically, raising his voice. "THIS, the if-not-murdered-then-nevertheless-absolutely-dead person, is the effect. We must inform the authorities. It is the ONLY decent thing to do."

"No cops! We didn't think this would happen. What do we know about stupid ATVs and how they may or may not kill someone? We meant to throw him off, scare him, scratch his paint. Remember? YOU said that."

Bipin frowned. "Suddenly your memory is conveniently flawless – how can that be? No matter. Whatever I said before, NOW I am saying something else. How in heaven's name could we have been so obviously, patently STUPID? And, holy cow, at the very least the cops will charge us with manslaughter."

"No cops!"

Bipin stopped pacing, placed his hand on Villis's shoulder. "Breathe three-part breath, my friend. Nose, chest, belly. Good for the panic. See, I am needing it now myself." Bipin demonstrated, drawing in a long, wavering breath, filling his chest but not bulging his belly as he normally did. He flushed, something Villis had never seen him do.

"Holy cow, I am feeling too alarmed to breathe into my belly. This is a terrible situation. Now listen to me, Mr. Villis Krastins, I understand how this arouses your most pressing VC – *Abuse of Power by Uniformed Men with Guns and the Oppression of Citizens*. Add to that your onerous police phobia and acute fear of incarceration, both of which have arisen from your inhumane backstory, and it becomes crystal clear that you could never bear another stint in prison. My friend, I SWEAR it – if I could do time in the Big House on your behalf, gladly I would. Nevertheless, we cannot pander to your plethora of anxieties at every turn of the screw. So, listen to me – in simple terms, we'll inform the police that we chanced upon this unfortunate fellow who has apparently had an appalling accident. We will neglect to mention the ramp, and neither will we say boo about our role in this melancholic outcome. The police will absolutely believe us."

"They won't."

"They will."

"Won't."

"And furthermore ..." Bipin picked up the ramp and pitched it wildly into the woods. "There! The evidence is vamoosed. Now, let's get a handle on ourselves and do whatever's what."

"Evidence? Oh my God." Villis slapped a hand across his mouth. "What about our notes? Stay out of The Pearl or else–"

"Or else – '*it will be the end of you*'?" Bipin looked gloomily at the asshole. "Who would've thought our bluff notes would turn out to be prophecies?"

"And incriminating evidence."

"Doesn't look good, holy cow, why did we put in that bit about being the end of him? I'm so very very regretful that we didn't stick with my initial inspiration and write 'or else we'll paint-bomb your ATV'. Now we have manslaughtered the poor asshole and it looks as if we premeditated the entire result. And if they find out how much I meditate–"

"If we report this to the police they'll do an investigation."

"They'll find the notes."

"Those notes connect us to him."

Bipin nodded, still flushing. "As any half-competent handwriting analysis will prove."

"And why would the cops believe us when we say our threats were only bluffs?"

"They will not." Bipin said this faintly. He put his hand to his head. "I may keel over ..."

Villis wrapped an arm around Bipin. "Think of all the wrongful convictions you read about in the papers."

"The cops always want a collar."

"That's right. They want a closed case so they can ..." Villis puffed out his cheeks. "We should check his pockets. Look for the notes."

"And for ID, too?"

"You do it."

"I have never touched a deceased person before."

"Do you want me to?"

Bipin closed his eyes for a moment. "No no no. I must do it. The ramp was my idea. And I picked the place, too." He shuddered. "Killer Hill. It's all so painfully obvious to me now."

Bipin bent over the asshole's body and gingerly patted his shirt pocket and then his pants. "I am not liking this. Please forgive me the intrusion, sir. Dear me, here is something. A notebook." Bipin slipped it out of the asshole's pocket and fanned the pages. "No dice. Blank pages."

"I think that's the notebook he wrote in when I was watching from the top of the Lopsided Ridges. He pulled a pencil from behind his ear, then a notebook, then he wrote something. You had your eyes closed. Check again."

Bipin shook the notepad and then fanned the pages a second time. "Nothing written anywhere. Must be a different notebook." Bipin stuffed the notebook in his fanny pack. "Now we must decide what to do with this killed body."

"We didn't mean to kill him," Villis said, though as he did so he was thinking: he had, in point of fact, imagined the asshole falling into a dark abyss.

Bipin nodded. "Manslaughter was most assuredly not in my heart."

"But you can bet on it – manslaughter WILL BE the charge."

"*If,* for argument's sake, no fuzz, then what? We cannot leave a killing victim lying about in the bush. And we must advise the next of kin, who are bound to be worried sick."

"It was an ACCIDENT."

"Semantics! Denial! I, for one, will face the music. But then ..." Bipin trailed off.

Villis pointed with his toe. "What we do is this: we put him and the ATV in the ditch by the road. When they find him, they'll assume he had an accident, which he DID." He glared at Bipin, daring him to comment. "And that'll be that."

"Who is *they*?"

Villis snorted, exasperated. "I don't know. Whoever, that's who. Whoever happens along."

"Precisely."

"Meaning what, exactly?"

"People happen along the road, all sorts. Housewives in Hummers. Business boys in Beemers. Teens in hoodies and beaters. Cranky old guys in pea caps driving Camrys at twenty clicks under the speed limit. If we dare to drag the cadaver to the ditch someone is bound to bear witness."

"We'll do it at night, then. *They* can find him the next morning."

Bipin winced.

"What! What?"

"Coyotes. You know full well what they do to the deer. We can't possibly leave this corpse exposed, either here or in the ditch. Even for one night." Bipin looked ominous.

Villis had to agree about the coyotes. More than once, in various parts of the woods, he and Bipin had come across body parts of deer – haunches for the most part, tufts of brown and white fur stuck to bones with dried blood. The asshole certainly did not deserve that. And what if the coyotes left a rib bone or femur or, worse, the skull, in the roadside ditch? On more than one occasion he himself had found deer bones (including skulls) in the ditch. And might not one of those cranky old guys in pea caps stop his car to relieve himself? (Villis had seen *that*, too.) What if the old guy, while following the golden streaming of his bodily fluid, happened to spot the asshole's skull poking up from between some thistles? And Villis himself, while strolling in The Pearl some day, certainly would not care to come across human bones plastered with hair the colour of Elvis Presley's.

He thought for a moment. At the very least they should do a better job of hiding the evidence – the ramp. Correction, not evidence, per se. No crime had been committed. He searched for the ramp between the trees where Bipin had thrown it, and finding it he flung it still deeper into the woods. Then he found it again, smooshed leaves overtop and dragged a log to weigh the thing down.

Bipin watched from the trail. "I suppose we could bury him," Bipin shouted.

Villis inspected his job. Check check check. No fuzz would ever find it. "Bury?" he shouted back, and then, catching himself, shushed at Bipin. "Don't yell." He scanned the scene, making sure no unwanted persons were eavesdropping.

He hurried back to Bipin and in a low voice said, "Bury? Bury him here?"

"Not here. It's too close to a trail. Someone might come along some day and notice a suspicious mound. No, we should bury him in the Resonating Nexus. The vibrations there should prove beneficial. In fact, now that we're on a roll, why not bury him under the moai?"

"Under the moai? Might work." Villis was thinking about coyotes and the shallow grave the guards had forced him to dig for Juozas.

"We'll wheel him up there in the wheelbarrow in the same way I wheeled you down after that hapless clash between Mother Earth and your coccyx."

"With the moai secured on top of the grave, no animals will be able to dig it up."

"And it will serve as a decent interment monument, despite its Styrofoam construction."

Villis frowned but said nothing. If Juozas did not have a monument, certainly the asshole didn't deserve one, even if it would be a fake. "I suppose we can push this to the road." He gave the ATV a slight shove, careful not to make it topple any further onto the asshole. It shifted easily. Not too heavy, after all, for such a clunky machine. "Give me a hand with this."

"Take care not to step on the deceased," Bipin said.

"Blah blah blah. What do you think I am? Some kind of ignoramus?"

Bipin came alongside Villis, and with both of them positioning themselves so as not to touch any portion of the asshole's corpse, they put hands on the ATV and shoved.

"Ugh. One ... more ... push ... ought to do it ..." Villis said. The ATV rocked, and then over it went, landing upright on its fat wheels with a laid-back bounce.

"See if it starts," Bipin said.

Villis found a key in the ignition and twitched it. Nothing.

"Try the handlebars."

"You try." Villis stepped back. The thing was probably out of gas. Or out of order.

Bipin climbed on, straddled the seat and then, tensing forward as if blasting off, squeezed the handle grips. Nothing.

Villis pointed. "Try again."

Bipin held his breath and for a second time squeezed the handle grips.

"Whoa!"

The ATV lurched a few feet, putt-putting like an old man passing gas. Then it stopped. Bipin straightened his Ray-Bans and tried again, this time managing to drive the thing forward fifty feet along the trail before stopping, turning and bounding back, faster. He pulled up alongside Villis, downshifting the motor until it purred.

"I am disinclined to say this, my friend, but this baby really sings, though it wobbles to the left due to its bent wheel. Hop on."

"No goddamned way."

"This machine will allow us to do this most unpleasant deed as efficiently as possible. Consider the ramifications of the task at hand. We must go to my shed, procure the wheelbarrow, wheel it back here, transport the dearly departed up the Lopsided Ridges to the Nexus, disassemble the moai, dig a hole deep enough to fit the asshole – who,

I might remind you, is larger than your average bear – then bury him with prayers, reassemble the moai, and at long last drive the ATV all the way to the road and tip it into the ditch."

"At night. We tip the ATV into the ditch at night."

"Nonetheless–"

"When the asshole doesn't show up at his home, someone is bound to miss him. Come looking. Oh my God! Next of kin." Villis was just now realizing this.

"Assuming someone knows where to look. It is possible the asshole told nary a soul where he was off to."

"I guess." Villis wasn't convinced. "But if someone does come they'll find the ATV."

"But no ATV driver."

"They'll think he's dead."

"Or run off to avoid responsibilities."

"That does seem in character."

"It will become an unsolved missing persons case. His likeness will appear on milk jugs."

"They only do that for kids."

"The asshole wasn't a kid? Holy cow, I guess everyone looks like a kid to me. I must be getting old." Bipin said this as if it were a revelation. "But if there is next of kin they will be dismayed about not knowing what has happened to their loved one."

Villis sighed, staring at the asshole's pale face, which was still slightly visible beneath the fern fronds. "Do you think he is somebody's loved one?"

Bipin placed a hand over his heart. "If not, then I suddenly forgive him everything."

"And if ...?" Villis said. "If he *is* somebody's loved one? Do you think they would want to know the truth? About how ..." he paused, searching for the right word, "how stupidly he died?"

"Don't you mean 'how senselessly'?"

Villis waved his hand impatiently. He couldn't, wouldn't discuss this any further. It *was* senseless. Any idiot could see that. And yes, how could they have been so stupid? But Bipin was a naive man, and this incident clearly brought to light the dangers of naivety. Fact: they had not intended to harm the asshole. Fact: no one would believe this. Fact: they would both die in prison.

"We need to focus," Villis said, hissing his *s*. "Stick with the situation at hand. We can talk about the next of kin later. For now, we stay calm. No panicking ..."

"I have not felt the panic since dearest Bapu was assassinated."

"That's not focusing."

"That's panicking."

"So? What will we do with the body while we're getting the wheelbarrow? What if someone comes along? Finds it, I mean, *him*, like this."

"Departed?"

"It could happen." Anything, it seemed, could happen.

Bipin patted the seat of the ATV. "All the more reason to speed things up by availing ourselves of this helpful transportation technology. Climb on behind me."

"We should cover the rest of the body, just in case."

"With what? The longer we dilly-dally the worse things are getting. For him, and for us."

"Bracken." Villis looked around. It would take armloads of bracken to hide the asshole. He was a gangly kid with those lanky Elvis legs of his splayed across the path and his arms flung wide.

"No one will pass by. In the forty years of our walking how many interlopers have penetrated The Pearl? Why, you can count them on the toes of one foot."

"Still. And don't forget the coyotes."

"They only prowl at night. Now hurry up. If we're going to do this deed, then let's just do it, for crying out loud, as you so frequently lament."

Villis puffed out his cheeks again and, because he couldn't help himself, tossed another frond at the body. It fell limply across the asshole's tummy.

"Much better," Bipin said. "Now, for the last time, let's get a move on."

Villis approached the ATV. Had it come to this, him riding an ATV through The Pearl? There was hardly any room behind Bipin. He was about to protest, saying the ATV couldn't possibly fit the two of them, when the truth of what was happening struck him – here was yet another unmistakable wallop from the forces of omnipresent irony. He snorted. Good God. Of course – of course! – he would jockey the ATV through the pristine forest of The Pearl. What else?

Holding onto Bipin's waist for dear life, bouncing along on wheels that slapped against the trail like sloppy slippers, Villis found himself thinking unexpected thoughts. He was not enjoying the ride (which was *exactly* as he'd expected), the ups and downs jostling his tailbone, which was responding to each bump with tiny, throbbing pulses. He was not enjoying the smell (which was worse than he'd expected), the chemical nip of gasoline itchy inside his nostrils. And the sound of the damned thing (with the source of the racket immediately beneath his buttocks) was a grumbling, vibrating nuisance, numbing the insides of his ears until he thought he would die.

But none of those thoughts was unexpected. What *was* unexpected was this – Villis had suddenly found himself, in spite of the offensiveness of his current situation, undergoing another vision of Palaeolithic man. How could that be? How on earth could a fellow have a vision amid all this confounded commotion? And yet, there he was, Palaeolithic man in the flesh, so to speak, in all his green and glowing glory, trotting alongside the ATV, the thick mess of his hair bobbing up and down, almost, it seemed to Villis, in time with the tiny, throbbing pulses from his own tailbone. And he was wearing what looked like Bipin's Ray-Bans, only this pair had a piece of white tape binding the bridge of them as if they had been broken and repaired.

And what's more, Frog was riding on his shoulder, hanging on, it seemed to Villis, with some Yoda-like feat of mind-boggling balance. Villis wanted to shout in Bipin's ear, *LOOK! It's Frog! He's okay! Froggy, ol' boy!* But he stopped himself – Palaeolithic man and Frog were invisible to all but himself. Had to be.

Villis let go of Bipin's waist and stretched one hand to see if Palaeolithic man and Frog had any tangible substance. But he couldn't quite reach. Palaeolithic man continued trotting alongside, taking no notice of his attempt to touch. And was he going crazy, but didn't Frog appear to be blinking at him encouragingly?

I love you, Frog, Villis thought, without really thinking.

I love you too, Villis, Frog thought back at him.

"Whoa! Sorry, my friend," Bipin said. A bump in the trail. Bipin had sped up and nearly bounced Villis off the ATV.

Villis didn't order Bipin to slow down. Didn't complain, as he normally would have. Didn't even hang on more tightly. He was too stunned.

Fact: Frog knew his name.

And Fact: Frog loved him.

Then he wondered, did Palaeolithic man love him too? He wasn't exactly the lovable type. In truth, when was the last time any living thing had said (or thought-said) those words to him? I love you, Villis. He couldn't remember. Decades.

And did *he* love Palaeolithic man? They hardly knew each other. And yet, Villis thought at the green man, I *do* love you.

It was so easy. So obvious.

I *do* love you.

Palaeolithic man smiled the tender smile from before and Villis felt love fill his mind, coming in a gush that was unquestionably (though how did he *know* this?) streaming from Palaeolithic man.

And then he heard someone speaking, in English, though with an Indian accent and a voice as buttery as a mouthful of caramels. It was Gandhi. Villis *knew* this, too, instantly, knew it with an almost blasé familiarity: oh hey, it's Gandhi – who else?

"Tell Bipin," Gandhi was saying, "I was tired and ready to die. God gave me an easy way out, quick, no suffering, when my body was still relatively okay. And tough as it was for onlookers, it was a dramatic exit that helped immortalize my life's work by making me a martyr. Not my idea, by the way, but I accepted it."

What? Villis thought. Say it again. He needed to be sure he had it right. But the only answer that came was a warm chuckle and one more word, "*Namaste.*"

And then they were gone: Palaeolithic man, blinking Frog and the buttery voice of Gandhi.

"Stop! Stop!" Villis whacked Bipin on the shoulder. Bipin downshifted and settled the ATV into a ready-rumble. He angled his feet for balance and halted the machine.

"I heard Gandhi!" Villis said this to the back of Bipin's head.

"What did you say?"

"Turn around!"

Bipin, screwing his spine into Sage Twist, spiralled easily and glanced back at Villis over one shoulder. "You were saying?"

Villis, having had an instant to think, was no longer sure he should tell Bipin about the vision. Bipin *would* believe him, that wasn't the problem, and it *was* an encouraging message; nonetheless, if Villis admitted to hearing Gandhi he would be agreeing, for the first time in their forty years of arguing on the subject, that people continued after they died.

"Umm," Villis said.

"Go on."

"I heard Gandhi."

"Gandhiji! Dearest Bapu? Holy cow, I'm flabbergasted. Gobsmacked. Knocked for six. When, just now? Amidst all this terrible hullabaloo?"

Villis nodded. "He had a message for you."

Bipin tossed off his Ray-Bans, not at all concerned that they landed on a rock. "For me?"

"He said he was tired and ready to die and that it was okay because he went without pain, which was better than dying from some awful disease, slowly, bit by bit, and when you think of it we all have to die, and either we go violently or by disease, and his way of going violently was actually not too bad for him from his point of view, albeit not so good for people like you who had to witness the blood and, as you said before, the anguish of it, and thereby wind up suffering significantly more than the deceased person, especially if you feel guilty about the manner of dying, as was the situation in your case since you didn't try to prevent his assassination as foretold to you in your so-called premonition dream, though I've always thought *that* was being a bit hard on yourself because who in their right mind expects dreams to come true?"

"He said all that?"

"More or less."

Bipin covered his face with his hands. His shoulders trembled.

"Are you crying?"

Bipin nodded from behind his hands.

Villis sighed. He had aroused the anguish of his friend's life. But he had meant well. "I'm sorry. Me and my big fat stupid mouth."

"It's okay, okay," Bipin mumbled.

"*Govniuk.*"

"No, no, no."

Villis slapped the ATV. "This stupid damned piece of crap."

Bipin lowered his hands, teary-eyed but smiling. "You blame this poor machine for everything. It is one of your most endearing qualities."

"I don't."

"You do."

Villis slid off the ATV and stomped over to where Bipin had flung the Ray-Bans. He picked them up, brought them back to Bipin. "Here." Then he fumbled his way onto the seat behind Bipin.

Bipin squeezed the handle grips and babied the ATV engine into a sound as buttery as caramels. "Hold on," he said.

Villis tightened his arms around Bipin's waist. "Always."

CHAPTER 13

Ditching the Evidence and
Thoughts on the Immeasurable Beyond

They buried the asshole in the Resonating Nexus, under the moai, about four feet down. Villis had wanted to dig the hole deeper, but the tangling root tips of the circling butternut trees gripped the soil like fingers, making shovelling a challenge. It was a good thing they had brought along a pick. Bipin was swinging it rhythmically, like a labourer in a chain gang, breaking through the packed surface of the ground and the criss-crossing roots below.

They worked silently, Villis with the shovel, Bipin the pick. This was unusual, this silence between them, but Villis was glad for it. Who could chat while burying a body? If he did speak he might blurt something – for example: this wasn't right, what they were doing, burying a body, not telling anyone. Not informing, as Bipin had put it, the authorities. But as this whiff of the authorities – like the acrid smell of gunshot smoke, of incarcerations and humiliations – pinched at his nostrils, Villis's worst memories and his bruised heart and the cells in his body that were lined up like the bunks at Camp TTK-6 heaved, and he knew that he would never be able to tell anyone what had happened with the ramp. I've done my time, he thought.

"At some point, we must give consideration to the next of kin," Bipin said, out of the blue. "It behooves us to relieve their suffering."

Villis grunted. One thing he had learned in Camp TTK-6 was how to relieve sufferings by organizing the chaos of the heart into contained reports, like lonely hearts letters never sent. A post office wall of cubbyholes loomed in his mind (he could actually see this when needed) into which he tucked these letters, unopened, the envelopes pale and unaddressed. Each letter was the documentation of a yearning denied; or a soul shredded at its source; or of shame that was like shrapnel deeply embedded – all these facts of his dire existence he had slotted into this dead letter office in his mind with the all-consuming goal of ignoring the harrowing voice of whichever truth was, at any given moment, the painful one. So too, then, could he file away this idea of the suffering of the next of kin, safely sealing the looming loved ones inside anonymous envelopes, which later he might or might not open. As need be.

He decided he had better change the subject.

He should ask Bipin if he thought the asshole had continued on in the same way as Gandhi and Frog appeared to have done. Gandhi was a saint and Frog an innocent. He was fairly certain that the asshole did not fall into either of those categories. But then, who knew? Maybe continuing on also applied to less-than-stellar persons. Villis thought of Juozas, Janis, Gregori and Endres. They were about the same age as the asshole at the time of their deaths. Hardly saints – he smiled slightly at this, remembering the good times – but surely worthy enough to continue on.

"What brings the smile, my friend?" Bipin asked.

"Nothing."

"More of your irony?"

"Could be."

Bipin rested the pick. "As I was swinging this pick, I couldn't help being reminded of dearest Bapu, spinning at his wheel in Sabarmati Ashram, relishing the self-effacing tedium of the working man's chore. I am still completely agog that he had a message for me. For eons I have prayed to him to bring me up to date on how he is getting along in the immeasurable beyond, and only now do I have my answer. But I am overwhelmed with wondering why he appeared to you and not to me. And why now?"

"I'd be insulted. I mean, about appearing to someone else."

"Wait, wait! Holy cow! Now that I think of it, I *do* know why he did it. He was answering *two* of my prayers at the same time! First prayer: Dearest Bapu, how are you managing in the afterlife? Second prayer: Dearest Bapu, how do I assure my friend Villis that there truly *is* an afterlife?"

"You prayed to Gandhi for that?"

"Oh no. Not just Gandhi. For that particular item, I have prayed to everyone." Bipin grabbed the pick and jammed it into the ground. "But why now? Why did he come to me now?"

Villis shrugged. Gandhi had said nothing on the matter of timing, and Villis didn't want to speculate.

It was clear to him that Bipin was struggling. Normally, he would have tried his trick of distracting Bipin with a wisecrack, but at the moment, and given the situation, nothing funny was popping into his head.

"Who am I kidding? I *do* know why," Bipin finally said with a sigh. "Dearest Gandhiji is not pleased with me. He has reappeared to remind me of his high principles."

"He didn't say anything about principles. And he didn't sound displeased with you. He sounded affectionate."

"He always sounded that way – even when giving corrections to one's bad behaviour." Bipin hung his head. "I am a bag of wind. I have learned nothing."

They stayed in the Resonating Nexus for the remainder of the day, smoothing the ground around the moai, scattering pine needles and bracken in haphazard patterns across the site in order to hide all hints of grave-digging. There was still some rubbish left behind by the asshole: a pair of leopard print sweatpants, an inside-out Blue Jays cap, three two-fours of beer empties and a battery-operated can opener – all of which they piled into the wheelbarrow for disposal.

"That's the last time we'll have to do this," Villis said. "Thank God."

"Amen, Brother," Bipin answered, removing the batteries from the can opener and tucking them in his fanny pack.

Villis stretched his lower back and groaned. He must have pulled a muscle, earlier, while they were towing the wheelbarrow hitched to the ATV. Villis had been convinced that the wheelbarrow, bouncing precariously behind them, would flip, and so he had constantly twisted to look back and check on it. They had towed it all the way from Bipin's shed to the bottom of the Lopsided Ridges, where they'd had no choice but to park the ATV and then hand-push the wheelbarrow the remainder of the way – the ridges were too steep to drive up.

Bipin hovered a hand over Villis's lower back. "But I am duty bound to point out – you are master of your own suffering. Once again, your unwarranted anxieties have manifested as physical pain."

"It could've flipped, the way you were driving."

"And you watching like an uptight mongoose could not have thwarted such a calamity."

Villis nodded at the wheelbarrow, piled now with beer crates, the shovel and pick, and the leopard pants draped overtop like the trophy skin from a jungle expedition. "Not a chance we can tow it back to your place like that. Stuff will fall. We'll have to push it the whole way."

Bipin swung the key to the ATV on his index finger. "I can be a safety-saint. No barrelling along in a madcap manner, risking unintended mayhem."

Villis rolled his eyes.

It took over an hour to make it back to Bipin's shed with the wheelbarrow. For once, Villis had been right – towing the overloaded wheelbarrow behind the ATV was out of the question. They decided to take turns pushing it, which meant they also had to alternate driving the ATV. Villis hated his turn in control of the all-terrain vehicle. He hated the clumsy lurching, the drone, the ugly false yellow of the thing that was like a fist punching the living green. He complained to Bipin, but Bipin advised him to consider the experience an exercise in compassion for the asshole, whom they had, after all, had a hand in terminating.

"And of all people, surely *you* driving the ATV is evidence of John Lennon's instant karma concept," Bipin was saying. Then he started to sing – "*Instant Karma's gonna get you, gonna knock you off your feet, better recognize your brothers, everyone you meet.*"

"I'm plenty compassionate, but only for people who deserve it. And anyway, how much instant karma do you think the asshole believed in?"

"One doesn't have to believe in it for it to work. It is simply and utterly a Law of the Universe."

"I hope you're right, because those bastards at Camp TTK-6 have a lot of payback coming to them." He paused, suddenly sad. Why wasn't he used to it, after all these years, how his anger was always filled in by sadness, like groundwater seeping into craters made by land mines? "Though I guess they're all dead by now."

"*Well we all shine on, like the moon–*"

Villis revved the ATV to escape Bipin's singing, shooting ahead of him on the trail. Bipin wasn't singing in his usual perky manner, exaggerating like a pop star; instead he was singing mournfully, drawing out the words *we all shine on*, making them unbearable. Surely shining on did not apply to those Soviet bastards. And if *that* was a Law of the Universe, then call him an outlaw. But then he remembered the ramp and how it had played a part in the death of the asshole. Maybe some degree of forgiveness was in order? Perhaps for accidental infractions?

They waited until the pit of night, when the dark was darkest, to dump the ATV in the ditch. The moon was a sliver of silver, no more than a wink. Looking up between the trees, Villis was glad the moon wasn't watching.

Bipin was driving, cautiously for a change, the headlamp of the ATV knifing the night with slashes of light. Villis was wearing a miniature LED flashlight fastened to an elasticized band that encircled his skull. Worried that the jouncing of the ATV might jiggle the gizmo loose, he had fastened it tightly before setting out – perhaps too tightly; the thing was giving him a headache. He didn't dare ask Bipin to stop. Bipin would insist on a supported headstand, on the spot, to rush blood to his aching brain.

Villis switched off the flashlight and tugged it down around his neck. He especially enjoyed the woods on a dark night in the summer when it was warm. For one thing, it was something hardly anybody did. Most people lived in cities, and even country dwellers turned on lights at night and burrowed inside their houses like dung beetles. Villis supposed they were afraid. As an anthropologist, he needed no one to tell him about humankind's primal fear of the night, scratched into the stubborn reptilian brain over eons of tooth-and-claw savagery. And he could see how the blue flicker of the television had replaced the prehistoric campfire. He supposed this was reassuring: regardless of wheels and cogs and other advancements; notwithstanding materialism, rationalism, the scientific method, nuclear bombs and pharmaceuticals; despite man's subduing of nature in order to extend the human race over the universe; despite everything – people were still afraid of the dark.

Villis had overcome his fear of the dark in Camp TTK-6, when nighttime had been the only time he had known the slightest piece of peace. Alone in his bunk, before collapsing into a sleep that was like a longed-for death, and despite the nearby snores and outcries from his prison-mates, his mind had wandered in that woozy zone between awake and asleep, expanding in the darkness like a free man, Mr. Nobody in a blackness where there were no guards to peer and prod, no ends of rifles – no one commanding his feet where to step, his hands what to touch, his eyes what to see.

But on this particular night in the woods with Bipin, Villis was thinking, for *some* reason, he was afraid. Some reason? Who was he kidding? After ninety years of living with himself he knew all his own tricks. It wasn't the darkness that had him worried but the possibility of a light abruptly shining on their clandestine doings. The quicker this business with the ATV was over and done with the better.

They cut the engine about a hundred feet from the road and pushed the ATV to the brink of the ditch. They waited for a moment, hunkering behind twisted thistles, checking for cars; long before any might appear they would be able to see headlights fanning a warning glow across the feathered tips of the trees that lined the road.

"Coast is clear," Bipin said.

Villis held his breath. Beside him, he could hear Bipin doing the exact opposite, breathing deep *ujjayii* breaths. Ocean breaths. He could also hear crickets – a million of them, ricketing, nestled in the night – and the toes of his own sneakers making a skritchy sound in the dirt, like an animal scratching.

"All right, my friend. It's time to fish or cut bait. Put up or shut up. Do or die."

Villis let out his breath. "At the count of three. We'll push it into the ditch, ass over teakettle." He put his hands against the back of the ATV, braced his legs. Bipin did the same.

"One ... two ... three."

Bipin heaved against the ATV, expelling a mighty rush of *ujjayii* breath. Villis bent his head and tightened his shoulders, just as he had done while a prisoner rolling logs, and pushed alongside his friend. The ATV trundled forward a few feet and then tipped, ass over teakettle, into the ditch.

"Geronimo!" Villis said.

"Mission accomplished, my friend. Though I am in no mood to make merry." Bipin high-fived him half-heartedly.

"Thank God that's done. Now we can have our normal lives back."

"Copy that, Good Buddy."

On the other side of the road, lights, round and silver, suddenly rayed across the asphalt like search beams from outer space, lighting up the dark, the ditch, the twisted thistles and the ATV, catching Villis in the eyes, blinding him.

"It's the fuzz!" Bipin whispered. "Make a run for it, my friend!"

Villis felt Bipin's hand clutching his arm, tugging. He stumbled backwards, scraped his knee, squinted into the light, then scrambled after Bipin. The headlights – from what could only be a police cruiser – spread a small sector of visibility across the road and the ditch, casting misshapen tree shadows, like a posse of skinny giants, into the woods.

Villis watched Bipin step away from the light and disappear into the blackness of the trees.

"Where are you?" Villis whispered.

"Over here."

Villis tiptoed toward the voice.

"Ouch."

"Shhhh."

"We'll be seen."

"I can't even see *you*, my friend."

"We should run."

"*Ujjayii* breath."

"Fuck off."

"That cop is taking his sweet time. He must be radioing for backup."

"Shit."

Villis felt Bipin's hand on his arm, patting. "Hush now, my friend. He's coming."

Villis couldn't see anything outside the sector of light, not even Bipin, who was pressing against his side. That meant the cop wouldn't be able to see them, either. But surely he would hear something Villis's heart was at this moment thumping so loudly, surely the cop's ears would pick up the beat of it. And what about Bipin's annoying *ujjayii* breaths? He poked Bipin. "Stop breathing," he whispered, as quietly as possible.

"Identify yourself."

The cop! There! On the road. Villis froze. He could feel Bipin beside him, as still as a pool of water.

There was another beam of light now, skinny like a stick, prodding the woods. The cop had a flashlight. Crapola bad luck.

"I know perpetrators are hereabouts. I note that you've ditched your ATV." The cop's voice was brusque. The voice of authority. Villis wished he could run, but it was too dark and he was too old. He felt Bipin's hand settle on his arm, warm, and surprisingly steady. Villis himself was freezing. Or else, why was he shaking?

"Are you hurt?" The voice suddenly softened, but only for an instant, then it was all business again. "If you need hospitalization I will have to call it in." Then soft again, "*Do* you?"

Villis heard steps coming toward them, crick-crunching across the asphalt, then a squashy-rustling sound as the cop scrabbled through the ditch. Pause. What was the cop doing now? Tap-tap-tap. Must be investigating the ATV. The tap-taps stopped, then footsteps again, almost silent now as the cop spidered his way into the soft woods, the stick of his flashlight still prodding, searching. Villis thought he would faint. Or throw up. Or both.

Bipin nudged him, pushing him slightly to the left, so that he was now tucked behind a tree. Villis leaned against it, resting his cheek on the bark. If this was the end, then at least it would happen in the woods. The flashlight beam was closer, closer. Soon it would find his eyes.

But then the light disappeared.

"Shoot," the cop said. Villis could hear the cop whacking the side of the flashlight, then rattling it. Then he heard him say, "Okay. That's all she wrote, kids. Looks like your lucky night. Now scoot on home to your folks. They're probably worried sick. And I hereby inform you that this said vehicle must be removed from these said premises within a period of no more, no less, than twenty-four hundred hours. And don't think this investigation is completed. There will be notes. I will be recommencing tomorrow. It is my stated intention to close this case with a successful conclusion to this episode hereby."

The cop stood for a moment in the light from his car. Villis could make him out clearly. A young fellow. Huge. Looked like a brick in his uniform, though he wasn't wearing his hat. And didn't he have a ponytail? What kind of cop was he? Villis saw the cop shrug and then walk out of the woods, the crick-crunch of his feet on the asphalt mixing with the sound of crickets.

Bipin whispered, "Blessing Number 14,039 – *Deus ex machina* saves the day."

"That was no act of God, just dead flashlight batteries," Villis whispered back, nervously, thinking now was not the time for chit-chat.

Bipin patted his fanny pack. "I should have offered the cop the ones from the asshole's can opener."

"And I should've asked Palaeolithic man to give him a kick in the goolies."

Villis heard the cop cross the road, click open his car door. "Take care, eh," the cop called out, almost as if he wasn't sure such a thing was possible. Then Villis heard the door click shut and the car drive away.

"Let's blow this popsicle stand," Bipin said softly. "Our kinfolks will be worried sick."

CHAPTER 14

Officer Bigcanoe and a Discussion About Philip K. Dick

They decided not to set foot in The Pearl for a week, just in case the cop did return, as he had threatened, to recommence the investigation, as he had put it. But Villis worried – was a week enough time? He mentioned this to Bipin.

Bipin nodded. "Given the short attention span of young people, I think a week is oodles of time."

"I guess." But he wasn't convinced.

"Holy cow! Now that you mention it – can we absolutely be positive that the cop was a young person? Don't forget, they all look like youngsters to us."

Villis considered, then remembered the ponytail. "Definitely young–"

"A babe in the woods?"

"No more than twenty-five. Tops."

"Twenty-five? We're having the luck! The cop is most definitely a member of 'Generation Tweet'. His brain will be geared to 140 words. Hah! I give him two days. Tops. Then he loses interest."

One week later they were back in The Pearl. Bipin had emailed Villis the night before, saying that they should try to look normal, just in case. Villis had agreed, though he wasn't sure what normal was.

It was a blustery day, the wind warm and swelling in waves – as if Mother Earth, Villis thought, was breathing *ujjayii* breaths. He had just passed the Second Bridge and was resting on a boulder, relaxing into the heat of the rock, watching Bipin heading toward him on the trail. Bipin had on his Ray-Bans, as usual, and his fanny pack, but – not as usual – he was wearing the asshole's Blue Jays cap. And instead of his customary water bottle, he had slung a beer bottle from his belt.

"How do you like my new normal look?" Bipin said.

"Good God! Take off that hat."

Bipin patted Villis on the shoulder. "Have you forgotten? The asshole's passed. He no longer needs it. In the immaterial realm, baseball caps are of–"

"It's a clue! Crap, Bipin. It links us to *him*."

"But sportswear is standard gear for normal guys."

Villis grabbed the cap from Bipin's head and shoved it into his own backpack. But then he worried: what if the cop came back, flashed his ID and demanded he dump the contents of his pack?

"Chuck it in the creek," Bipin said.

"Brilliant idea, Einstein."

"I was only trying to be helpful."

"Do you think the cop has a taser?"

"Alternatively, you could hurl it in the ditch."

"They're supposed to hurt like heck."

Bipin held out his hand. "Give it here."

"I heard on the news, they tasered an eleven-year-old kid."

"I'll hide it."

"And they tasered a tourist who was lost in the airport. To death."

"I'll thrust it down my trousers."

Villis wasn't sure. "He might conduct a strip search."

"The cop is gone. Let's go, my friend. Blessing Number 232 – one of my favourites – *All things will pass*."

But barely moments later, and after walking a few hundred yards farther, they came upon the cop, perched on the creek bank at

Frog's Bend, dangling his bare feet in the water, reading.

Villis zipped his lips and motioned Bipin off the path, tugging him behind a honeysuckle bush.

"Can you make out the title of the book?" Bipin whispered.

Villis hissed, "How is that relevant?" Bipin was about to answer, clearly gearing up for one of his long-winded explanations, when Villis cut him off. "Never mind. Let's just get out of here."

"Before he sees us?"

"Exactly."

"Too late."

"Hey! You, behind the bush. Who's there? I mean, stand and identify yourselves."

Bipin stood up, unhitched his beer bottle and pretended to drink. "Just imbibing a brewski, Officer."

The cop leapt to his feet, tossed his book aside and at the same time bent to tug on a sock. "Who else is there?" He gave Bipin the once-over and then nodded at the honeysuckle.

Bipin turned to Villis and gestured. "You've been ousted, my friend. Might as well face the orchestra."

Villis stood up, dropping his backpack and discreetly toeing it behind the honeysuckle. "Nice day, Officer, for a picnic in the woods." He pointed vaguely in the direction of the cop's shoes and book.

"These premises are not for picnics. And drinking outside is illegal."

Bipin looked stunned. "It *is*? What a bizarre directive. I drink outside incessantly."

Villis said, "What he means is he drinks a concoction made from a greens powder. Non-alcoholic. One hundred percent."

The officer strode toward them. "I'll have to confiscate said brewski." He pointed at Bipin's beer.

Bipin held it out happily. "Be my guest. I don't relish beer. It travels directly to my waistline. Have you read about the Wheat Belly? I was–"

"What he means is he *does* like beer, *of course*, or why else would he *have* a beer with him." Villis looked pointedly at Bipin, silently warning him to keep his mouth shut. "It's just that–"

The cop pulled a notepad out of his pocket. "Name?"

"Whose?" Villis and Bipin said together.

The cop flipped a page, checked something, then cocked his head at them. "Last Tuesday, August 7, where were you two gentlemen partaking?"

Villis widened his eyes. They hadn't thought of this, of coming up with an alibi. Dumb *govniuks*! If, over the years, he could have brought himself to watch crime dramas, he might have remembered about the importance of an alibi. He tried but he couldn't think one up on the spot, so he kept quiet, silently praying (though prayers were for the susceptible masses) that Bipin's answer would not arouse the cop's suspicions.

"We were at the casino," Bipin said.

The cop nodded, scratched in his notepad. He seemed satisfied with the answer.

"Which one?"

"Flamborough–"

"–Mohawk," Villis answered at the same time.

Bipin prayed with his palms. "First Flamborough, second Mohawk."

"Why two casinos?"

"We weren't feeling the luck at Flamborough."

The cop nodded. "Yeah. I like Mohawk better myself."

"Is that because you are a First Nations citizen?" Bipin asked.

"Officer Tomas Bigcanoe." The cop waved his ID.

Bipin beamed. "That explains the ponytail."

Officer Bigcanoe pulled his shoulders back. "It's our tradition."

Bipin beamed more broadly. "Of course, everybody knows that. Would you like to know my traditions?"

Officer Bigcanoe chewed his lip. "Name?"

"Bipin."

"Bipin?"

"Bipin Patel. I'm Indian too."

Villis blurted, "He means, India Indian, not your kind ... not, ah ..."

"First Nations."

"Right. First Nations. I know something about that. Them, I mean.

I'm an anthropologist. Was. Was one. I mean, I'm too old now. I mean ..."

"Name?"

"Villis."

"Villis?" The officer looked skeptical. "Really?"

"Villis Krastins. It's Latvian."

"Where's that?"

Villis was about to explain when Officer Bigcanoe interrupted. "Ir-revelant. Stick to the business at hand."

"What might that be, Officer Bigcanoe? Something to do with last Tuesday, when we were categorically nowhere near these vicinities, absolutely no way we were in these woods, which we hardly ever come to, in fact, what a blast! Now that I think of it, today is the very first time we have ever perambulated in here, or anywhere near here or–"

"What he means, Officer, is – what happened last Tuesday?"

"An ATV was apprehended in a ditch."

"What's an ATV?" Bipin said this with such an exaggerated tone of innocence that Villis was certain Officer Bigcanoe would smell a skunk.

"Really?"

"What he means, Officer, is–"

"Can't he answer for his self?"

"What I mean, Officer, is ... Holy cow, I don't know *what* I mean. I'm a geezer. We forget things. In fact, what did I just say?"

"Cows are sort of like sacred in India, right? I don't get that." Officer Bigcanoe looked interested.

Bipin bowed his head. "It's our tradition."

"Is the ATV still in the ditch?" Villis asked, trying to sound innocent, though not in Bipin's exaggerated way.

"Said vehicle was compounded Wednesday morning at ..." Bigcanoe checked his notes, "Oh-ten hundred hours."

"Well then," Villis said.

"Well then what?" Officer Bigcanoe shot Villis a suspicious look.

"Well then, we'll be off."

"Did either of you two see this ATV? Ever seen the driver?"

"Was the driver a girl or a boy?" Bipin asked.

Officer Bigcanoe looked confused.

"We never saw *any* drivers," Villis said. "Girl ones or boy ones. And we never saw any ATVs. Isn't that right, Bipin?"

Bipin nodded. "What is the title of the book you were reading?"

Bigcanoe flushed. "I wasn't reading."

"Well then–"

"There are tracks all over these woods," Bigcanoe said. "From the ATV. I've been all through here. Seen them for myself."

"It's our first time here, remember," Bipin said. "Today."

Villis nudged him in the arm. Then he made a cuckoo sign at Officer Bigcanoe to let him know Bipin wasn't all there.

Bigcanoe gave Villis a sympathetic look. "My granddad used to be like that. Old-timers Disease."

"Like what?" Bipin asked.

Bigcanoe cleared his throat. "I stopped commuters on the road this week, pulling folks over, asking anybody if they saw this ATV, or the driver, or anything else of a suspicious nature. Nobody saw nothing. Except ..." Bigcanoe paused as if he was waiting to deliver a punchline, "except for this." He read again from his notes. "Sixteen drivers reported seeing, on more than one occasion, a very old man picking up garbage from alongside the ditch." Bigcanoe looked questioningly at Villis, then Bipin. "And further to that, it says here, some reported the same said old man behaving in inappropriate ways, for example, flipping the bird at passing drivers for no apparent reason."

"Ho ho," Bipin laughed. "That would be Villis."

Villis nudged Bipin again.

"So, what is the title of the book you were reading?" Villis asked.

Bigcanoe threw up his hands. "*Do Androids Dream of Electric Sheep?*"

"Yes," Bipin said. "They absolutely do."

"That's Dick," Villis said.

Officer Bigcanoe grinned. "You read Dick?"

"Love him."

"Dick is the best. I was just at the part when Rick Deckard is wishing he owned a real animal instead of a fake electric sheep.

Electric animals are mostly all anyone has for pets since mostly all the real animals are gone. Anyways, Deckard is remembering how, when he was a kid, the animal obits reported every day how a new species was going extinct, foxes one morning, badgers the next, and then, how in Canada there was still some forests left, and every now and then someone would find a small animal here, and that would be breaking news all over the world. And since I was sitting here, reading those exact words, in a forest in Canada, I was thinking – how cool is that?"

"Cool indeed," Villis said.

Bigcanoe flushed again. Then he suddenly about-faced, found his socks and wriggled them on. "Now what about this garbage-picking business?" His voice was stern again.

"Ir-revelant," Bipin said.

Bigcanoe looked thoughtful. "Then what about the ATV driver?"

"I wonder where he is?" Villis asked, thinking this was a question an innocent man would ask.

"There are no indications whatsoever of the whereabouts of the driver, of any, or either, unknown gender, of said compounded ATV."

"Then you don't know where the driver is?" Villis said. "Or who?"

Bigcanoe nodded. "No one has filed a missing persons report. No one has come forward to claim the ATV."

"Maybe he ran off to avoid his responsibilities," Bipin said.

"Could be," Bigcanoe agreed. "I was thinking the guy might have been pissed. I mean, inebriated. Didn't want me to charge him with impaired."

"That too."

"There could've been two of them. Kids, I was thinking. I heard some kind of whispering that night."

"Surely not whispering," Villis said.

"Most likely the rustlings of furtive night creatures," Bipin added.

"This is the woods in Canada, after all." Villis forced himself to chuckle.

Bigcanoe put his notebook back in his pocket. "It was yellow. The ATV. You sure you never seen it?"

Both Villis and Bipin shook their heads.

"I guess," Bigcanoe said, "since no persons have been reported missing. And no one has brought forth a claim for said ATV, I guess it's fair to say–"

"No crime has been committed."

Bigcanoe nodded. "You guys can get back to your ... whatever."

"And you can get back to your Dick," Bipin said.

CHAPTER 15

Celebrity Impersonators and the Time Portal

"That was a close call," Villis said, after they had put distance between themselves and Bigcanoe. "But you heard what the cop said? No missing persons report. In a week! No one has noticed the asshole missing. What does that suggest to you?"

"No loved ones?"

Villis nodded. This was good news. And it made sense. Fact: some people are so obnoxious no one loves them. Sad, he realized, but then, the asshole's lack of significant others wasn't his problem.

"I didn't know you were a sci-fi buff," Bipin said.

"I'm not."

"Are you implying that you pulled that one out of your donkey?"

Villis nodded. "What should we do now?"

"Would you consider Palaeolithic man an alien?"

"He's not real," Villis said, though even as he did, he felt as if he were betraying a friend. "Certainly not in the conventional sense."

"Maybe Palaeolithic man saw an alien – in the murky reaches of the inconceivable past."

"What are you going on about? Aliens?"

"I was just musing – maybe Bigcanoe, since he is a sci-fi buff, would appreciate my hypothesis about alien beings engaging in carnal relations with cave peoples, such as your Palaeolithic man, and thereby fast-forwarding the evolutionary process."

"Bigcanoe won't be back. At least, I hope not."

"Peace and quiet, once again interweaving with the breezes throughout our exquisite Pearl. Now that the worm is turning for the better, perhaps we will win the *So You Think You Can Think* competition."

"I'd forgotten about that. I'd still like to go to Easter Island."

"Before you bite the big one?"

Villis snorted.

"At least, if you do die–"

"–not *if*. When."

"*When* you do die, you can continue trotting through The Pearl alongside Palaeolithic man and Frog."

Villis rubbed his face. The skin crinkled over his cheeks like crumpled paper. What had happened to the stuff that used to be beneath his skin, the pliable, podgy substance that sprang back into position? Now when he poked his skin, it creased into wrinkles that stayed put, like a linen shirt hot from the dryer. He was losing layers. Soon, skin and skull would be all that was left.

"I hope I look young after I'm dead." He was thinking of how well Frog had looked, balancing on Palaeolithic man's shoulder. Frog had looked distinctly youthful – his green colouring more vivid, his waistline trim.

Bipin clapped him on the shoulder. "Collagen, my friend. That is what has gone AWOL. But never to fret. Everyone is more eye-catching after they're dead. That's one of the perks."

They decided to hike up to the Resonating Nexus and visit the moai. Though Villis didn't say, "Let's check the grave," *that* was his main reason for wanting to go. Coyotes may have sniffed out the asshole's earthly remains. And it had been a week since the you-know-what incident. Thank God that idiot cop, Tomas what's-his-name, hadn't found the moai during all his snooping around The Pearl.

They walked silently, Bipin first, then Villis; single-file-Indian-style, as Bipin had put it. Villis had given up explaining to Bipin that the expression "Indian-style" was what people nowadays called "politically incorrect". Bipin always waved Villis off with, "Am I not an Indian?"

It was a relief to stop scanning for Captain Early's signs and to know that they would discover no new damage from the ATV. For the first time all summer, Villis felt as if The Pearl was itself again, and familiar warm fingers of peace were unpicking the knots in his shoulders.

Then Bipin suddenly blurted, "Bloody H. E. double hockey sticks."

Villis, who was bending to appreciate a cluster of slender white morels, glanced up. "Bloody hell what?"

Bipin nodded. Some distance down the path there was a clump of young men. How many? Villis squinted. He couldn't count them. They were circling, it seemed, like pagans, but not quite. One? Two? For certain, three. And was that chanting?

"Who are they?" Villis whispered.

One of the group turned toward them and shouted a warning. The others stopped circling, stopped chanting. Not three, after all. Four. And there was something decidedly odd about them. It was how they were dressed, each one differently, but in some form of white garb. Like the morels, Villis thought. One, with shoulder-length hair, was wearing a white tunic tied at the waist; the second was bare-chested with a white cloth like a cumbersome diaper between his legs; the third had round wire-rimmed glasses and was wearing a white Nehru shirt; and the last one – how on earth could this be? – had a blue-black slick of hair and a white jumpsuit with what looked like sparkles.

"Elvis!" Bipin said.

"The asshole!" Come back to life? Or was this a vision, like Frog and Palaeolithic man? Villis glanced at Bipin. Whatever it was, Bipin was seeing it too. Maybe they were both dead.

"Instant karma!" Bipin said, stepping toward the group. Then he laughed. "No no no. I curse my baroque imagination. It *is* Elvis, but not *our* Elvis."

"Shhhh!" Villis said. "Never mention you-know-who."

Bipin clamped his hand over his mouth. "Oops." Then he

whispered, "But it is, most emphatically, a second Elvis."

The group of four walked toward them. None smiled.

"Brace yourself," Villis said.

"*I believe it to my soul*," Bipin started to sing.

Second Elvis snapped his fingers. "*You're the devil in nylon hose ...*"

"*'Cause the harder I work*," Bipin continued.

"*The faster my money goes–*"

"For crying out loud!" Villis shouted this so loudly he surprised himself.

Second Elvis stopped singing, then said, sadly, "You ain't no friend of mine."

Bipin folded his hands at heart centre. "*Namaste.*"

The young man wearing the diaper returned the gesture. "The good man is a friend of all living things."

Then the young man in the white tunic and long hair raised a hand and blessed them. "Do unto others as you would have them do unto you."

Villis stared at the fourth young man – the one in the Nehru shirt, like a hippie without colours – and waited for him to speak.

"All we are saying is give peace a chance," Number Four said.

"Oh brother." Villis stopped himself – only just – from rolling his eyes.

"I am the walrus, Brother," Number Four added, peering seriously through his round glasses.

"Holy cow!" Bipin said, pointing from the first young man to the fourth. "Elvis. Gandhi. Jesus. John Lennon!" Then he flung his arms around Gandhi. "Oh, dearest Bapu, I have missed you so."

Gandhi disentangled himself from Bipin's embrace. "Dude! I'm not really Bapu, like."

Bipin stepped back. "Absolutely, I figured that out. But I thought we were playing 'Let's Pretend.'"

"We're celebrity impersonators," Jesus said, running his fingers through his long hair. "We met on Facebook."

"We formed a Friend group," Elvis added. "We call it 'Like Likes Like'. Get it?"

Villis frowned.

"Everything is clearer when you're six foot in the ground," John Lennon said mysteriously.

Villis drew in a quick breath. "Young Man, just what do you mean by that remark?"

John Lennon took off his glasses and started polishing them on the sleeve of his Nehru shirt. "Shit, I don't know, man. I only memorize the quotes. Lennon, man, he was *always* on something. He said, like, crazy shit."

"Like Likes Like! I get it!" Bipin beamed, turning to Villis to explain. "It's my Flock-together Principle, or surely some manifestation of it."

"What's that about flocks?" Jesus said.

Villis interrupted before Bipin could explain. "You four are not supposed to be here."

The impersonators looked at him with varying expressions of disbelief and pity.

Gandhi puffed out his bare chest. "A small body of determined spirits fired by an unquenchable faith in their mission can alter the course of history."

Bipin clapped. "Why, I was *there* when Bapu uttered those glorious words!"

"What?" Gandhi said. "How could that be? I'm dead, aren't I?" Gandhi glanced at Jesus for confirmation. Jesus made a 'how-should-I-know?' face.

Bipin was about to continue, when Villis interrupted again. "You four are not supposed to be here."

"Wroooong, Dude," Gandhi said. "We got an invite." He waved his hand at Elvis. Elvis withdrew a card from inside his jumpsuit and handed it to Villis.

Villis read the card, blowing out his cheeks, thinking, Damn! It was from the asshole. He recognized the handwriting. And the lousy spelling.

You are cordilly invited to attend the premeer demonstration of the Sacred Super-charged Cosmic Time Portal under the Easter Island Monolift. Be there! Or be square.

Elvis 1.

Villis handed the card to Bipin. Bipin read it, his eyebrows shooting up like flags.

"Elvis 1?" Villis blurted this out without thinking and then immediately wished he hadn't. Surely, in this situation, Captain Early would advise playing one's cards close to one's chest.

The other three impersonators looked to the second Elvis to explain. He struck an Elvis pose – lip curl and a pelvic thrust.

"Thank you, thank you verrry much. I'm Elvis 2. Elvis 1 was the one that started the group on Facebook, but I was all shook up to be Elvis, on account of this." He flicked his hair. "So everyone said I could be Elvis too, get it? Elvis 2. And Elvis 1 could be Elvis 1."

Jesus, John Lennon and Gandhi nodded. John Lennon tugged the collar on his Nehru shirt. "A dream you dream alone is only a dream. A dream you dream together is reality."

The others linked arms, suddenly serious.

"Hey, Babe," Elvis 2 said. "I think it was Yoko who said that."

Jesus made the sign of the cross.

"Dude! No cross thing – Jesus wouldn't do that," Gandhi said, hitching his diaper. "We agreed, like."

"Yeah, that's just sick," Elvis 2 added.

Bipin handed the card back to Elvis 2 and said, matter-of-factly, "You don't need a time portal for time travel."

Villis flashed Bipin a look. "What he means is there are no Easter Island monoliths anyway near here."

"Righto," Bipin said. "You'll have to go to Easter Island."

"Dude, how far is that?" Gandhi asked.

Jesus looked fit to be tied. "*Fuck* Elvis 1! I knew we shouldn't trust him."

Villis tried to sound magnanimous. "Too bad, fellows. There's a Judas in every group."

"Jesus was all right, but his disciples were thick and ordinary," John Lennon said. "Still, I believe in Elvis 1. I think it's these two old codgers who are having us on."

"They ain't nothin' but hound dogs."

Gandhi sighed. "I do not like your Christians. They are so unlike your Christ."

The impersonators turned and scrutinized Villis and Bipin.

Bipin held up one hand. "I'm not a Christian."

Villis said, again, as clearly and emphatically as possible, "There is no time portal. No Easter Island moai–"

"Moai?" Gandhi said.

"I misspoke myself."

"Cool beans," Jesus said, slapping Villis on the shoulder. "You are one badass old guy."

John Lennon put an arm around Bipin and pulled him in like a brother. "Now, what's that you said about not needing a time portal? Sounds to me like you know something about time travel."

Bipin slipped away from John Lennon and folded to the ground, Lotus position, moving as effortlessly as beach sand through fingers. He closed his eyes, rested hands on knees, palms up, breathing deeply, and then, or so it always seemed to Villis, he disappeared inside himself. Bipin had been meditating since he was twelve years old. He had tried to teach Villis, and Villis had earnestly wanted to learn. He envied Bipin his inner life. But whenever Villis had tried to meditate, he had either run into his anxieties marching like fascists across his imagination, or else he had started to snore. Nonetheless, Villis was proud of his old friend – there probably wasn't a better meditator anywhere on earth.

The impersonators were quiet. Thank God, Villis thought. It would give him time to figure out a strategy: how to force these fools from The Pearl; how to keep these morons from finding the moai. And the asshole! Crapola – even gone, *still*, he was causing trouble. Villis wondered again about John Lennon's instant karma concept. Darkly, ironically, sarcastically, he thought – here was his chance to ask John Lennon about it directly. Serves me right, Villis thought. It was his hands that had placed the ramp. His thoughts that had tumbled the asshole – correction, Elvis 1 – into a dark abyss.

A minute passed. Given the situation, it felt longer. Bipin was barely breathing, was unblinking, his face so relaxed he looked like a boy. The impersonators remained quiet. It seemed, in fact, that they were behaving respectfully. In fact, Villis thought, you might have said the impersonators were impressed. They were obviously falling under Bipin's spell. He and Bipin would never be rid of them now.

Villis clapped, but, of course, even as he did so, he knew this would not rouse Bipin. Bipin could meditate through a hurricane. A nuclear bomb blast. Through the dripping of a tap.

"Dude," Gandhi said, "what happens if you poke him?"

Villis sighed. "Go ahead."

"No way I'm touching him," Gandhi said.

"I'll do it." Jesus stepped toward Bipin, placed a hand on his head. "Bless you, my son, for you have sinned."

Bipin flicked open his eyes. "Hallelujah! I'm saved!" Then he closed his eyes again.

Jesus jerked back his hand. "Shit!"

"He's kidding," Villis said.

"Fu-ck!" Jesus whistled. "For a minute I thought I had powers!"

Elvis high-fived Jesus. "Way to go, Bro."

"Part of me suspects I'm a loser, and the other part of me thinks I'm God Almighty."

"Good quote, John," Gandhi said. "I haven't heard you do that one before."

John Lennon smiled benevolently. "Well, right you are."

Villis thought he would explode. "Bipin! Enough!"

Bipin opened his eyes. "Hey, kids! Who wants to know where I went?"

"How could he have gone somewhere?" Gandhi said, looking at the others. "Did I miss something?"

"Where did you go, sir?" Elvis 2 asked politely.

"I journeyed to Easter Island, back in time to when they were constructing the monoliths."

"Cool beans," Jesus said. "Aliens moved them, you know. That's how they did it. Did you see any? Like, aliens?"

"Aliens did *not* move them," Villis said. "They were rolled on felled timbers by large groups of men who cut down every last tree on the island. Erosion! Massive loss of soil! Pissing in their own pool–"

"Hold it there, Dude. How do *you* know? Were *you* there?" Gandhi said, looking skeptical.

The impersonators all looked toward Bipin.

"Well, sir," Elvis 2 finally said, "*you* were just there. Was it aliens? Or timbers?"

Bipin blinked. "Aliens."

"Beauty!" Gandhi said. "Teach us how to do that. Time Travel 101."

"Yeah." The impersonators flocked around Bipin.

"It takes a long time to become proficient enough for time-travelling," Bipin said.

"Proficient?" Gandhi asked.

"How long?" John Lennon added.

Bipin appeared to calculate. "Twenty years, give or take."

Jesus slumped. "I say we look for the time portal."

"Check it out," Gandhi agreed. "Action expresses priorities."

"Yes is the answer," John Lennon said.

"I say we go this way." Elvis 2 pointed. "Too bad Elvis 1 didn't give us a map."

"I have a GPS," Jesus said hopefully.

"The dude was supposed to meet us," Gandhi said. "I wonder, like, what happened to him?"

They all four nodded sombrely.

"Perhaps," Bipin said, "he has disappeared into the time portal."

CHAPTER 16

Atonement

Villis waited until the white of the impersonators dwindled into the green of the trees before turning to Bipin. "For crying out loud! Why did you tell them you saw aliens?"

"Actually, I didn't even go to Easter Island. That part I conjured for the sake of convenience. It takes at least ninety minutes of meditation before one can time-travel."

"Young people today know nothing about history. And now, thanks to you, 'Generation Tweet' are secure in their continued ignorance."

"I was striving for your much-vaunted principle of political correction. Don't politicians support dim-witted misconceptions in order to woo the public?"

"Why would you want to woo those idiots? At least they've gone."

"For now."

"For good. But we'd better not chance going up to the Nexus. They might follow us, secretly. Discover the moai."

"And topple it in an attempt to access the time portal."

"What a moron that Elvis 1 was, inviting those lunatics into The Pearl."

"Do you think we should consider them as his next of kin? What if we tipped them off as to the asshole's fate without revealing our culpability?"

"And exactly how do you propose we do that?"

"Anonymous phone call?"

"Traceable."

"Anonymous email?"

"Ditto."

"Anonymous letter posted from another country, written using cut-out letters from a newspaper glued to the page forming the words and sentences?"

Villis frowned. This idea was so dumb it didn't merit a response.

Bipin sighed. "It's so difficult to be clandestine in these modern times." He sighed again. "And this conversation is doing nothing to relieve the grip of guilt that has been grasping my groins ever since our terrible lapse in judgment."

"Maybe we can put notes in our last-will-and-testaments that explain everything that happened with the ramp and the accident. Then the truth can come out *after* we're dead."

Bipin brightened. "And surely that will not be so long from now, given our acute old ages."

Villis turned in the direction of the Nexus. It was still a good thirty-minute walk to there. The impersonators were obviously city kids, play-acting in the woods. Not a chance they were bush savvy. No drive-through fast food joints here, kiddos, or wireless access; no texting for directions, or tweeting random sentences. Those kids wouldn't last thirty minutes in The Pearl.

But to be on the safe side, and because he couldn't shake images of scrawny coyotes rooting for the asshole's remains, Villis suggested they rendezvous after sunset at the Second Bridge and trek to the Nexus protected by the night.

"A first-rate proposition!" Bipin said. "That will give me a chance to test-run my spanking-new motion-powered flashlight. It's slogan is, *Shake, rattle and glow!*"

As it happened, while waiting for Bipin that evening at the Second Bridge, Villis fixed on the full moon above the creek, which seemed to him a meticulous cut-out streaming silver through the midnight.

He thought of Palaeolithic man. Why on earth, he wondered, was he *always* thinking of him? It was as if Palaeolithic man was becoming real by virtue of this fact – that he was always thinking about him. What would Palaeolithic man have made of the moon? He would not have known that it mirrored the scattered golden gleamings of the sun. He would not have imagined it as a place men might rocket to someday. But surely he would have felt it gorgeous.

Fact: Palaeolithic man would have seen the moon he himself now saw. Theory: Palaeolithic man might have stood at this very spot where he himself was now standing – without the bridge, of course; and in those antediluvian days the creek would doubtless have been a robust waterway wriggling with fish; and the scores of flora and fauna that would have overflowed the planet then had long since suffered extinction. But nevertheless, Palaeolithic man might have stood at this very same spot and gazed upwards at this very same silver hole cut out of the sky. He would have been, at times, grateful to the moon; at times, fearful of its perplexing power. He would have felt at one with it, as he felt at one with animals, with the rain that smeared the skies, and with the over-brimming Earth itself. At one. Atone.

"I'm sorry," Villis said out loud. Sorry for everything. Especially the asshole. He shaped a telescope lens with his thumb and forefinger and stared through it at the moon – so much time had unravelled since Palaeolithic man had looked upon it. A spiralling, trackless snake of time from then to this minute. How much time did mankind have left? Not much, Villis thought sadly. We've pissed in our own pool. The green Earth, the blue oceans, the white of the ice caps, all the colours that one could view from the moon were waning.

Maybe he should pray to the moon for aliens to visit? Maybe they could teach men how to live at one upon the Earth. *Govniuk* idea. Believing in aliens was worse than believing in gods. His thinking! Gone cuckoo! *Durak* – what was happening to the straight lines in his head? All those steadfast grids of reasoning; what goes up must come down; cause and effect; one plus one; I think, therefore I am – wobbling now, widening, the spaces between filling in with wonky wonderings. Why why *why* was everything so confusing? Bipin often said that suffering in humans was caused by fear, pain and confusion. Fear and pain, Villis got those. But up until recently, he would not have added confusion to Bipin's list.

I am an acutely old man, he thought. With a lot of crapola under the bridge. Too much. And though he was ashamed to acknowledge this about himself, he simply never had the courage for the truth when the truth came bearing suffering in its arms like a newborn, wailing. He hoped that Bipin could forgive him this, his worst weakness. Then he realized, not without some relief, that things would be better for Bipin when he was out of the picture. What was one less old dog, dead and gone, more or less? At least then Bipin would be free to tell the truth. Free to honour Gandhiji's high principles.

He had on his LED headlamp. He switched it off. Palaeolithic man would have managed in the woods at night without it. Then he switched it back on. How else could Bipin find him?

He began distracting himself, pivoting the lamp, knocking beams of brightness about the woods; against the undulating bark of a maple, making it glimmer silver; against a rock, polishing it with light; across tufts of grasses gracing the creekside, casting feathery shadows upon the water, until he heard a rattling heading his way.

Bipin. Shaking his flashlight.

"Will you have to do that the whole time?" Villis asked, hoping the answer was no.

Bipin stopped rattling. "Only when I super-duper-charge it. After that, it's good for ten minutes of unremitting illumination."

Unremitting illumination. That was exactly what he needed, Villis thought, to clear up his confusion. He did a mental calculation. The Nexus was a half-hour walk away. That meant three rounds of Bipin super-charging, give or take. He sighed. "One more shake, then let's go."

Bipin went first, though Villis protested. A bad idea. Bipin was barefoot. He might slash his soles on unexpected hazards. Shit happens – Villis quoted the slogan from the 1970s – and weren't these last few weeks in The Pearl ample evidence of that?

But Bipin insisted on going first in order to fully prove his new flashlight. "My light will ease through this darkness like a smile through uncertainty," he said. "Or else it will extend only a few feet before feebly collapsing into nothingness."

"That's how I feel," Villis said, meaning the part about feebly collapsing.

Bipin turned and washed the flashlight light across Villis's chest. "My friend, this is your last year of confusion." Then he turned away and continued along the trail.

Last year? Villis wondered – did Bipin mean he would die soon? Had Bipin had a premonition of his death in the same way he had received advance notice of the death of Gandhi? Was this Bipin's cockeyed way of preparing him? Villis felt a squeeze in his chest at the exact spot washed by the flashlight beam. Oh God. Premonitions were not possible. (*Time isn't.*) Who could know something before it happened? (*Time isn't.*)

Then Bipin turned again. Beamed the light again. "Google it."

They walked silently, listening; to crickets chirping in waves rising up; and from high in the trees, to the falling *whoo* of owls; then here and there, to other night birds cooing – doves? – and to harrumphing bullfrogs in the boggy patches that smelled of mushrooms and mosses; and from between trees, knee-level, to the skritchy-scratching comings and goings of creatures that lived the night and slept the day.

And then they heard something unexpected. A voice. Familiar, but barely.

"Wait up. I mean, halt! Or freeze, you know."

"Tomas Bigcanoe," Bipin whispered. Then louder, cheerfully, as if he were pleased, waving his flashlight in a merry way, Bipin said, "Good evening, Officer."

Tomas Bigcanoe's voice, closing in on them through the shadows (though still no view of the officer himself), sounded relieved. "Hey, it's you two again."

Tomas Bigcanoe flicked on his flashlight and crossed the beam of it with Bipin's light, like crossing light-sabres, Villis thought.

"I ascertained lights in the woods. I was on patrol. Well, okay, not patrol, but doing a stakeout on the road. In my cruiser."

"What were you staking for, Tomas?" Bipin asked.

"Uh."

"Nefarious characters?"

Tomas Bigcanoe studied his fingernails. "I was, um, not doing anything, right – just around this neck of the woods – it's cool here. And then, like I said, I ascertained your lights in the woods. Thought it might be something to do with the as-yet-still-unresolved criminal investigation pertaining to the crashed yellow ATV. You guys don't know any more about that, do you?"

Villis and Bipin shook their heads.

"Criminal?" Villis said.

Bigcanoe looked reconciled. "Ah, I guess not. No, not really criminal. Still no *haveous corpseus*."

"*Habeas corpus*," Villis corrected. "Latin."

"Really?" Bigcanoe looked baffled. "I always thought it was, like, we-have-us-no-corpses-yet." Bigcanoe narrowed his eyes, sighed.

"It's tough being an officer of the law," Bipin said.

"You don't know the fuck of it. Beg your pardon, I meant–"

"I'd rather be the cop than the poor sap the cop nabs," Villis interrupted.

"Me too, Brother, me too," Bigcanoe said. "Ah–" Bigcanoe held his flashlight above Villis's head so that a funnel of light shone done on him. "So? What are you two old uncles up to in the bush at this time of night?"

"Sky-gazing," Bipin said.

"Taking in the air," Villis added.

Bigcanoe squinted at the sky. "Any UFOs?" Then he added quickly, "But no one believes in those, right?"

"People are always getting gods and UFOs confused," Bipin said, sounding mildly irritated. "Not believing in, or believing in – it doesn't change anything."

Bigcanoe frowned. Aimed his light down. Pointed at Bipin's feet. "No shoes. What about cuts, sticks? Bugs?"

Bipin raised his left leg sideways, like a tree branch, angling the bottom of his lifted foot level with Bigcanoe's shoulders, so that the officer had a view of his sole. "Good as gold. You should remove those boots of yours. Walking in the woods wearing footgear is like making love to Mother Earth while wearing your underpants."

Bigcanoe laughed. "You sound like an Indian. We're all over the Earth Mother."

Bipin flicked a pine needle off his sole then lowered his leg. "I *am* an Indian."

Bigcanoe clapped him on the back. "Mind if I come along with you guys, on your, you know, walk?"

"It's lonely being a cop–" Bipin said.

"Yes," Villis cut in, meaning yes he minded if Bigcanoe came along.

But Bigcanoe misunderstood and aimed his flashlight down the trail. "You don't know the half of it ... This way?"

Villis lagged behind, keeping an eye on the heels of Bipin and Bigcanoe (who had kept his black boots on); one pair of heels silver in the light of his flashlight, the other pair gleaming like dark eyes. They were chatting as if they were long-time school chums, their chatter drowning out the crickets. Villis supposed if he were forced to take a lie-detector test he would have to admit that he was jealous – *he* was the only person Bipin talked to that way.

And where was Bipin taking them? *Not to the Nexus, not to the Nexus* – Villis sent this thought along the beam of his flashlight to permeate Bipin's silver heels, hoping it would travel up Bipin's legs to his brain. Which begged the question, what exactly had that crazy old Indian *done* with his brain, letting his guard down like that with a cop? A cop! A cop who would ask snoopy questions about the ass-hole. Now, if Villis were forced to take a shot of sodium pentothal he would blurt that this particular cop was not much of a sleuth, but still, Villis couldn't contain his suspicions. What had Bigcanoe been doing in that cruiser of his? Stakeout? Likely story. Villis would swear this under oath – in his opinion, Officer Bigcanoe had been snoozing in his cruiser.

Thankfully, Bigcanoe was a dope. But a dope, nonetheless, being led up there smack dab to damning evidence. Better catch up, Villis decided, and redirect their chummy midnight stroll to anywhere but the Resonating Nexus. Maybe Bigcanoe would appreciate a snack of power bars on the First/Third Bridge?

Villis trotted until he came alongside them, just in time to hear Bipin ask Bigcanoe why he had become a police officer.

Bigcanoe stopped walking when he realized Villis had joined them and directed his answer to both of them. "I, like, wanted to help people that got hurt. You know, by others. Innocent victims, right?"

"You seek justice," Bipin said.

Bigcanoe laughed, but he didn't sound amused, more as if he sensed something ironic about the statement. Villis thought, How could that be? Irony required a certain fineness of intellect.

"Justice. Yeah, I guess. Justice."

"Did you find it?" Villis asked, not kindly, not that he cared, but because he was certain what the answer would be. Justice, phooey.

Bigcanoe shook his head. "Mostly what I found was power."

"The abuse of," Villis said quickly.

Bigcanoe sighed. "Not all the time. And mostly in little ways. But yeah, guys in uniforms getting kicks from controlling people, seeing the looks on their faces, pushing them around."

Bipin patted Bigcanoe on the shoulder. "But you have always exercised compassion."

"You mean kindness?"

"Not a concept they teach you in police academy," Villis said.

"Shh," Bipin said. "He's just a boy."

"I try. Yeah, I really do. Thanks for noticing. But, well–"

"We don't know the half of it?" Villis chided.

"You're what my granddad used to call a seven-day stew," Bigcanoe said to Villis. "What did cops ever do to you?"

"You don't know the half of it," Villis said.

"Shh," Bipin said again.

"But, yeah, I'm thinking of quitting. The force, I mean. I don't think I'm cut out–"

"Because you don't like the taste of that type of power," Bipin said.

Bigcanoe nodded. "I've had to take some unsavoury actions. You know, the demands of the situation and all. But, um, stuff that was not cool."

"Illegal?" Villis said.

"Doesn't matter. Legal, illegal, things I didn't have no choice about."

"Confess it to the moon." Bipin waved his hand at the sky. "Release it with an out-breath, which is the only way to divest oneself of toxins."

"Really?"

"Go for it," Bipin said.

"Waste of time," Villis said at the same time.

Bigcanoe took a breath then rushed his words. "I did a strip search. I mean, more like, I assisted in a strip search. A whole bunch of them. Wrong, though. Very, I guess ... sick."

"Strip search?" Villis said, feeling his stomach pitch. What had invaded The Pearl now? Something worse than wheels, worse than white-robed lunatics – the GULAG was strolling beside him, black boots, high-and-mighty.

"Women," Bigcanoe whispered. "They didn't do nothing wrong. At the G20 Summit in Toronto that summer. You watched it on TV, right, the riots and stuff?"

Villis nodded. He and Bipin had together witnessed what had happened in the ordinary streets of Toronto back then, from the chesterfield in Bipin's home theatre. They had watched on Bipin's plasma television as democracy had been swatted (like a butterfly) to the pavement and pinned beneath boots. Blocks of black-clad policemen, their faces obscured beneath visors that Villis thought made them look like robots, had thrummed their shields with clubs, just as he imagined medieval thugs might have, a dreadful beat-beat-beat, drumming backwards confused citizens wearing blue jeans and T-shirts bright beneath the July sun (who were there – Villis could tell by their signs and their faces – because they cared about things: poverty, climate change, human rights); citizens faltering backwards, protesting – *Hey! These are our streets, too!* Villis had watched as the black block of policemen had wailed down on the citizens as if they were dangerous and not citizens in T-shirts who cared about things: kindness to animals, green energy, global fairness. Had it come to this? That's what Villis had thought as he watched the black wail over the colours. Had it come to this, *here*, in this Canada to which he had run believing that he would be safe from official thugs? Had it come to this – citizens were now considered dangerous?

Villis put out his hand. "I need a breather."

Bigcanoe offered his arm. "I get it."

"Do you?" Villis said, regretting that his words came out feebly, wishing instead that he could have shot them at Bigcanoe's black boots as if they were bullets, as if *he* had power and was not merely an old man suffering with the past.

"Tomas," Bipin said, kindly, as if he were blowing bubbles. "Take off your footgear. Refresh your toes in the cool moss of the path."

Bigcanoe hesitated, and then, balancing on one foot, then the other, yanked off his boots and socks.

"Is that how they did it at your strip search?" Villis said. "The women? Did you make them take off their shoes and socks first? Did you bend them over? Did you conduct a cavity search?"

Bigcanoe's shoulders drooped. "Procedure. It was procedure." He hung his head, mumbled, "I'm trying to forget."

"Good luck with that, Kiddo," Villis said. Then he felt ashamed. Was this a leftover from that cold night when the man with the pencil behind his ear had humiliated them? Or was this some new shame, one begun here in The Pearl, now, as he himself had only just humiliated Bigcanoe?

"I didn't have no choice," Bigcanoe whispered.

Villis couldn't stop himself (where was his compassion?). He didn't care. It had to be said. "You *did*. You *always* do."

Bigcanoe looked at him. He wasn't crying, but he could have been. It was dark in the woods, and tears needed light to be seen. But nonetheless, it seemed to Villis that the officer was struggling.

Bipin picked up Bigcanoe's boots and socks and handed them to him. "'Soldiers, don't give yourselves to brutes; men who despise you, enslave you, who regiment your lives, tell you what to do, what to think, what to feel.'"

"Gandhi?" Villis asked.

"Jesus?" said Bigcanoe.

Bipin waggled a finger. "Charlie Chaplin."

Bigcanoe tied together the laces of his boots and slung them over his shoulder. "Never heard of the dude. But I guess what he says, the part about giving yourself to brutes, like – that's pretty much what I did. I'm sorry. Yeah. I'm really fucking sorry."

Villis passed his light across Bigcanoe's face. Not enough to blind him, but enough to see if he was kidding. He looked into the officer's eyes and saw there only the pain of truth. He switched his LED light off. "How about we turn off all the flashlights," Villis said, "and make it dark enough to see UFOs."

"You don't believe in UFOs," Bipin said, switching off his shaker flashlight.

Villis looked at Bigcanoe, who was still slumping. "Believing or not believing doesn't change anything," he said softly.

Bigcanoe turned off his flashlight. The woods were dark again, save for the slight silver wash of the moon. Villis breathed a deep *ujjayii* breath, letting himself drift in the darkness as if he were Frog riding the current of the creek.

Palaeolithic man, he thought, what did you see on a night like this in the dark sky? Justice? Compassion? Aliens? Gods? He turned to Bigcanoe. The officer's features had blurred into the night, but Villis could tell from the slope of his shoulders that he was struggling less.

"Thanks," Bigcanoe said to Villis.

"You don't know the half of it," Bipin and Villis said together.

Bigcanoe may have smiled (Villis couldn't be sure), then he turned and started along the trail, picking his way tentatively (Villis was certain of this) like a man drawing the earth in through the soles of his feet for the very first time.

CHAPTER 17

Stupidity From All Directions

"Halt! I mean, stop-stop-stop." Tomas Bigcanoe, first on the path, held out a hand to prevent Bipin and Villis from passing. "Up ahead. Lights!"

They had been walking for ten minutes in silence, other than the occasional *heads-up* warning from Bigcanoe. When Bigcanoe put out his hand, Villis had just been thinking that Tomas wasn't doing such a bad job leading them through The Pearl. He seemed to be at home in the woods. Must be because he's Mohawk, Villis thought. And he made a mental note to tell that to Bipin later, as an example of political incorrectness.

But now, apparently, the kid was seeing lights in the woods. Villis craned his neck to look where Bigcanoe was pointing, and squinted.

"Crapola," Villis said. Bigcanoe had sharp eyes. Young ones. There did seem to be an eerie glow of whitish light, low to the ground, up ahead in the clearing where The Pearl's biggest patch of trilliums bloomed in the spring.

"What do you think it is?" Bipin asked, swooping past Bigcanoe and up the trail.

Villis and Bigcanoe trotted to catch up. As they drew closer to the light, Villis could see it more clearly. It wasn't concentrated, like headlights, or wavering, like a fire. It was, instead, a placid haze of white, as if a bit of the moon had fallen into the clearing, Villis thought. Then he rolled his eyes at himself.

Bigcanoe hugged them into a huddle. "Shh! Holy shit – but that there could be, might be, may be an unidentified flying object. Shitshitshit!"

Bipin shook his head. "That object is absolutely not flying."

"It's made landing. You know, it's, like, put down. That's what they do. In secluded rural areas under cover of the night. Man-o-man-o-man-o-man! I wish I had a video camera. SHIT."

"Doesn't your cellphone record video clips?" Bipin whispered.

"Oh for crying out loud!" Villis said.

"Yeah-yeah-yeah-yeah-yeah!" Bigcanoe started digging in his pockets. "Here it is. Here it is." He pulled out his cellphone. "Okay. We'll advance toward the light. No. *I'll* advance–"

"We'll provide backup," Bipin said. "Hand me your firearm."

"For crying out–"

"On second thought," Bipin said, knocking himself on the head, "give the gun to Villis. I'm a pacifist."

Bigcanoe crept a few more steps toward the white light. "No weapons," he hissed, patting the holster on his hip. "Won't work against superior alien technology." Then he crouched like a cat stalking along the dark tunnel of the trail, his brick shoulders silhouetted against the light glowing from the clearing.

When Bigcanoe was out of earshot, Villis whispered to Bipin, "Guns! UFOs? For Pete's sake, don't encourage him. We want him OUT of here! ASAP."

"Maybe the aliens will abduct him."

Villis rubbed his eyes. They were dry, despite the moist air of the woods – not the sort of eyes that looked for the unseeable. He decided to keep quiet. At times, there was simply no talking to Bipin.

Bipin poked him in the arm. "Cop alert. The boy is returning."

Bigcanoe was hustling along the path toward them, no longer a cat, but hurtling like something hunted. When he reached them he was panting. He hugged them into a huddle again.

"Check it out, oh GOD! There's *four* of them. And they look so human! But WOW! What they've done is fucking, excuse me, awesome! They've taken on *human* forms. Morphs. Like bodysnatchers. That's a theory – that aliens take on human forms. Shit shit shit! But not just any fucking, excuse me, ordinary people, but human forms of famous guys. Yeah-yeah-yeah-yeah-yeah! It makes sense, right? Right! Aliens can probably only get intel about people that are famous."

"Are you saying the aliens look like celebrities?" Bipin said.

"Fucking A-list! Jesus. John Lennon. And Elvis. ELVIS!"

"I thought you said there were four," Villis said.

"Yeah-yeah-yeah. Number four. Some funny little dude in a diaper outfit."

"A-list. But notice – all dead," Villis said.

Bigcanoe gasped. "Shit! I hadn't put two and two together."

"Maybe they're ghosts," Villis said.

"They *are* all dressed in white!"

"And the light is white," Villis said.

"Go into the white light," Bipin added. "Customary directions provided to the dying."

Bigcanoe chuckled nervously. "No such thing as ghosts. Right?"

"That's not what I hear," Villis said.

Bipin switched on his flashlight and waved it in the air. "Hey, boys. Come on down!"

"Don't!" Bigcanoe pulled on Bipin's arm.

"Let's run while we can still make it," Villis said, sounding ominous. "Whatever those creatures are, who can trust them?"

Villis started to run away, hoping that Bigcanoe would follow. He was thinking, if he scared the crapola out of Bigcanoe maybe he wouldn't dare set foot back in The Pearl. But Bipin! What was he doing now? Shaking his flashlight, charging it as he ran, not *away* from but *toward* the light. And there was Bigcanoe, lumbering after him. Must have been his cop instincts kicking in. Villis switched on his LED headlamp. No point risking tripping. But he wouldn't run. Absolutely not. Sore knees. And something else. Hadn't Bipin promised? – "*My friend, this is your last year of confusion.*" Maybe that meant his heart was about to give. In fact, the instant he thought this, his heart twinged as if confirming its vulnerability. Better not strain the ticker. He didn't want to die at this particular moment. He didn't want to miss watching dopey Tomas trying to figure out whether the idiot impersonators were ghosts or aliens.

When Villis reached the clearing he found Bigcanoe, Bipin and the impersonators staring at each other. Gunslingers at sunset. The white glowing lights were not an alien landing craft (what an imagination that Tomas had) but solar-powered landscape lights – the kind people use to illuminate their driveways – arranged in a wide circle. In the centre of the circle were two tents.

Villis stepped into the circle of lights and scowled at the tents. Everyone looked at him expectantly, as if they had been waiting all along for him to arrive and to speak.

"What the hell?" he said. "No camping allowed in these woods."

Bigcanoe stepped into the circle alongside him and folded his arms across his chest. Villis thought – though grudgingly – that this was brave of Bigcanoe, considering his fear of ghosts.

"Identify yourselves," Bigcanoe said, with only a slight tremor in his voice.

Jesus stepped forward. "Let he who is without sin cast the first stone."

Bigcanoe frowned, rested his hand on his holster.

"You may say that I'm a dreamer," John Lennon said, linking arms with Jesus.

"But he's not the only one ..." Jesus added.

Elvis 2 fell to one knee. "We're caught in a trap, I can't walk out."

"Because he loves you too much, babeee," Jesus added.

Gandhi shook his head. "That last bit doesn't make sense, Dude."

Bigcanoe held up his hands. "Stop! Talk normal. Who the hell are you guys? I mean, let me see some identification."

Gandhi patted his diaper. "No pockets, Dude."

Bigcanoe let out a lingering breath. Villis thought that Bigcanoe was beginning to relax. He must have been thinking that "dude" wasn't the sort of word that either aliens or ghosts would use. And Gandhi had used it twice.

"You unidentified persons are trespassing on these herein prohibited lands," Bigcanoe said, in the same stern voice Villis had heard him use on the night they had ditched the ATV.

Elvis 2 said, "We can't go on together with suspicious minds." Then he pulled a card from inside his jumpsuit and handed it to Bigcanoe. "Honey, you know, I've never lied to you. Check it out. We've got an invitation."

Bigcanoe raised an eyebrow. "Honey?"

Elvis 2 curled a lip. "Keeping it real, man."

"Reality leaves a lot to the imagination," John Lennon said.

Gandhi high-fived him. "Good one, Dude!"

Bigcanoe shone his flashlight on the invitation and read. "You've been invited to a time portal?" His eyes went wide. He turned to Villis. "I am so into time portals!"

The impersonators grinned and then spontaneously, as if of one mind, like lemmings, Villis thought, gathered around Bigcanoe and clapped him on the back.

"Dude, you can help us look for the portal," Gandhi said.

"Yeah," John Lennon said, "we'd all love to see the plan."

Jesus grinned. "Seek and ye shall find."

Bigcanoe's face lit up. He flipped open his cellphone. "Speaking of seeking ... take a look at this." He fiddled with the phone and handed it to Jesus. "It's a picture I took here a little over a week ago."

Jesus looked at the picture and nodded. "Cool beans. Elvis 1's ATV. Yellow. Check it out." Jesus handed the cellphone to Gandhi who handed it to John Lennon and then to Elvis 2. They all looked and nodded.

Bigcanoe pumped his fist. "A clue! I mean, a solid lead – like, a break in the case."

John Lennon snorted. "If you go carrying pictures of Chairman Mao, you ain't gonna make it with anyone anyhow."

"Chairman who?" Gandhi said.

"What case?" Jesus asked.

"Who's Elvis 1?" Bigcanoe said, taking out his notebook.

Gandhi raised his hand like a schoolboy. "I know, I know. Elvis 1 is our, like, host. He's the dude, whatever, that invited us here. But he, like, ditched us."

Bigcanoe looked instantly suspicious. "Ditched? Exactly *how* do you happen to know that?"

"When you talk about destruction, don't you know that you can count me out–" John Lennon said.

Villis interrupted, "No one is talking about destruction."

"Maybe Elvis 1 was Raptured," Elvis 2 said. "The Rapture Index was in the heavy pre-tribulation range last month. If he's a Believer he may have been suckered up to heaven, leaving the rest of us to die in the upcoming apocalypse."

Jesus looked annoyed. "What kind of a dick god would do that?"

"Imagine there's no heaven. It's easy if you try."

"*Who* is Elvis 1?" Bigcanoe repeated, enunciating. "What's his real name?"

Jesus, John Lennon, Gandhi and Elvis 2 shrugged. Then Elvis 2 said, "We don't know nothing about him. It's against the rules, Babe, to use real names – we only know each other's impersonator names from Facebook."

Bigcanoe threw up his hands. "How do I purportedly close this case? Who was driving the currently impounded yellow ATV? Where did said who abscond to? What criminal deed was said who perpetuating in the woods?"

Gandhi pulled a cellphone from a tuck in his diaper. "I have a pic of said who. Here. We took it at our last *Like Likes Like Elvis Luau*. Elvis 1 is the one wearing the coconut boobies."

Bigcanoe studied the cellphone photo and nodded excitedly. "Very very very excellent. I can go on this! Maybe get a positive I.D. Contact next of kin, see if they know where he is. I'll be needing you to send this to my cell for indentificationing purposes. I'll send you my contact info–"

Villis plucked the cellphone from Bigcanoe. "Just curious," he said, though he was hoping he could figure out how to delete the photo.

But the cellphone was cryptic; juvenile icons instead of reliable words. As Villis searched for a pictograph that might indicate "photo delete", he was thinking that this generation was regressing to hieroglyphics.

Bigcanoe held out his hand for the cellphone. "If you don't forward me that aforesaid pic I'll have to abscond with this herein as evidence."

"Evidence of what?" Villis asked, handing back the phone.

"Foul play."

The impersonators chuckled, but said nothing. Bigcanoe made a note in his book. "Okay. I'm out of here. Like I said, gotta investigate. Find out stuff."

"Some kind of druid dude, lifting the veil?" John Lennon said, peering over the tops of his round glasses.

Bigcanoe waved goodbye and then stepped outside the circle of lights, slipping into the darkness.

Gandhi chicken-danced, pumping his elbows. "That's some bizarro dude! And did you catch what he said – fowl play? That's so beauty. Fowl play. *Cluck cluck.*"

Elvis 2 chicken-danced as well. "Hey Babe, it's so kick-ass. The yellow ATV – but *no* Elvis 1. That so proves that Elvis 1 has for sure beat it through the time portal."

Jesus looked wistful. "I wonder if he'll come back. And, like, where in time did he fucking go? I'd go back to the fucking Dark Ages so I could fucking fight with a mace." He pulled out his GPS and flicked it on. "I am so taking this with me when I go through the portal. See if it, like, still works in the year 1000."

Villis looked around the campsite for something to sit on. Maybe if he sat down he wouldn't explode. Or implode. How could anyone stand while stupidity from all directions bowled him over? Had he been sucked through a wormhole into a parallel universe where all semblance of intelligence had become extinct? He caught himself. He would not think that. He must *not*. *That* was thinking the way *they* thought. Kooky crapola. Parallel universe? Wormholes? Good God, there was no rational explanation for such intensity of stupidity.

"There is no time portal," Villis said, slowly, maintaining control.

But at the same time Bipin said, "We'll help you look for it.

Tomorrow. Rendezvous back here, ten o'clock sharp." Before Villis could protest, Bipin pulled him by the elbow. "It's high time we blew this gin joint, my friend. Ten o'clock comes swiftly."

Villis stomped, grumbling, after Bipin, shutting his eyes past the landscape lights, and then opening them into the cool black of the woods. The last thing he heard as they turned down the path toward home was Gandhi saying, "Gin joint? Coolio. Vintage, right?"

When it was safe to speak, Villis could barely contain himself. "Help them *look* for a time portal! Is craziness catching? Have you forgotten the ramp, what's under the moai?"

"You mean the monolift? What *is* under it? I have forgotten."

"You don't forget anything."

"I have forgotten that I don't forget anything. And you should too. We are geezers, remember. I say we employ the tried 'n' true senior-moment-memory-lapse excuse to our advantage."

"I'm going home. And tomorrow I am *not* helping anybody look for a time portal."

"Suit yourself. But your toes are poking over the brink of Erroneous Conclusions from which you are likely to free-fall. By encouraging the time portal delusion we prevent Jesus, John Lennon, Gandhi and Elvis 2 from fretting about foul play. As long as they believe the asshole is cavorting in other time zones they will not think him pushing up daisies. They will become our allies against the inquisitive Tomas, who suspects the demise of the asshole and is not as block-headed as you deem him to be."

"Humph." But he knew Bipin had a point.

Bipin went on, "What we'll do is this. First thing tomorrow morning at the smiling of the violet dawn, I shall steal up to the Nexus and plant false evidence that will subsequently give rise to the erroneous impression that Elvis 1, a.k.a. our own dear asshole, has somehow passed safe and soundly through the time portal."

"What evidence? Never mind. I don't want to know."

Bipin patted him on the shoulder. "Even if I told you, you would forget. Blessing Number 10,780 from 1998 – *Thank you for forgetfulness because it allows us to laugh at the same punchline over and over again.* After I've planted the evidence, we'll pick up the boys and wander with them haphazardly hither and thither about The Pearl. Then at some point, as if by pure happenstance, we'll lead them to the Resonating Nexus and their sought-after time portal monolift."

"Stop calling it a monolift."

CHAPTER 18

The Impersonators Consider the Time Portal

After the dawn had stretched its smile, violet, across the horizon, and then drifted upwards against the blue, high enough to lounge across the green backs of the leaves in The Pearl like a drowsy god, and at exactly fifteen minutes to ten o'clock in the morning, Villis watched as Bipin strode toward him through the trees – barefooted, Ray-Banned and (as Villis could tell) raring to go. Bipin was fanning a piece of paper. And shouting.

But shouting what? Bipin's lips were moving, smiling, moving, and yet – no sound. Villis sighed. Here was additional evidence of his diminishing capabilities – his ears shutting down, the drums inside them beaten upon so many times with life's drumsticks they had stiffened like his knees and were no longer supple enough to flex beneath the delicate strokings of a slight sound wave.

He waited. Close enough, soon enough, he would make out what Bipin was going on about.

"Holiest of holy cows, my dearest friend and soulmate." Bipin was now twenty feet away. "We are the Chosen Ones!"

"You've converted?"

Bipin crinkled his eyes. "Good one! Check this out. As our new friend fake-Jesus would say, this is cool beans." With a grand gesture, Bipin fluttered the paper into Villis's hands.

Villis read out loud, "'Hey, Bipin and Villis. Fasten your seatbelts! Kick yourselves into hyper-speed. Rev your search engines and install another motherboard in your brains, because you've been selected to compete for humongous cash money in *So You Think You Can Think* – Canada's favourite reality TV CRAZE.'

"Humongous?" Villis said.

Bipin snapped the letter back. "Apparently they want a photo op with us at the moai. I guess the picture I included in the application of the two of us standing in front of it did the trick. Yikes. It says here they're coming tomorrow morning."

"Coming where?"

"My place, I presume. I entered my address on the application."

Villis groaned. "Jesus, John Lennon, Gandhi, two Elvises, a dumb cop and *now* a pack of reality TV guys, all poking around The Pearl."

"Bigcanoe is not dumb. And how do you know it's a pack of TV guys? It says here the executive producer is coming." Bipin coughed. "And oh, it says further, a cameraman, sound guy and, um, social media coordinator."

"We DO NOT take them to the moai. We refuse. Or lie. That's it! We lie, say the moai got blown down in a windstorm."

"Lie?" Bipin looked worried. "I'm abysmal at that. You'll have to do it."

"With pleasure."

The impersonators seemed surprised when Bipin and Villis stepped into their campsite at ten o'clock sharp. John Lennon was cutting wood discs off the end of a campfire log with a handsaw; Gandhi was swatting bugs; and Elvis and Jesus were murmuring in one of the tents.

"Dudes," Gandhi said, ceasing his swatting, "there are people in the world so hungry that God cannot appear to them except in the form of bread."

John Lennon finished cutting a disc and stacked it with a pile of others. "We-e-ll, you know – we haven't had our breakfast. Our supplies got eaten while we were sleeping." He waved with the saw at what looked like shredded cereal boxes scattered near the firepit. "Bears."

"Check it out," Gandhi said. He picked up one of John Lennon's wood discs and threw it like a Frisbee. "In case the bears come back. We'll hit them with these."

"Oh, brother," Villis said. "There are no bears in The Pearl."

Jesus and Elvis, on hands and knees, crawled out of the tent and scowled at Villis and Bipin.

"What the fuck is The Pearl?" Jesus said.

Bipin shrugged in an exaggerated way and then zipped open his fanny pack. He pulled out four power bars and handed them around. "Feast on these. Sufficient protein and calories to get you through the morning, and yummy to boot."

John Lennon smiled. "Imagine all the people, sharing all the world."

Elvis 2 ripped his power bar open with his teeth. "You have made my life complete and I love you so."

Jesus and Gandhi nodded and grinned and dug into theirs.

"I love you too," Bipin said.

"He doesn't," Villis said.

"But I love all humankind, and animals, too. And the plants. Rocks and shells, nematodes and bacteria and–"

"Cool beans about the bacteria," Jesus said. "But loving all mankind sucks."

They set out to hunt for the time portal, with Bipin in the lead. Villis noted that the impersonators were glued to the old Indian like teenaged girls gaggling after a pop star. Maybe he was dazzling them with a celebrity story, perhaps telling them about the time he had his picture taken with Brando, or when he taught Bowie how to do Cow Face pose, or Bono where to buy vintage Ray-Bans online. Villis, bringing up the rear, told himself to focus on the task at hand, which was to hike to and from the moai without complications; nonetheless, it was niggling at him, this observation that Jesus, John Lennon,

Elvis 2 and Gandhi were infatuated with Bipin. Villis knew why – it had nothing to do with intriguing celebrity stories, but rather with the fact that Bipin actually did love them. The impersonators, despite their limited intelligence, had to be sensing this love. And who could help responding to that?

Well, Villis thought, better they love him and ignore me. He preferred to be ignored. Didn't he? Fact: people had been ignoring him for thirty years, ever since his body had begun to turn grey. He wasn't sure why this was so, and he couldn't remember why he himself had overlooked old codgers when he was young. Was it because old people, closer to death than birth, were fading, and therefore difficult to see? Were they like autumn leaves, losing their colour, paling and thinning through the skin until the veins and skeleton showed and they crumbled altogether?

He looked again at Bipin. What was he doing now? Demonstrating a straddle-leg headstand for the impersonators in a flat spot at the edge of the trail. No one ignored Bipin. Why was that? Villis wondered.

Bipin folded neatly out of his headstand. Jesus, John Lennon, Elvis 2 and Gandhi applauded. Then they set off again, the impersonators in their white clothes billowing around Bipin like clouds trailing the sun.

Villis peered into the deepest part of The Pearl. He was hoping to catch a glimpse of Palaeolithic man and Frog. Too bad he couldn't conjure those two at will. Conjuring friends at will was an antidote to being ignored.

"Whoa-ho, my dear fake-celebrities!" Bipin had stopped and was indicating vaguely. They were in the dell at the base of the Lopsided Ridges, at that very same place, coincidentally, where Bipin and Villis had first encountered ATV man singing *Shake, Rattle and Roll*. "Let us ascend and see what's what. Not that I have any specific reason for thinking that what's what may be anywhere near there, but what the hay, these three ridges – holy cow, don't they appear to be lopsided, as if Mother Earth burped a long time ago? – in any case, these ridges are Sirens bidding my feet to mount–"

Bipin *is* a terrible liar, Villis thought. "What he means," he interrupted, "is that we may as well go up there."

The impersonators looked at each other as if they were waiting for some subtle signal of herd verification, the way field cows did. Then all at once they started climbing the ridges.

Villis caught Bipin by the elbow. "Let them find it for themselves," he whispered.

Bipin nodded. "May I share with you something intriguing? Even though I love all humankind, I love some humans better than others – which is scarcely a quality of Godhead, but given how stupendous some people are, it's tough not to." Then he leaned sideways and kissed Villis on the shoulder.

Villis flushed. Colour in his cheeks, he could feel it. Colour swirled up by Bipin's kiss. Years ago he would have found such a sign of affection mortifying, but now he understood – this was the flush not of embarrassment, but of life rising from as deep as the marrow in his bones. That was how to keep an old person from fading.

Villis watched the impersonators clamber up the hill. Such bodies. Moving without knowing they were moving. Those kids had no idea what was in store for them in the future. *Future future future* – a word Villis now realized sighed with melancholy, as if it were a depleting feather pillow, worn open and holey, pouffing out tufts of goose down like the white hairs from an old man's head. Those kids had no idea what was in store for them when those movements of theirs, graceful and taken for granted, became a noisy business of cracking joints, muscles nagging and tendons complaining that they had given too much at the office.

Elvis 2 was the first to reach the top of the ridge, followed by the others. They stopped there. Villis could tell by the way they craned their heads that they had discovered the moai.

"Let's go," he said to Bipin.

"And be one with whatever comes."

When Bipin and Villis made it to the top of the ridge the impersonators were already surrounding the moai, circling it, Villis thought, like pagans again. Villis scanned the clearing between the butternut trees, checking for signs of the asshole's remains that may have been brought to the surface by coyotes or some such calamity. But the ground around the moai was pure, flat woodland. No sign of anything.

When the impersonators spotted Bipin and Villis they shouted all at the same time. Villis nudged Bipin. "Remember. Act surprised."

"Copy that," Bipin said. Then he threw up his hands. "My my my word! What have we here? Villis, do you know what this monument is, so unexpectedly discovered in the depths of these woods where we have never before been, and where we have certainly never before seen any such bizarre and mysterious primitive monolith as this?"

"Why, no, Bipin."

Jesus pumped his fist. "Sweet! This has to be it."

"The time portal, the time portal, beauty!" Gandhi said.

"Projecting our images in space and in time," John Lennon said, bending to take a closer look at the base of the moai.

"Return to sender, address unknown." Elvis 2 bent beside John Lennon and scratched at the ground. Then he frowned and scratched harder. "Dudes, there's something here."

Villis clutched Bipin's arm. "God! He's found the asshole."

Bipin shook his head. "Wait for it."

"Huh?"

Elvis 2 tugged at something, then brandished the something as if it were a sports trophy. "Thank you, thank you very much. Don't step on my blue suede shoes!"

Villis let out his breath. Not the asshole.

Bipin was beaming. "*Voilà*. The evidence, as planted by yours truly this morning at dawn."

"The blue shoe from the road?"

"Didn't I tell you it would someday come in handy?"

The impersonators passed the shoe around as if it were a holy relic. Jesus cleaned it with the hem of his robe.

Villis whispered to Bipin, "Fake nonchalance." Then he drowsed over to the impersonators as if he had just woken from a dream. Bipin darted ahead, not in the least nonchalant.

"A shoe," Villis said to Jesus, keeping his tone noncommittal.

"It's a fucking miracle."

Gandhi said, "Providence has its appointed hour for everything. Dudes, this is Elvis 1's very own shoe. I remember the first time he wore them."

"It is?" Bipin and Villis said together.

John Lennon nodded solemnly. "Yes is the answer and you know that for sure."

"Wow!" Bipin said.

Even Bipin seemed genuinely surprised. Villis thought, clearly, this was not just any garbage shoe casually picked up from alongside the road, but *the* shoe that had once contained the foot of the asshole. Maybe the same foot, Villis couldn't but imagine, that had poked up, D-E-A-D, out of the leaves at the site of the crashed ATV. How could that have happened? And yet, shouldn't he have been used to this by now, to Bipin's weirdish magic (what else could he call it)? Wasn't this seeming coincidence with the shoe further evidence of Bipin's indisputable connection with the World Wise Web?

"The shoe is a fucking sign," Jesus said. "From Elvis 1 to our group. He, like, left it behind to fucking inform us that he has for sure time-travelled underneath this thing here."

"Dudes – how does it work?" Gandhi squatted and stared at the base of the moai. "Do you, like, think there's a toggle switch?"

The impersonators clustered around the moai and began to peer at it. Jesus brushed it with one finger. Then he started to tap.

"Maybe it has a secret control panel," Jesus said. "Like in James Bond. You have to tap to get the mechanism to open."

John Lennon and Elvis 2 joined in with Jesus's tapping. "You tap the top," Jesus said to Elvis 2. "John does the middle, and I'll do the bottom."

Villis pulled Bipin aside. "We have to make them stop tapping. They'll tip the thing over."

Bipin looked insulted. "Not a chance it will topple. I'm renowned for the longevity of my props."

The only one not tapping was Gandhi. He was sitting on the ground, cross-legged and in what seemed to be a contemplative mood, though Villis thought this was doubtful.

"What's on your mind, Bapu?" Bipin said.

"Dudes – I was thinking. What if Elvis 1 didn't go off somewheres time-travelling?"

Elvis 2, John Lennon and Jesus stopped tapping.

Elvis 2 frowned. "He said he was going to."

"But can we trust him?" John Lennon said, picking up on Gandhi's suspicions. "Elvis 1 could be a Facebook scammer."

The other three impersonators were silent for a moment. Then Jesus said, "But what about the fucking shoe?"

"Beauty point," Gandhi said.

"And hey, Babe, he *has* disappeared without his ATV," Elvis 2 said. "He would, like, never leave it behind. He loved that thing."

The other three nodded again.

"Maybe something happened to him," John Lennon said.

Villis jumped in. "Maybe he was Raptured."

"Dude," Gandhi said, "that's the lamest thing I ever heard."

"Fucking right about that," Jesus said. "If Elvis 1 was Raptured he wouldn't go without his shoes. Those kicks must've cost him a shitload."

"What about aliens, then?" Villis said.

"Abduction." John Lennon shuddered. "It happens."

"I have an idea," Gandhi said.

"Stop the presses," Villis said.

Gandhi shot him a look and then shrugged and went on. "Let's stay here as long as it takes to, like, time-travel ourselves through the time portal. Then we can, like, go and look for Elvis 1."

"Maybe he's trapped in another time dimension," John Lennon said. "Absolute elsewhere."

Elvis 2 sat down beside Gandhi. He patted the ground beside him. The others sat down too. Then Bipin. Villis sighed. They were all watching him.

"Why are we sitting?" Villis said, settling down between Jesus and John Lennon.

"Dude – it's like, whatever, obvious."
The impersonators all nodded.
"Are we not simply waiting for the portal to open?" Bipin asked.
The impersonators beamed at Bipin.
"He, like, so fucking gets it," Jesus said.

CHAPTER 19

Villis Has an Unsettling Vision of the Future

By Villis's guess they had been sitting for an hour. He had finally needed to stand and stretch his legs. The others, it seemed, were comfortable where they were, though Gandhi had been scratching at a mosquito bite on his chest.

"The bears, like, ate the bug stuff," Gandhi said.

"Raccoons, maybe," Villis said, although there wasn't much point in clarifying facts for Gandhi. Solar panels on the north side of the roof, Villis thought, embarrassed for Bipin, who must've noticed that phoney-baloney-Bapu appeared to be the dumbest of these four dodos.

Villis wished he could signal Bipin to join him. They needed a plan (one that didn't involve ramps) to lure the impersonators away from the moai and out of The Pearl. He couldn't stand this sitting around playing time traveller with the boys for much longer. Forget that his knees were seizing and his back was throbbing – his head was the body part giving him the most trouble. He was bored out of his mind. No one was saying much of anything. The impersonators were – what was the opposite of eloquent? He couldn't remember. The word started with "in" – incoherent? Not that. But definitely a word beginning with "in" and having – he tried to find it in his mind – having three or four syllables. In-blah-blah-blah-blah. He let it go. Eventually the word would appear in his head, floating there, like a half-erased chalk scrawl on a blackboard. But keeping to the point, the impersonators were hardly loquacious types (he was pleased with that word, even though it wasn't the right one), Generation Tweet, no doubt about it. Generation Tweet had smashed the art of conversation into pathetic fragments beneath the incessant tapping of fingers on keypads. Funny, that. Maybe *that* was why they called it digital communication. He had to remember to tell that to Bipin.

He will remember to tell that to the boys. Juozas and Janis are excellent listeners and always appreciate a good joke. And don't they have that funny twin habit of finishing each other's sentences? It's a darn good thing, too, that the twins are good listeners, because when Gregori gets going, watch out! What a chatterbox! But interesting. Isn't Gregori always reading the encyclopaedia and reporting on historical events – on kings, pharaohs and all manner of world dominators like Genghis Khan and Napoleon? Sometimes Villis has to tell him to shut up, in that affectionate way they have with each other, because no one else can get a word in edgewise. And, of course, if he doesn't intervene, Endres gets all hot under the collar because *he* wants to talk about politics. History is water down the drain, Endres is always saying. Are we not men of the future?

Talk talk talk. There is never enough time in the day for him and the boys to say all they have to say to each other. Sharp observations, ironic jokes, daring predictions, provocative theories, weaving like ... like a ...? Three syllables, beginning with – with the letter "t"?

"Villis?"

"What is it, Juozas?"

"Come, my friend, and sit down with us near the moai."

"Who the fuck is Juozas?"

"Dudes, he's looking like a space cadet."

"Absolute elsewhere in the stones of his mind."

"Maybe he's, like, starting to slip through the time portal."

Villis hears bells.

Listen carefully. Concentrate. No, not bells – wind chimes. He opens his eyes. Feet, lined up, right there. Lots of them.

He is lying on his side, his cheek pressed to ... what? Tiles! What has happened to the ground? Cold, hard tiles! Not even tile, but plasticky stuff. Wind chimes are beautiful, though, as if the breeze is flirting. He rolls on his back. Looks up. Wind chimes, hanging from the steel girder of a ceiling. Where's the sky?

Above the wind chimes a monster fan, mechanical, its skewed knives hacking the air, is troubling up a false breeze and forcing the wind chimes to flirt.

He stands up. How do you like them apples? No trouble from the old knees. But forget knees. Where the hell is this?

The lined-up feet belong to strange people. The people are wearing miniature shoe pendants – blue ones – hanging from fine silver chains around their necks, and as well, white mittens. Mittens, but whacko – no thumbs. Is it winter? No one notices him. No one talks. They are lined up in a wide corridor with windows along both sides that overlook the woods. Signs above the windows say: *Silence, please. You are about to enter the sanctuary.*

He looks out a window. Not winter. The woods are a harmony of greens. Then why the mittens?

He taps a woman standing nearby. "Excuse me. Why is everyone wearing mittens? And why no thumbs?" The woman doesn't respond. Doesn't appear to have felt his tapping.

A voice. The lined-up people tense. They obviously hear it too. A loudspeaker.

"Welcome, Pilgrims. The sanctuary doors will open in sixty seconds. Please be reminded that touching of any of the trees and other green-aura life is strictly forbidden. Should your life-sensory mittens touch any Plant Being an alarm will sound immediately and you will be ejected from the sanctuary and fined. Likewise, the alarm will sound should you remove your mittens in an unlawful attempt to foil the life-sensory alert system. We ask that you maintain a tranquil demeanour at all times so as not to aggravate the rare species of birds, butterflies and other Insect Beings that are the revered guests within this sanctuary. Further, remain on the path without exception. Deviating from the demarcated pray-way will cause irreparable damage to the graceful bio-lace of the sanctuary and your immediate ejection. Those pilgrims standing nearest the doors, please step back and allow room for the doors to open – we invite you all, upon entering the sanctuary, to breathe deeply and draw into your lungs the sacrosanct and rejuvenating green-aura airs of one of Mother Earth's most precious biospheric masterpieces, The Pearl, North America's last undisturbed, wild woodland."

The Pearl?

His Pearl! He closes his eyes, opens them, hoping the scene before him will change. If this is a dream then he is the dreamer, and *that* makes him god of this craziness, so he ought to be able to think it away.

Think think, something else – The Pearl the way it really is. What what what is this? *Where* is this?

Bewildered, he follows the people into this whacko Pearl.

It is the woods, all right – more or less – with what must be the so-called "pray-way" threading through it. The pray-way (what kind of term is that?) is a trail, though it is unlike any trail made by himself and Bipin; it is unnaturally neat and too straight along the edges to have been created over time by the meandering feet of friends. It is covered completely with some uniform substance. Garden mulch? He sniffs. Doesn't smell like mulch. He wants to touch it, but the people are moving along the pray-way and he remembers that touching is forbidden.

Trees. More or less the same, though not quite. No broken branches, no dying bits, no ripples of fungus up the bark like rolling reams of felt. And the trees are as symmetrical as church steeples. Someone's been pruning them. Kooky, that, pruning trees in a woods. And how odd that the voice had described this place as undisturbed and wild. It was hardly that.

The birds sound like birds, thankfully.

There is some commotion, a quiet murmuring coming from ahead on the pray-way. He pushes through to see. A group of pilgrims are clustered, watching something – a cardinal, hop-hop-hopping across the path. Several of the pilgrims are plainly crying. Several are on their knees.

The bird watches back at them with the black beads of its eyes. Then it hops into the woods and hides beneath something with fronds.

Why doesn't it fly away?

The pilgrims make solemn gestures and beam, and it seems to Villis that they are enraptured by the sighting of the cardinal.

He pushes ahead along the pray-way. Everything is flat. If this is The Pearl, where are the ridges, the dells and ravines? The creek with Frog's Bend? Then he knows the answer. This is only a small piece of The Pearl, a shaving off the top of it – all that is left – the flatland above the crest of the Lopsided Ridges where the moai is. He turns in a circle, looking for it. Sees that The Pearl begins over there, at the doors, and ends over there, just beyond ... what?

The moai?

He runs. No one seems to mind. Damn crapola, how is this? – the knees are good! And it *is* the moai. More or less, though painted in earth tones: the lips of the face, deep red; the eyes, green. And taller. There are trees surrounding it, in a circle. He checks the bark, the leaves. Butternut! No doubt about it. But are these the same butternut trees? He will cry. But, no – how *can* they be?

There are benches positioned discreetly with views of the moai, with people seated upon them, staring, either in deep contemplation or boredom, he cannot tell. He finds a spot and sits down. There are information signs on stands in front of the benches.

This is the third replica of the original moai, worshipped by the First Devotees of Elvis Presley, and erected at this site in the sacred woods of The Pearl during the early 21ˢᵗ Century, by Vinous the Latvian and Bipin the Purifier. It marks the Place of Resonating Nexus, believed by the followers of Elvis Presley to be a vortex of exceptional life-verve. Very early followers of Presley also believed the Nexus was a time portal through which He traversed other time dimensions, returning from time to time to impart his teachings. The Resonating Nexus is also the same place where the holy Blue Suede Shoe was discovered, considered the First Miracle of the Transmigration of Presley, though questions about the historical accuracy of the time portal have recently arisen (following the installation of the third replica) when the skeletal remains of a male human were discovered beneath it. Testing of the bones dated them to the Early 21st C Wireless Epoch, leading Presleyan scholars to speculate that rather than a time portal, the moai marked the gravesite of Presley himself, whose bones, it is now hypothesized, were secretly removed from their original burial site at Graceland and transferred here by The First Devotees.

Villis stands up. Nonsense! He shouts this. Nonsense. But nobody so much as glances at him.

I'm leaving. Does he shout this, or say it to himself? Never mind.

He pushes along the pray-way, heading to the second set of doors. This whole place has a wall around it, he now notices, but no roof, only the steel girders, criss-crossing. He squints at the spaces between the girders. It looks like a blue checkerboard. Is that the real sky? Who can be sure of anything?

At the exit there is a pile of wooden discs that look as if they have been sawn from logs. Villis takes a good, long look. Not wood, it seems, but some plasticky stuff. There is another information sign:

Please take one of these replica log-smackers as a souvenir of your encounter in The Pearl. Log-smackers were thought to have been used by early Presleyans to repel attacks by mega Grizzly Bears that ran rampant in The Pearl during the period of the First Devotees.

Villis tries to knock over the log-smackers, but finds he cannot. No matter how hard he hits them they do not budge.

What is happening? What has happened?

Villis heard bells.

Listen carefully. Concentrate. No, not bells.

He opened his eyes.

Feet, lined up, right there. Bare feet. Familiar. Bipin's? Yes. And the bells – not bells, but the carabiner on Bipin's water bottle, tapping.

He was lying on his side, his cheek pressed to – what?

The ground. Dusk now. A campfire, cozy. Over there.

He propped himself on one elbow. Bipin helped. Young men dressed in white chatting around the campfire. Janis and Juozas? Gregori? Endres?

Bipin gave him a drink. He closed his eyes, sipped, opened his eyes. Four young men in white, still there, but not them. Only – Jesus, John Lennon, Elvis 2 and Gandhi.

"What's going on?" he said to Bipin.

"The boys wanted to remain in the Nexus overnight and see if anything happened."

"Has anything? Happened?"

"You tell me."

Villis pressed his eyeballs with the heels of his hand. He didn't know what to say. He was suddenly inarticulate (there it was, the word he couldn't remember earlier). Irony, he thought. Himself, now the inarticulate one – rendered so by an experience for which he had no words. If he told Bipin, Bipin would insist that what had happened was a premonition, similar to the assassination dream he had dreamt about Gandhi. Similar, it seemed in more ways than one, for hadn't Villis just seen (foreseen?) the end of The Pearl as he loved it, just as Bipin had foreseen the end of Gandhi?

Well, *if* what he had just experienced *was* a premonition, he would have nothing of it.

"I'm getting old," he finally said.

Bipin smiled, nodded, patted him on the shoulder. "My friend, you've seen the light. What you have so succinctly articulated happens to be none other than Blessing Number 1, from 1972 – *Thank you for getting old, since it means I am getting to live.*"

CHAPTER 20

Dealing with the TV People

The next morning, Villis was still debating with himself about what had happened – dream, delusion or descent through a time portal? He was waiting in Bipin's kitchen for the TV people to arrive. When they did, he would put them off about the moai, without, he hoped, putting them off about himself and Bipin as contestants for *So You Think You Can Think*. The reality show was still a dumb idea. And the chances of two geezers (one with dwindling capabilities) outsmarting younger brains were slim to nil. But then, when you considered the models of youthful intelligence that had recently invaded The Pearl (describing them as less-than-stellar would have been a kindness), perhaps two geezers tobogganing down the sunset slope of life did have a chance of winning the humongous cash money.

The TV people would be young. Well, of course, *everybody* was younger, but would the TV people be very much younger? And would they be idiots? He yawned, thinking he may as well assemble Bipin's juicer. If he could remember how. He had spent a rough night. Had he slept a wink? Who could, after what he had – what? – *experienced* yesterday in the Resonating Nexus. Was "experience" the correct word?

Dream, delusion or descent through a time portal? Villis supposed people would dub all three *experiences*, but would those same people be thinking the thing through? Shouldn't experiences have some connection with reality?

The juicer wasn't going together. And he ought to put on the coffee. But then he remembered he was at Bipin's and Bipin didn't believe in caffeine. What time was it? He would have checked the clock but Bipin didn't believe in those either. *Time isn't*, as Bipin was always saying. And in any case, Bipin could tell time, even without a clock. Except today, apparently. Where was that Bipin? He was never late. The TV people were due any minute now. It had to be the impersonators keeping him.

Bipin had decided to spend the night in the Nexus, babysitting the boys. Villis had declined to join them, excusing his old bones as too cranky for camping. Bipin had offered to walk him home, but Jesus had whined about man-eating bears and what might happen if Bipin left them unprotected, after which John Lennon had boasted, we-e-ll then, if he had a saw he could cut log discs to throw at those bears, but, imagine, no possessions, because he had left the saw at the tents. Then Elvis 2 had cracked a joke about Bipin the Bear Bopper, and Gandhi had said, "Dude – live as if you were to die tomorrow."

In the end, Villis had said he preferred to walk home by himself – didn't he know The Pearl, even at night, like the back of his hand? Like the sound of his own voice resonating in his head? (Though he hadn't said *that* to the impersonators.)

Old bones. Soon, his would be all that was left of him, buried someplace. Not that he cared where. He would be dead and gone. Then he remembered Frog riding Palaeolithic man's shoulder. Where were those two now? Dead and gone? Not quite. Or so it seemed.

Maybe he *should* care. Maybe it did matter where your bones rested. After all, when a man's earthly goods lay layered in the landfill, and his face had dulled in the picture frames of his descendants, maybe he *would* be glad that some artifact of himself was deposited in this world that he loved so much. In that case, he decided, plant me in The Pearl.

Then there were the bones of the asshole to consider – Elvis 1, beneath the moai. Now *there* was a point, he thought, that favoured the case for defining yesterday as a descent through a time portal. *If* yesterday's – call it a "happening" – had in fact been a transit through a time portal into the future, then he could stop worrying about coyotes digging up the asshole's bones any time soon – assuming one accepted the alleged facts on the sanctuary's information sign as accurate.

But just how far into the future had he time-travelled, assuming he had? Far enough for the world to become kookier than it was now. Or so it seemed.

And what had the passage of time done to his name? Vinous the Latvian? Though he could not but acknowledge a tingle of contentment that his name had lived on, he was not happy about the misspelling. Was this perversion of his identity related to some mistaken notion that he had an excessive fondness for wine?

Nonetheless, immortalization for alcoholism was far from the worst thing about the descent-through-a-time-portal theory. *If* he truly had visited the future, then the future was, as fake-Jesus would have put it, fucked. At least as far as The Pearl was concerned. "Fucked" was the strongest word he could think of to describe what had happened in the future to The Pearl. It was exact and depressing. According to yesterday, the future would imprison his beautiful Pearl in a girded cage; pickaxing this growing, breathing, rollicking land out of the planet like a piece of raw emerald, falsely cutting it, unnaturally polishing it and then mounting it in a dollar-store ring.

Therefore, and because he was still a man who thinks-therefore-he-is, he must reject descent-through-a-time-portal as an explanation for yesterday. It was clearly an unbearable speculation, despite the relief of knowing that the asshole would remain buried for eons.

That left dream or delusion.

Villis poked around Bipin's kitchen for something useful to do. Usefulness argued against delusion. Surely as long as a person could *do* things (cause and effect) that person was not deluded.

He tried the juicer again. Still no go. Too many pieces puzzling across Bipin's countertop, the mystery of their coming together as baffling as yesterday's whacko doings in the woods.

Correction. In his head. Fact: the head was the place where dreams and delusions played. He selected a gizmo from the juicer and turned it over in his palm. Which way was which? Confusing as it was to admit, and only on pain of death, he would have to say that what had happened yesterday had *not* happened in his head. But then, wasn't that the textbook definition of delusion: believing something was real when it couldn't be? He felt a prick. Was that the blade of the juicer gizmo? Or panic?

Perhaps, given the situation, dishonesty was the best policy. Villis draped a tea towel over the juicer pieces. He could just as well delude himself about being deluded.

Dream it was, then. Dream it must have been. Though it was like no dream he had ever dreamt.

The TV people pulled up in Bipin's lane driving a white van with the *So You Think You Can Think* logo emblazoned on both sides. Villis went outside to head them off, determined to block them from entering the house and hinting for coffee. Or juice.

There were four of them, young men in jeans and white T-shirts, the T-shirts stamped on the front with "*So You Think ...*" and on the back with "*... You Can Think*". The show's logo, a tilted black question mark superimposed on a pink sea sponge, glared from beneath the words. Villis squinted. Not a sea sponge. A brain.

The first young man had a clipboard and one of those phoney-type smiles that Villis mistrusted. The other three tagged behind him, gingerly picking their way up the path to the front door as if they had never walked on anything but concrete and asphalt. Villis noted their inappropriate footwear: spotless white runners with yellow blazes. City slickers. He felt a smug certainty – those boys wouldn't walk far in the woods.

"Good morning, sir," the clipboard said, holding out his hand to shake. "You must be Mr. Bipin Patel."

Villis raised an eyebrow. "Do I look like a Bipin Patel?"

The clipboard blushed. "Ah."

"Think." He wanted to add "before you open your mouth" but bit his tongue. The less said, the sooner they would leave.

The clipboard checked his clipboard, reposted his phoney smile. "Of course. My mistake. You're the lucky Mr. Villis … Mr. Villis …" He glanced again at the clipboard.

"Krastins."

"That's Latvian," the first of the other three said.

"Thanks for that," Villis said.

"You're absolutely welcome."

Good God, Villis thought. Too thick for sarcasm.

"We're hyper-pumped about shooting the moai," the clipboard said.

Villis folded his arms across his chest. "About that. It blew down. Last night. In the wind. No point going all the way up there." He pointed at their shoes. "Trails are muddy."

The four looked downcast. Then the third young man said, "We'll stand it back up. We can still get the shot. No problemo."

"And who minds a little mud? Not us, right, guys?" the clipboard added.

They all nodded enthusiastically, though Villis thought the fourth one looked doubtful.

"It broke," Villis said. "The moai. Nothing much left to stand up."

Number Three said, "No problemo. We'll shoot the pieces. Man, we drove all the way here in killer traffic. We gotta get something."

The others commiserated.

There was an awkward silence. The TV crew stared at the front door as if they expected it to open sesame. Villis was about to make up a story about the house being toxic due to household pesticides when the crew turned away from him. With their juvenile ears they had clearly heard something he hadn't. It was Bipin, coming out of the woods, beaming, waving, leading – like the Pied Piper – the impersonators, who all looked relieved and a little less white.

"Good morning, good morning, reality people. Welcome, welcome. *Namaste.* Please, have you eaten? Would you like some juice? Come in, come in. I was just about to prepare breakfast smoothies for myself and my four phoney friends here." Bipin flung open the front door and marched inside, followed by the eight young men (Villis noticed that the impersonators were uncharacteristically quiet) all in white, like goslings, Villis thought, traipsing after a tall, dark, skinny mother goose.

Inside, Bipin handed around bowls of granola, then concocted fresh veggie juice (he assembled the juicer with a few deft manoeuvres, Villis noted), followed by goat milk kefir smoothies with blueberries and maca powder. The eight young men sat resting their elbows on Bipin's harvest table – like testy apostles at the Last Supper, Villis thought, only not quite – shovelling granola and giving each other the eye and wiping kefir from their lips.

The TV boys soon sorted themselves out. There was the producer of *So You Think You Can Think* (clipboard kid); the cameraman, sound guy, and the social media coordinator. Villis had no idea what a social media coordinator did; he wondered if it might have to do with arranging parties for reporters.

The social media coordinator aimed his cellphone, clicked a picture of his kefir smoothie, hunched as if he had scoliosis, finger-punched the phone's tiny keyboard and finally groaned. "There's no cell service here! I can't send my tweets. Shit."

The producer flicked a nervous glance at Villis. Villis thought the producer was expecting him to criticize the social media coordinator for swearing, but Villis decided maintaining a stony silence was more effective.

The producer said, "A minor glitch. Simply line up your tweets and send them later. None of our followers will know that it's not real time."

"Followers?" Jesus said.

"In any case," Bipin said, "time isn't."

The TV crew exchanged a look among themselves.

John Lennon said, "Life is what happens when you're busy making other plans."

"That's Lennon, isn't it?" the social media coordinator said, glancing at the sound guy for affirmation. "From his last CD, *Double Fantasy*, before he was assassinated."

The sound guy stopped chewing and blinked. "Album, not CD."

"Double Fantasy?" John Lennon said, tensing. "I don't think so. It was for sure *Walls and Bridges.*"

The social media coordinator looked surprised. "Chill, Buddy. It's common knowledge. Wiki it."

Gandhi scoffed. "Yeah, right."

The cameraman suddenly stood up. "Gotta get the gear. Let's get her done before the light changes. And I need to be back in T.O. for my poli-sci thesis class."

"Is that the same as sci-fi, Babe?" Elvis 2 said.

The cameraman ignored Elvis 2. "Who's coming with?"

"But it's blown down," Villis said.

"It is?" Elvis 2 said.

"We are absolutely not fibbing," Bipin said.

"What's blown down?" Gandhi added.

"The moai," the TV crew answered together.

"No fucking way," Jesus said.

"But, dudes – we were just there. It's like, intact. Totally."

The producer perked up. "Are you certain?"

"Fucking-A."

The producer, sound guy, cameraman and social media coordinator stared at Villis and Bipin, their faces grim, like judge and jury. "You two fellows are fibbing," the producer said.

"Who's fibbing?"

It was Bigcanoe, standing in the doorway, in uniform, his ponytail tucked up in his cap, the bricks of his shoulders packing the entrance.

The producer swept a hand at Villis and Bipin. "These gentlemen, Officer."

Bigcanoe grinned. "Hey, Uncles, how's it going? I seen the van in Bipin's laneway. Seemed suspicious, like, you know, a unbeknownst vehicle and all. But that's not why I came. I've had a humongous break in the case."

"Case? What case?" the social media coordinator asked, pulling out his cellphone and tapping the keys.

Bigcanoe kept quiet, looking expectantly at Villis, obviously pleased with himself.

"A break?" Villis said, trying to keep a nervous wobble out of his voice.

"Like I said, B-R-E-A-K, as in through. I did a little old-timey detective-ing, plus cyber investigations on Facebook and whatnot. And don't forget I had that pic of the guy as he was beknownst to Jesus, John Lennon and Gandhi–"

"Jesus? Jesus, John Lennon and Gandhi? What the hell's going on here?" The producer started snapping the clip on his clipboard. "What are you people smoking?"

Bigcanoe raised an eyebrow at the producer, then held out his hand for the clipboard. He continued, "I got an I.D. on the guy. Name's Roland, uh ..." He handed the clipboard back to the producer and fished out his notepad. "Roland Kaduhh, pronounced Kad-*duh*, as in duh. Anyhooow, Mr. Kad-*duh*–"

"Did you find his next of kin?" Villis interrupted.

"Any loved ones?" Bipin added.

"Negatory. There's none. Parents long dead. No sibs. No spouse. This guy didn't even have any friends."

"You get by with a little help from your friends," John Lennon said.

Jesus, Gandhi and Elvis 2 exchanged sad glances.

"He was, like, our friend," Elvis 2 said. "Sort of. Right, guys?"

"I fucking hardly knew the dude," Jesus said.

"I mostly remembered him because of the coconut boobies," Gandhi added.

"No loved ones?" Villis said. "That's too bad. Life's like that. But what can you do?"

"Nearly everything you do is of no importance," Gandhi said. "But it is important that you do it."

"Could you repeat that? Slower," the social media coordinator said.

"Lived in a motel room, few belongings," Bigcanoe went on, ignoring the social media coordinator, reading from his notes. "Worked as a night security guard. Hasn't shown up to work since the aforementioned incident in the ditch. Same goes for the motel. Motel-worker-guy says Roland had been going on lately about some place called Easter Island, which, according to my research, is in Gull Lake, north of Bobcaygeon. Said he was planning to go there. Said he'd be gone for a while. Maybe he'd stay there. That's all she wrote."

Gandhi nudged Jesus with his elbow and winked. He mouthed the words *time portal*, but it seemed no one noticed him doing so, other than Villis

"Then there are no grief-stricken kinfolks?" Bipin said. "No one suffering? No one to send a midnight telegram to with the unsettling news of a mysterious disappearance?"

"Nope."

Bipin beamed. "I am so unbearably relieved."

"What about the fowl play?" Elvis 2 asked.

"Yeah." John Lennon looked concerned. "Who's gonna take care of the guy's chickens?"

Bigcanoe scrunched his face at Gandhi. Villis wanted to tell him not to waste any brain cells trying to figure these guys out. "What they mean–" Villis started to explain about fowl play, but Bigcanoe cut him off.

"Chickens? Ir-revelant. As for foul play, the evidence is unsupporting of such a said conclusion. No sign of struggle. No body. And don't forget the whispers. I heard two guys talking that night, just off in the woods a bit. Maybe Mr. Kaduhh had at least one friend, after all."

"Or he was so lonely he talked to himself," Bipin said.

"*Sergeant Pepper's Lonely Hearts Club Band*," John Lennon started to sing.

Bigcanoe waited for John Lennon to stop before continuing. "Way I see it, the most logical conclusion – what we have here is a lonely, loser-type dude who gets drunk, ditches his ATV, then coincidentally goes off to some island in northern Ontario for an unbeknownst but most likely ordinary reason."

"Is it case closed, then?" Villis asked, crossing his fingers behind his back, even though he didn't believe that crossing fingers helped.

Bigcanoe tucked away his notepad. "Looks like. I guess we'll sell the ATV at the next police auction."

"*Who*, exactly, are you talking about?" the producer asked. "What case is closed?"

"The case of the missing Elvis 1," Elvis 2 said. "But don't ask me where he's gone, because my lips are sealed, Babe."

The producer was suddenly intense. "Elvis?"

Elvis 2 locked his lips.

Bigcanoe folded his arms across his chest. "I don't care anymore. Like I said, case closed."

Then Gandhi said, "Dudes, the time portal. And don't forget the blue suede shoe. He for sure went through the portal."

"Time out," Jesus said, making the time out sign used by coaches. He whispered at Gandhi, though loudly enough for everyone to hear, "Remember what we fucking agreed to?"

"This could be breaking news." The producer poked the social media coordinator. "Phone it in to the station."

The social media coordinator snapped his cellphone at the producer as if *he* were to blame for the lack of cell service. "News flash. Minor glitch, remember?"

"Remember?" Gandhi said. "I don't remember."

"You do," Jesus hissed. "No talking about the you-know-what."

"Time portal?" Gandhi said.

Jesus slapped his own forehead.

Bigcanoe whipped out his notepad. "Time portal. Did you find it? Have we located a locale for the said same time portal indicated therein on the invite from said identified missing person, Elvis the First, a.k.a. Roland Kaduhh?"

The impersonators were silent, stirring their kefir smoothies.

Bigcanoe snugged his hand across his holster. "I can reopen this case. Do you understand, like?"

The producer and the social media coordinator said, "Do it," at the same time. They seemed to Villis happy, almost ecstatic. At the very least raring to go. The producer signalled the cameraman, who sidled toward the door, jerking his chin at the sound guy, who wheezed back from the table and followed the cameraman outside.

John Lennon and Elvis 2 raised their hands.

"Are we under arrest?" Elvis 2 said, snapping his fingers. "Is it time to do the jailhouse rock with me?"

Gandhi perked up. "A *no* uttered from the deepest conviction is better than a *yes* merely uttered to please, or worse, to avoid trouble."

The producer hustled to the door and shouted to the cameraman and the sound guy. "Get the gear and get back in here!" He turned to the impersonators and smiled his phoney-type smile. "Would you guys mind repeating that last bit for the camera?"

CHAPTER 21

Going Viral in The Pearl

One half-hour later they were parading through The Pearl on the path to the time portal and, as Villis brooded, certain catastrophe. Bipin had pulled Villis aside and whispered, "Holy cow." The impersonators were without a doubt impressed by Bigcanoe's firearm and would lead him to the moai with or without the blessing of Bipin and Villis. Bipin had made the case that it was vital they go along to oversee the situation, but not to worry, once the reality people had their photo op they would absolutely vamoose. "And no question, my grumpy friend," Bipin had gone on, they could distract Bigcanoe from sleuthing at the moai by chatting him up about Dick.

Villis was walking last, stalling, trudging, picturing himself as the poor sap who scoops up the horse doo-doo at the tail end of the parade. But lagging behind was making no difference. No one cared about his dragging feet. All of them – motormouths. Yak. Yak. Yak. None of them had self-control enough to listen to The Pearl. Except for the sound guy. The sound guy *was* listening, walking in front of Villis, moving his microphone (which looked to Villis like a salami in a furry sock) high and low as if the contraption were inhaling sounds. Villis wanted to ask him what he was recording. Was he collecting the chip-cheep of the crickets, or the give-and-take of the red-winged blackbirds that balanced atop the tall grasses like gullible optimists? Was his electronic apparatus soaking up the sound of their foot-steps pad-padding in a kindly way upon the trail, this gaggle of men coming and going, as Palaeolithic man had come and gone, and then his descendants after him, and then their descendants, and then more folks after those? Eons of pad-padding upon this land, while the Earth had endured.

But would it? Villis worried. Endure? Could it, now that the padding footsteps had mostly been displaced by cars and trucks, and roads choked the land with asphalt straps, and stagnant mounds of discarded tires persisted like bunions, and the smog of burnt petro-leum smothered the air while acid burned the oceans as if a mad professor's laboratory had run amok, and the ice caps that frosted the globe were dissolving into the sea, and in the span of time between grandfather and grandson one-third of the world's cities would probably drown beneath salt water like Atlantis – could the Earth endure all that? Villis could not shake the shadow of his unset-tling walk through the Future Pearl. Could not shake the sense of the Earth, overburdened.

Fact: it had happened before. Five times. Mass extinction events. Hadn't 64 percent of the megafauna died out in North America during the late Pleistocene Age? Mammoths and mastodons, western camels and dire wolves, giant beavers and giant peccaries, short-faced bears and sabre-toothed tigers, shrub-oxen and tapirs and giant ground sloths, all snuffed by the explosive combination of climate change and too much human hunting. The same thing is happening now, Villis thought, we're in the sixth mass extinction event, and half of all species on Earth will be gone forever by the end of the twenty-first century. Which ones? he wondered. Polar bears and emperor penguins, salamanders, fireflies and whales, turtles and coral and salmon and trout, and birds, lots of birds. What would the dawn be like without birds singing? And this time, he thought, the climate change is caused by us. We're committing terracide. Or perhaps matricide was the better term.

When they reached the Lopsided Ridges, Villis was the last one to clamber up. He climbed reluctantly, following Bipin's straight back and Bigcanoe's shiny ponytail, and the scattering line of young men wearing white, and the sun-bounce off the cameraman's camera and the bobbing of the furry salami.

At the top Villis stretched his lumbar muscles and scanned the Resonating Nexus for trouble. All seemed well. Better than well, he noticed with relief. The butternut trees still circled the moai like green queens. And with the war won, the asshole's garbage gone and summer cresting the Lopsided Ridges in a wave of gigantic life, Villis suddenly found it ridiculous, the idea from his strange dream, of walls *here* – of bland corridors, flightless birds and The Pearl scooped out of the planet like a real pearl from its oyster shell. Now that he was here, even with these youngsters, he couldn't help feeling a kiss, perhaps from the green queens themselves, fall delicately upon his cheek, pledging that here, at least, as always, there was peace.

This shouldn't be too bad, he thought, settling on a boulder (which was probably a glacier erratic, he realized with pleasure). A few pictures, a little video, some chit-chat and they would all go away. For good.

"What's this?" the cameraman asked. He was stooped at the base of the moai, peering through the lens of his camera, filming. Snooping, Villis thought – busybodies, these city people.

The producer squatted beside the cameraman. "People! People! Check this out!"

"Don't touch it!" the cameraman said, still filming. "You could contract Hepatitis C."

The producer yanked back his hand.

Villis stiffened, and not in his back or knees but in his heart. ATV man. What else could it be? But what part of him? Villis hoped, please not his head. He waved frantically at Bipin. Mouthed to him to *Come here*. Bipin came, looking stricken.

The young men were clustered around the moai, murmuring and shaking their heads. Bigcanoe slapped his cap back on and flipped open his notepad.

"Hey, cop guy! Write this down – he just found a fucking bone!" Jesus said.

"Dude," Gandhi said, speaking to the bone, "who *were* you?"

"I don't believe in killing, whatever the reason," John Lennon said.

Villis pushed Bipin toward the moai. "You go and see. I can't. I can't do it. I just can't. I–"

Bipin nodded. "Remember, I'll serve your stint in the Big House." Then he shot over to the moai and pushed his way through the knot of young men.

Villis closed his eyes. He would faint. Keel over like a stupid old fool. He put his hand to his chest, concentrated on his heart. Okay, he said to his heart. Do it now. Stop beating.

But it wouldn't stop, and so Villis opened his eyes, and to his surprise saw that Bipin was no longer stricken but laughing to beat the band and holding something up. A bone. But ...?

"It's not a you-know-what bone, my friend. Come quickly and render your professional opinion. You're the expert, but to my amateur eyes I'd say this belonged to some super-duper critter."

"A megafauna?" Villis shouted, warily, afraid to believe it.

Bipin nodded. Villis hurried over. The young men parted and let him pass.

Villis took the bone in his hand, turned it over, examined the surface, which was smooth and somewhat pitted. He noted the colour – ivory with highlights of amber. Dusty, very old, too big to be human, too big to be anything alive on the planet nowadays. No doubt about it.

"It's a fragment of a rib bone from a woolly mammoth, an animal larger than the largest elephant alive today," Villis said.

He blew dirt from the bone. After all these years searching. After scouring the soil, buffing in his heart the decades-old dream of discovering a bone from one of those magnificent, mysterious, massive creatures that had once moseyed in The Pearl like stout housewives – finally, in this odd and unexpected way, his dream had come true. Villis started to cry. As he tasted his own tears he thought, how could this be? Though he could not turn on the waterworks for his four lost friends, for Juozas, Janus, Gregori and Endres, he could for this silly old bone.

"Dude," Gandhi said, "did you, like, know that thing personally?"

"Are you getting this?" the producer snapped at the cameraman. The cameraman waggled his hand affirmatively and then motioned to the sound guy, who dangled the furry salami close to Villis's face. Villis cried more quietly. He didn't want his first tears in sixty years amplified.

Bigcanoe draped an arm around Villis's shoulder. "I'm with you, Uncle. It's how my people feel whenever we're faced with the sufferings of Earth Mother's innocent children."

"How could an animal that fucking big be fucking innocent?" Jesus said. "That thing must've been a super-predator."

"Woolly mammoths were herbivores." Villis sniffled.

Bipin interrupted, "What he means to say is, they were vegetarians."

The social media coordinator threw up his hands. "Jesus, I could have tweeted that."

"Do you think *I* give a shit?" Jesus said.

"I say it's like, what do you call it, a souvenir from Elvis 1," Elvis 2 said. "He's sent it to us through the portal. From caveman days."

John Lennon pumped a fist in the air. "Before Elvis there was nothing."

The sound guy swung the microphone around to John Lennon and then nodded at the producer. The producer signalled the cameraman, who swung the camera around as well. Then the producer leaned toward John Lennon. "Sir, are you agreeing that this discovery of an ancient bone from a long-extinct woolly mammoth is in fact a souvenir deposited here in these deeply secluded woods by a time-travelling Elvis Presley, who has apparently visited prehistoric times via the time portal beneath this arcane and mysterious monolith?"

John Lennon nodded. "I believe in everything until it's disproved."

Gandhi looked bemused. "Hey, like, dudes, I thought it was a monoLIFT."

The producer cleared his throat. "Ladies and gentlemen, there you have it. Breaking news from deep within the secluded woods–"

"The fucking Pearl," Jesus cut in. "The two old guys call it the fucking *Pearl*."

"Ladies and gentlemen, there you have it – breaking news from deep within the hyper-secluded woods known to insiders as The Pearl. Elvis lives."

"Whoa, that's an anagram," Bipin said. "LIVES. ELVIS."

"Amazing, folks! An anagram! The word *ELVIS* becomes the word, *LIVES*. Spell it out for yourselves. Further dramatic evidence. Elvis Lives. He is alive and well and sending souvenirs from another dimension of TIME. We can only hope that, someday soon, Elvis will see fit to send us a postcard from the outer limits of prehistory."

The producer nodded at the cameraman, who lowered the camera.

"Outer limits of prehistory," the social media coordinator said. "I could've tweeted *that*, too."

Villis took off his shirt and snugged it around the bone.

Gandhi reached for it. "Dude, like, who says *you* get to keep it?"

"I agree. This bone is the property of *So You Think You Can Think*," the producer said. "After all, we found it."

Villis didn't know what to say. It had never occurred to him that on the longed-for day when he finally found a mammoth bone someone would steal it from him. "Uh-uh," he said, hugging the bone to his chest. He was keeping it, even if he had to fight every last one of them.

The cameraman held up his camera. "No problemo. It's all here for the record. Video proof that *I* found it, fair and square."

"Which means," the social media coordinator said, "*So You Think* keeps it."

Elvis 2 stepped forward. "It came from Elvis 1, so *I* should be the one who gets to keep it."

Jesus frowned. "Why the fuck do any of you want a dead bone?"

John Lennon knelt at the base of the moai and started scrabbling in the dirt. "Possession isn't nine-tenths of the law. It's nine-tenths of the problem. I say let's dig around and find more bones. Then we can all have one."

"No!" Bipin and Villis shouted together.

Bigcanoe cocked his head at them. "Why not? Is there some

reason unbeknownst to those of us standing herein why we should not pursue a course of further digging for said mammoth bones?"

Villis shook his head and sent Bipin a begging look.

Bipin paddled the air, sweeping his arms upwards like the hands of a clock swinging to the midnight hour. He held his arms above his head, unbending for a moment, waiting until he had everyone's attention, before sliding them downward into a praying position above his heart. When he spoke they were all listening, especially the social media coordinator, who, Villis thought, was looking almost frantic with excitement.

"We most certainly should refrain from pursuing a course of further digging since such activities will undoubtedly perturb the portalistic vibrations of the moai."

"Portalistic?" Bigcanoe said.

"Perturb?" said Gandhi.

Bipin nodded solemnly. "Furthermore, I am suggesting that I transition into a trance and contact Elvis 1, the man himself, and ask him to whom he has sent this bone."

The producer signalled the cameraman and the soundman. "Are you getting this, guys, ARE YOU GETTING IT?"

The cameraman and the sound guy aimed their equipment at Bipin, who had dropped into Full Lotus in front of the moai.

"Jesus Jesus Jesus! Does anyone have a goddamned pen and paper?" the social media coordinator said. "Christ, it's like goddamned Christmas morning with no goddamned way to get this stuff down."

"*I* still don't give a shit," Jesus said.

"Sometimes the old ways are best," Bigcanoe said, ripping a page from his notebook and handing it, and his pen, to the social media coordinator.

Villis slipped away from the others, returning to the boulder to rest his bones. He was squeezing the mammoth fragment against his chest, feeling the length of it through his shirt, mentally measuring it – fifteen, sixteen centimetres, at least – then easing off squeezing, suddenly mindful of how brittle old bones could be. He turned to Bipin. His heart had stopped pounding. A relief. Now that he had finally found this smidgen of mammoth he wanted to live at least long enough to study it.

From where he sat, he could just make out Bipin's eyes, which were closed. Deep in meditation. Or at least pretending so. The impersonators were gathered around Bipin in an arc of white, like spoonfuls of unrisen biscuits awaiting Bipin's yeasty bubblings of hope. Villis could read it on their faces. The impersonators weren't very bright, but still, they had hope. Gullible optimists, like the red-winged blackbirds. Wasn't this how he himself had once been, swaddled, as he remembered it, in youth and a winter-white overcoat, like a dollop of butter in mashed potato, sitting in an arc around the campfire with Juozas, Janis, Gregori and Endres in those adrenalin days when they believed destiny was a thing men strode toward, rather than the steamroller it had turned out to be?

Villis sighed. Hope? Nope. He had shooed that pest away a lifetime ago. And yet, as he enjoyed the truth of the mammoth bone through his shirt, he realized: hadn't he always hoped for this?

The cameraman and sound guy trained their technology on Bipin like snipers. The producer and the social media coordinator shouldered their way into the arc of the impersonators – Jesus tried to block them with his elbows – and now waited eagerly alongside the others, the fronts of their white T-shirts facing Villis, asserting *So You Think* ... Villis chuckled. What would Captain Early advise? Make a run for it? Take his precious fragment of a woolly mammoth's rib and run as far and as fast as he could?

And miss this? Not a chance.

Bipin was speaking, not in his usual voice but with one that Villis knew came from a place secreted within him. It was as if Bipin were drawing his voice from the deepest of wells, where the water at the bottom was ancient. And his accent was more pronounced, his voice brimming with India.

"Blessings to you, my friends," Bipin said, then paused. The young men, all of them, Bigcanoe too, hearkened to his words. Bipin continued, "Blessing Number One. Thank you for getting old, because it means you are getting to live."

Villis cradled the bone, thinking that Bipin was probably right about that.

The young men murmured while the social media coordinator scribbled on Bigcanoe's paper.

"Blessing Number Two. Thank you for many stairs to climb, since they are the *only* way we can progress from one level to another."

Villis thought of the Lopsided Ridges. Right again, Bipin, old boy.

"Blessing Number Three. Thank you for annoying neighbours, for they allow us to practise our ability to love."

The impersonators glanced at the television crew, who smiled sheepishly. Bigcanoe slung an arm around the sound guy.

Bipin's breathing had slowed to almost nothing, a patient tide ebbing through his belly. "Blessing Number Four. Thank you for sinners, because, by comparison, they make the rest of us seem like saints."

"It's a fucking Sermon on the Mount," Jesus whispered.

Gandhi pressed a finger to his lips. "Dude. Can it."

"Is there more?" John Lennon asked. "The more I see, the less I know for sure."

"Blessing Number Five. Thank you for confusion, because it is necessary to mix contrasting ingredients together in a messy muddle before you can reap the sweet reward of a cake."

Bigcanoe bent over Bipin and blew gently across his hair. "Do you think the old guy's okay? Maybe we should stop him. Maybe he'll hurt himself. I don't know what to do. I never know what to do–"

"Blessing Number Six. Thank you for doubt, because the incessant jabbing nature of it digs in the soil of our psyches in the same way a shovel digs in the ground, preparing the depths of our souls for the seeds of change."

The sound guy nudged the microphone nearer to Bipin then motioned to the cameraman, who dropped into a squat and levelled his camera at Bipin's face. Villis glanced at the producer, who seemed suddenly more excited than before.

"Do you think there's a chance he'll keel over?" the producer said. "It makes for good footage. Maybe even, you know ..." He made a choking motion at his own throat.

"Blessing Number Seven. Thank you for death, because it means we do not have to pay taxes any more."

The producer punched the sky with his fist. "I'll get my promotion for this!"

Villis, still hugging the mammoth bone, went to stand with the others. There was one more thing Bipin needed to clarify. "Uh, Bipin. About this bone – did Elvis 1 send it?"

"And hey, Babe," Elvis 2 interrupted, "were your messages from Another Time, like, coming from the King himself?"

Bipin crooned. "*Well I said shake, rattle and roll ...*"

Elvis 2 did a hip wiggle. "Everybody, let's rock! The old guy is, like, channelling Elvis 1!"

"Are you guys getting this? For Christ's sake don't miss anything!" the producer said, hopping.

Jesus waggled his hand over the producer's head. "Love your enemies, bless them that curse you, do good to them that hate you."

"*It's now or never ...*" Elvis 2 crooned beside him.

"*Imagine there's no countries, it isn't hard to do, nothing to kill or die for, and no religion too,*" Lennon added to the singing.

Gandhi did a runner's lunge in front of John Lennon, as if, Villis thought, he was honouring John Lennon's quote. But Gandhi was having trouble keeping his balance, which Villis found ironic, given how centred the original Bapu had been.

"Quick, pan to the guy in the diaper," the producer shouted.

"Be the change that you want to see in the world," Gandhi said, wobbling in front of the camera, hitching up his diaper.

Bipin suddenly sang louder than the others – "*You won't do right to save your doggone soul – and this bone is for Villis, this bone is for Villis, Viiii-lliiiis, shake-rattle-and-ROOOLL!*"

Villis unwrapped the bone from his shirt and lifted it to his face. Sniffed. What did an old bone smell like? Endurance. Continuity. The Earth. The Pearl. His home. Life. A good smell. Clean. Correct. Villis lifted the bone higher and waved it above his head, watching the others (who were now all singing different songs but somehow doing it in harmony with each other), watching John Lennon and Jesus with their arms knitted like buddies in a pub, and watching the television crew that was a scattering of ants, circling the others, filming, filming, recording the craziness. His beloved Pearl. A mess in the woods. A circus. Complete confusion. What was it Bipin had said? We need the muddling mixings of contrasting ingredients before we can enjoy the sweet reward of a cake.

Villis fed his lungs with the green of The Pearl and decided to sing too, raising his voice at least as high as the others. "*God bless Latvia, our beloved fatherland, where the Latvian daughters bloom, where the Latvian sons sing. Let us dance in happiness there, in our Laaat-viiiaaa!*"

The producer grinned at the social media coordinator, who was scribbling again on Bigcanoe's paper, while the sound guy darted over to Bigcanoe just in time to record him belting out, "*And God Bless the Mo-hhhhawk Nation. And Go-oood Blesssss The Pearl!*"

"It's the *fucking* Pearl!"

The cameraman lowered his camera and grinned at the producer. "*This* is gonna go viral."

CHAPTER 22

How Bipin and Villis Ended Up on Easter Island, Anyway ...

"There aren't any trees here." Villis checked his GPS and then turned 360 degrees, scanning the landscape that was as lumpy as an unmade bed. They were in Ahu Tongariki, gazing up at a row of fifteen colossal moai aligned like chess pieces sizing up some distant game.

"No, my observant friend," Bipin said, shading his eyes with one hand. "But there are hardly any roads here, either."

Fact: as far as Villis could tell, there was only one road suitable for cars on Easter Island, and even that was not much more than a wide-ish path, and certainly nothing like the asphalt arrow that hurtled alongside the green frill of The Pearl. And what was more, with the forests long gone – gobbled an eon ago by human idiocy – no trees had been exterminated to make this particular road. He was pleased with himself for thinking this. It was getting easier to see the silver lining without always needing Bipin to spot it for him.

"We're here and I'm still alive," Villis said.

Bipin started whistling Beethoven's Fifth.

"But too bad you broke your Ray-Bans," Villis went on.

"Didn't you report seeing Palaeolithic man wearing them, taped together, that time you saw Frog riding on his shoulder?"

"I did."

"*That* was a premonition of my broken sunglasses, and, as such, certain proof that time isn't."

"And what about your blessing notebook? It's in a plastic baggie in some filing cabinet in L.A. What's that proof of?"

"That airline security systems are misguided."

"Maybe the GPS can find your notebook," Villis joked.

He switched off the GPS and handed it back to Bipin for safekeeping. He hadn't wanted to bring it, but Bigcanoe had insisted. "You're going to weird places," Bigcanoe had warned, "you could get lost." To which Villis had countered, "We're going to two islands, small ones. What kind of idiots get lost on an island? Walk as far as you can. You'll always come back to where you started."

"A good deal has happened since we found out about lonely Roland," Bipin said.

"There was a reason he was alone."

"Nevertheless."

"Fact: there's no point in leaving explanatory notes in our wills about what happened to the asshole. No one cared. No one cares."

"Except for you and except for me. But there is no sense in leaving notes for ourselves. We know the truth and can never forget it."

"We went viral."

"Nor can I forget that, my eternal friend."

At first Villis had not believed that the footage of what happened in the Nexus could have done such a thing – "gone viral", as the cameraman had put it. Villis had even wondered aloud what the term meant.

"My delightfully uncool friend," Bipin had answered patiently, "*going viral* refers to contagious communicable gossip disseminated via the you-too?-tube, which contaminates people's precious time with a rapidly spreading plague of nonsense."

Nonsense, indeed; Villis had thought this at the time. Couldn't possibly happen to them.

And yet, only two days after Bipin defined it, and four days after the heady scene in the Nexus with the time portal, the singing, the mammoth bone and the blessings from Elvis, the nonsense had begun. It had happened while he and Bipin were doing the rounds on the road. Villis had just skewered a gooshy, half-chewed hamburger with his chopsticks when a tourist bus off-gassing diesel groaned to a stop on the shoulder of the road. He had raised the hamburger as a warning to the driver – *you can't park that thing here* – but the driver had parked anyway. Then the door of the bus had squealed and split and out gushed ladies in a rush of cheap pink and perfume like bubbles in a tub. One especially overwrought woman, apparently the leader, was holding aloft a golden, plastic bust of what Villis knew, judging by the instantly recognizable hair-peak and lips, to be Elvis.

"Hey! You two are the famous two old guys from the YouTube," the leader of the women said. "And we brought our Elvis all the way from Wawa to bestow upon the time portal."

"Over my dead body," Villis said, jabbing the half-hamburger at the plastic Elvis.

Bipin's eyes rounded. "Freudian choice of words, my friend."

But the leader lady was adamant. "The time portal is the place where Elvis is channelling through and whatnot. We seen it for ourselves on the YouTube. We figured this bust here will totally concentrate the vibrational forces and help Elvis find his way and whatnot. So take us to the portal, pronto – them's the short and the curlies of it."

Villis shook his head at Bipin. *Don't you dare.*

"No can do," Bipin said.

The woman was undeterred. "We'll find it ourselves, then, won't we, gals?" She hoisted the bust over her head, rotating it so that Elvis's golden eyes scanned the woods. "Where do we begin to bestow, Elvis boy? Show us, your loyal fans or whatnot, the way."

And so it had gone. In no time there were Twitter followers and a Facebook page, called *Time Portal to Elvis*, with over 95,000 "LIKE"s. Pictures had been posted online, mostly of the moai and of Bipin doing poses, though there was one of Villis holding up the mammoth bone, a little reluctantly, but not without a touch of pride. The description beneath the photo read: "This is Vinous, finder of the bone." Vinous? They had spelled his name wrong. Villis was still unnerved by his dream (or was it a vision?) of The Pearl in the future. They had called him Vinous there, too. He had worried – maybe *this* was where it started, the mistake with his name. Maybe the vision thing was coming true?

A few days after the busload of women from Wawa had pulled up, the entire *So You Think You Can Think* crew had returned – pumped from the giddy success of their YouTube viral video – and begun broadcasting a web series with worldwide distribution, featuring tours to the Nexus and re-enactments of the dramatic moment when the cameraman had dug up the mammoth bone. The impersonators, who had nothing better to do – and so had never left The Pearl – abided in the Nexus like supernovas, becoming web-stars, sustained on food donations and the adoration of fans, happily blinging their white costumes with logos in return for bags of corporate swag. More buses had come, and vans, too, plastered with the slogans of TV stations and encumbered with satellite dishes like awkward mono-ears. Cars like tin cans packed with bickering families had come too, and trucks hawking sausages off tailgates had come as well; all of these vehicles were cramming the shoulder of the road alongside The Pearl, until someone decided police were needed to direct traffic. And so Bigcanoe had stepped in, waving and smiling, and in between comings and goings had scribbled in his notepad until his notepad had filled up.

People searching for time portals had come, as had folks with erotic fantasies about cavemen. Archaeologists had arrived, armed with trowels and on the hunt for mammoth bones. The archaeologists had been especially interested in the ground beneath the moai (and above the asshole) but thankfully – and Villis had been surprised that he had felt such gratitude – the women from Wawa had bestowed Elvis's golden bust directly at the foot of the moai and then set up a round-the-clock vigil of shoulder-to-shoulder pinkness to protect the vibrational forces. This, in turn, had prevented the archaeologists from digging for bones and, by default, from unearthing the asshole. Despite this, Bipin had been called to break up a scuffle between the leader-lady and the head archaeologist – which was the moment when someone had broken his Ray-Bans.

And while all of that had been happening in The Pearl, Villis and Bipin had been repeatedly chauffeured in a stretch limo into Toronto to appear as celebrity contestants on *So You Think You Can Think*. At first Villis had found the limousine disconcerting. Inside the vehicle the mauve disco lights gave him a headache, and the passenger compartment was so big that he had rolled around its interior like a dime in a dryer. But Bipin had advised him to do Corpse pose on the long bench-seat and imagine the mauve lights as fingertips massaging his aura. Villis had thought, what the hell, and given it a try. After a while he had begun to enjoy himself, and in no time had felt centred enough to sit up and make faces through the tinted windows at people zipping by in other vehicles.

Bipin had tsk-tsked at him. "My friend, making faces at others is an unevolved behaviour."

"Don't knock it 'til you try it."

"What the hell," Bipin had said, and made a goofy face at a teenager staring dumbly out the window of a passing SUV. "Ho ho, I admit it. In the privacy of our stretch limo I am enjoying this minor moment of mischief."

Villis had smiled. "Some situations, my friend, call for a little mayhem."

So You Think You Can Think had gone better than Villis had expected. Things he had thought he should have minded he hadn't. Take the high-definition TV makeup, for example. Even though it amalgamated in his wrinkles like putty in wall cracks, he was able, in a moment of mischief, to imagine that the attractive girl brushing his cheeks was in fact sweeping him with kisses. He even told her about Latvia, about the nice things: his mother's sweet *piragi* (the girl had asked for the recipe, can you believe it?); the ice-blue of the Baltic Sea, especially in February; how Old Riga was more beautiful than Vienna. He had said, "You would've liked my friends. We were all so handsome then."

She had patted his lips with a tissue and said, "You're handsome still, Mr Krastins."

As it turned out, the *So You Think You Can Think* questions had been easy and the other contestants none too bright. Villis couldn't help pointing out to the makeup girl that even though his ninety-year-old brain was a tad slow, it was nonetheless chock full of dazzling answers. And once he had the hang of answering questions in Bipin's cockeyed philosophical manner, he was able to fling witticisms like a kid flipping baseball cards. For example – Question: Why do women wear high heels? Answer: Because men don't. The audience clapped. Question: Why do people stare at car wrecks? Answer: So they will have a story to tell when they get home. Ha ha! Why do people yell at the TV? Because it's easier to yell at the TV than it is to solve a problem you can't touch. After this answer, Villis had waited almost a minute for the audience cheers to die down, puffing up his chest, all the while squinting into the lights, noting that his knees were holding up, his voice was firm and his face surely twenty years better beneath the high-def foundation. This wasn't so bad, after all, these eager faces smiling at him. Loving him, it seemed.

After six shows he and Bipin had racked up a jackpot valued at $100,000.00. On the last night it had come to a final Think-down between themselves as top team versus the second-place competitors – two valets from a classy hotel who always rested theirs hands, palms up, on the *So You Think You Can Think* podium as if waiting for tips. The final assignment was, as the host had put it, a mind-blowingly awesome turn of the tables, where the top team would pose a super-killer question of their choosing to the second-place team. The audience, by clapping like crazies into a sound meter, would determine the winner.

Bipin winked at Villis and then posed the question, calmly, warmly. "My perspicacious, *So You Think You Can Think* friends, and all you trusting persons watching from the land of TV, our final question for the hotel boys is this: Why can't people simply love?"

Villis could tell by their scrunched faces that the hotel boys were confused. He was thinking, good for you, Bipin old man – finally, a question worth asking. No more foolishness about high heels and televisions. He couldn't wait to hear the jewel of wisdom that Bipin was bound to impart. And the audience, for the first time in the show, did not shout out answers. It seemed everyone was stumped. Everyone was waiting for a jewel.

Then one of the valets brightened. "I know, I know. People can't simply love because – they're mean."

The audience applauded.

"Uh-uh, off beam," Bipin said.

"Because they're selfish?"

Bipin shook his head. "Wide of the mark."

The second valet blurted, "People can't simply love because they're stupid!"

"Or afraid!" the first valet added.

"Afraid not." Bipin waited for the audience to settle down, then he looped an arm around Villis. The audience leaned forward en masse so that it seemed to Villis as if the TV studio was tilting.

Then Bipin bobbed his head and began – "People cannot simply love, because love is not simple. Love is not simple because for something to be simple it has to be a single, unmixed thing, like a sheet of paper with no writing, or a beach with no surf. For love to be love, there must be at least two elements to mix together, and this mixing together by its very nature creates something new, composed of a little from one, a little from the other. So to ask people to simply love is to ask them to love in a way that is contrary to the very nature of love; and that is why they cannot do it. Because to simply love is not to love at all; the only way to love is to do it in a whirling, weaving, everlasting, madcap, icewine, no limits, bellyflopping, deep-diving, sunbeaming, Bollywood dancing kind of way."

"No fair! That was a trick question," the first valet shouted.

"What's Bollywood?" the second valet added.

Then the audience had, as Villis described it later to Bigcanoe – "Gone nuts. And then we won the jackpot."

"What will you do without your notebook?" Villis was saying, turning away from a moai to watch Bipin cram the GPS into his fanny pack. It would be a shame if Bipin had no place to record today's blessing, particularly since this was their first day on Easter Island. The notebook had been confiscated two days earlier at the Los Angeles airport, on their way to Tahiti, when a security official's chemical-detecting wand had sniffed something alarming along the ruffled edges of Bipin's notebook. "It's only curry," Bipin had said when the wand had begun beeping. But the official, stone-faced, had plop-zipped the notebook into a plastic sandwich bag.

Bipin patted his fanny pack. "Not to worry. The World Wise Web has already given me my next notebook, #40, well in advance. I have it with me now." He chuckled. "I am striving against smugness, my friend – and it's only to you that I feel emotionally comfortable to confess this – but when the World Wise Web gave me #40 I had an intuitive inkling that something nefarious would happen to #39. Thus, the WWW delivered my new notebook in advance so that I wouldn't miss a single blessing."

"But you've lost almost one whole year's worth of blessings. All the ones in #39. How many is that? Hundreds?"

"They are not lost, my friend. The World Wise Web has simply taken them back and given them to someone else. And besides, I am giddy with the idea of it – can you imagine the security personnel in L.A. going through my notebook? Ho ho, what will they think when they come to Blessing Number 13,890 – *Thank you for diversity and non-conformity because uniformity is not only boring and unattractive, it makes for an easy target.* Why, that challenges the entire ethos of Homeland Security."

"Just exactly when did the World Wise Web give you #40?"

Bipin looked surprised. "I'm flabbergasted you do not remember, my friend. We must increase your B12. Why, you were observing me at the moment I received it. It was lonely Roland's notebook. Endeavour to picture it. The one I found in his pants pocket when we discovered his you-know-what body."

"Right." Villis did remember. All too well. "Then I guess that's okay."

But he wasn't sure. Did he want a reminder of the asshole every time Bipin noted another blessing? Irony, again, it seemed – his hidden misdeed with the ramp forever embedded in Bipin's blessings like a piece of grit in an oyster. He sighed. Wasn't Bipin always saying that was how a pearl formed? No grit, no pearl.

"Which reminds me," Bipin said, "I have yet to record yesterday's blessing. Must be the lagging jet. Blessing Number 14,101 – *Thank you for curry, which, despite having a notoriously potent lingering odour, is still the best flavour combination in the world.*"

"That's not much of a blessing," Villis said.

"Not every day is a banner day." Bipin pulled Roland's notebook out of his fanny pack, rifling the pages just as he had the day they found it. Villis snooped over his shoulder. The pages were empty, the notebook obviously new and unused.

"Holy cow!" Bipin said. "The first two pages are stuck together." He fiddled with the pages, unsticking them. "Why, will you have a goose at this? There is something written down here, after all. Roland has recorded real words."

"What's he say?"

"It's a list. Huh. He has entitled his list ..." Bipin squinted, "the writing is scratchy, but, yes, he has entitled his list: *Dumb-ass Things.*"

"Figures."

"Yes. Dumb-ass. I am certain of it. Though he has spelled dumb D-U-M. Dum-ass. Sounds French."

"Anything else?"

"He has written a gigantic number 1, and then beside it in caps: 'CRAZY OLD PAKI HAVING A FIT IN THE WOODS. NO TURBAN. WHAT THE FUCK?' Ho ho, he means me. He has called me a Paki. How on earth could Roland have mixed me up with the good people of Pakistan? But *wait*, this gives me the inspiration for today's blessing. Blessing Number 14,102 – *Thank you for confusion, because it makes us ask thought-provoking questions, such as 'What the fuck?'*"

"I fail to see how '*What the fuck?*' is a thought-provoking question."

Bipin snorted. "*That* one is obvious, my friend. You, too, must be lagging from the jet. Why, '*What the fuck?*' translated into less colloquial terms, means: 'What the sexual intercourse?' Roland, in his haste to write his note, obviously omitted the verb, which can only be *is*. Thus his question, '*What the fuck?*' translated correctly is: '*What is the sexual intercourse?*' The answer to that is also obvious. The sexual intercourse is nothing more, nothing less, than a manifestation of the life force travelling from the genitalia, up the spine and out the top of the head. So what Roland is really asking is, '*What is the life force?*' and that, my friend, is a most thought-provoking question."

"What the fuck?"

"What the fuck indeed. What the fuck *is* the life force? That is exactly what I am talking about. The life force is something you have to get into sync with. It's the only way to wield its energy, to swing it around you like Obi-Wan's light-sabre. When a person wields the life force it organizes the confusion."

"Another one of your kooky theories–"

"All one has to do is synchronize one's self with the present. The present is the only point for getting the life force. The past is played out, like a disconnected electrical circuit. No power. And the future is not yet played. An unconnected circuit. No power. Only the present moment is wired into the life force. Wire your feet into the circuit of the moment, and the life force will whoosh through you like a current through a light bulb."

Fact: sometimes Bipin made sense. And fact: he, Villis, could still change the subject, if that subject was close to an uncomfortable truth. Such as, how much life force had he squandered in his lifetime wiring himself into powerless circuits, brooding about the past, fretting about the future?

"Lucky for us about that email from Brando's son," Villis said.

"*Lucky* is not a big enough word for that, my minimalist friend. Neither are *good fortune*, *fluke* or *windfall*, or *jammy*, or *as sure as eggs* or *striking oil*, *hitting the jackpot*, *acing it*, *curling the mo* or *coming up roses*. Why, that email from Brando's son was nothing short of cosmic munificence."

Perhaps. Yes. Villis was willing to concede this – something else he was also beginning to get the knack of. Or maybe it wasn't that he was learning how to concede, but that things weren't bothering him as much. Had he become less congested? Ever since he had sung with the others in the woods, sung about his beloved Latvia – *Let us dance in happiness there* – something seemed to have sailed out of him along with the high notes of the chorus.

Besides, anybody would have marvelled at the email from Brando's son.

It had appeared in Bipin's inbox a week after *So You Think You Can Think* had reneged on paying their jackpot. The day after the show had ended, an archaeologist poking in the Resonating Nexus had discovered that the moai was made of Styrofoam. In the wild days following the archaeologist's outraged exposé of this fact, Bipin's credibility as an Elvis channeller completely collapsed. The crowds had stampeded out of The Pearl, declaring the time portal a fake. Villis and Bipin had gone viral as frauds and laughingstocks (though neither of them had minded), and The Pearl was mostly quiet again except for a few lingering fanatics. The pale lawyers from *So You Think You Can Think* unsheathed their yellow markers and highlighted clauses in Bipin and Villis's contracts that stipulated, as far as Villis could understand it, some mumbo-jumbo about misrepresentation and moral conduct. And so their jackpot, and by default their travel fund to Easter Island, was rescinded.

Until the email.

Hello, Bipin. I am a son of Marlon Brando. I am staring at my dad's favourite photo, of himself standing with a skinny Indian man. My dad always said that the Indian man told him wise things, but he never told me what those things were. And he couldn't remember the Indian's name. I never imagined that someday I might figure out who the man with my dad was. But I have. It's you.

About a month ago, I saw you and your old friend, Vinous, on YouTube. Right away, I recognized you from the photo. I followed your story online. Crazy. All those people coming for the time portal. I do believe there is some power in the Resonating Nexus, even if the moai was just a Styrofoam one. I like the Impersonators, especially

Jesus, because you never know what he's going to say. And I was happy when Bigcanoe announced that he was quitting the police force to write a book about aliens. But last week, when that stupid game show took away your money for your trip to Easter Island, that was when I decided to write you.

I live on a private South Pacific island not far from Tahiti, which is only a few hours' flight from Easter Island. I was thinking – since you were acquainted with my father, you might accept my invitation to you and Vinous to visit me on my beautiful island. I am hoping you can tell me the wise things you told my father. I'll arrange e-tickets, business class, the entire way, from Toronto onward, and return. Go to Easter Island first, and then, on your way back through Tahiti, come and stay with me for as long as you like. I live in a paradise. Similar to The Pearl, only tropical.

By the way. There are no roads on my island. Make sure you tell that to Vinous.

Villis was pleased about no roads in the tropical paradise, but it bothered him that Brando's son thought his name was Vinous. Ever since that picture of him had been posted on Facebook – "This is Vinous, finder of the bone" – people had been calling him that. No matter how many times he corrected them. VILL-is, not Vin-ous. Never matter, the name had stuck. And he still hadn't shaken his dream/vision of the future Pearl. With all the nonsense in the Nexus about Elvis and the moai, and added to that the mixup with his name, and the vision of Palaeolithic man weeping as the lights went out on Earth, it seemed more and more likely that what he had glimpsed had not been some queer delusion but a true peek into a distant tomorrow.

But here was the thing. Why hadn't he glimpsed the GULAG in advance? If he had seen that particular preview (before he and Juozas, Janis, Gregori and Endres had been bagged by the NKVD and pitched into the open-pit dump that was Camp TTK-6) he would never have joined the Forest Brothers. And he would have chained his friends to their bedposts and poured wax in their ears against the sad cries of Latvia before letting them join too. There. A coward. So be it. But he and the boys would be old men together.

And anyway, what could he do now to prevent the abysmal future of The Pearl? He was ninety years old. So what was the point of the vision? Still – and thankfully – the archaeologist had exposed the moai as a fraud. Villis hoped that this alone would be enough to spoil the conversion of the Resonating Nexus and his beloved Pearl into the artificial abomination of that future so-called sanctuary, with its roof and fans and hard-edged pray-way. Even though he knew hope was irrational.

(What was it Bipin said about hope? It was *supposed* to be irrational. If it were rational, it would be certainty.)

Villis stared up at the fifteen moai. Here he was, at Easter Island. His hope had become a certainty. In some ways the moai reminded him of himself. They were old men. Survivors. Fashioned from the rocky womb of Mother Earth against their wills, with some aspect of the life force having passed into their portly stone bodies from the hands of whatever anonymous chisellers had done the chiselling; who were then arranged upon the hard ground for unknown purposes, positioned so that they could look in one direction only. Pensive. Evasive. Brooding. Staring down their mulish noses at the paradise into which they found themselves embedded, indifferent. And yet, Villis thought, despite all this, in a funny way, he found the moai adorable. Maybe it was their tummies, rounded like those of toddlers, that made him want to hug them.

He clamped one arm around Bipin. Hugging Bipin was as good as hugging a moai. Better. "You said this was my last year of confusion. I googled it. Like you said to."

"And?"

"The last year of confusion was 46 BCE. As declared by Julius Caesar."

This had been a surprise to Villis, to discover that the "last year of confusion" was not one of Bipin's super-duper metaphors but an actual year. And 46 BCE, he had learned from his research, had been a very long one – 445 days in total, with extra months inserted between November and December.

It had happened, as Villis had read online, because Julius Caesar had been irritated with calendar problems. In Caesar's time, the Roman Empire had used calendars based on the lunar year of 354 days, instead of the solar year of 365 days. This shortage of eleven days in the lunar calendar meant that over time the four seasons – which came and went according to the movements of the sun and *not* the moon – drifted out of synchronicity with the lunar calendar. By 46 BCE these eleven days of drifting had accumulated to 80, making the imperial calendar almost three months out of step with the sun and thus out of step with the natural rhythms of the world. The fall harvest came in summer. Winter set in before September – which was confusing for the Romans, as Villis understood it, because they found themselves celebrating the harvest festival while crops still bloomed in the fields.

Caesar, in a brilliantly pragmatic move (in Villis's opinion), switched his empire over to a solar-based calendar. But before doing so, he had to synchronize the actual year with the actual seasons – in other words, find those lost 80 days. So, dictator that he was, Caesar blithely inserted 80 days into 46 BCE, extending it to 445 days, making it the longest year ever, while declaring to his grumbling constituents that this was *the* last year of confusion.

Villis thought, too bad he himself didn't have that kind of power, to extend the length of a year. If he did, he wondered – what year would he lengthen? All he could come up with were years he would like to have shortened. The war years. The GULAG years. But this year, he wondered, this year in The Pearl, with all that had happened – what about lengthening this one? Yes? Yes.

"Holy cow," Bipin said. "Isn't googling fantastic? See what enthralling titbits of extra-contextual information one can discover with minimal exertion and a keyboard? Caesar's last year of confusion was an alignment with the movements of the natural world, which can more essentially be construed as an alignment with our favourite spiritual concept, the life force, which only moments ago you and I were discussing–"

"You were discussing. I was listening."

"Right you are, my precise friend. But you see what I'm angling at – to align with the life force you need to align your consciousness, align your chakras–"

"Your jazz fingers?"

"Ho ho. Funny. Line up your essence with the presence, I mean, the present."

"I thought you meant I was going to die soon."

Bipin shook his head, gave Villis's shoulder a squeeze. "I have no idea, my dearest friend, when you're going to bite the big one. But I do know that this is your last year of being confused in your heart and mind. All your sufferings from the past, your four poor dead friends, the brutal injustice of your incarceration, all those mornings without finding the disc of carrot in your soup, the unrelenting cold and the beastly bunks, and then your obsessions and concerns for the future – for the tender green perfections of The Pearl, for our poor Mother Earth who is soaking and parched and trembling and coughing, though she is still so achingly beautiful – all of this will end for you and you will be on your way to starry galaxies of certainty and silver."

"Is that the kind of wise thing you told Brando?"

"No no. I told Brando to smile more. He was all the time too gloomy. Bad for the photo ops."

"Smile more. That was it?"

Bipin pulled his backpack off and unzipped it before answering. He let slip the soft smile of a fond memory. "I also told him that the next evolutionary stage of humanity was to advance beyond our incessant hoarding of consumer goods – cramming our space with dead things that hinder the free flowing of the life force – and to finally under- stand that we need virtually no things to be happy. When I told him this, Brando smiled, which I took as his acceptance of my first point. And I knew he had accepted my second point when, not long after our photo was taken, he bought his beloved island sanctuary, where he went to live without clutter, planting himself in green vibrations, bathing his brain in the wash of palm leaves, listening to the earth through the soles of his feet and generally being peaceful in a piece of the planet not yet dominated by plastic and asphalt and steel."

"Like you and me in The Pearl."

Bipin nodded. "A wise man follows his own advice." He rustled in his backpack and pulled something out. The blue shoe.

"Why on earth did you bring that? No, don't tell me, let me guess. You want to bury it beneath a moai, a real moai, in honour of ..." Villis paused. In honour of whom? Surely not Real Elvis or Elvis 2. Surely not the asshole. "In honour of–"

"In honour of YOU."

"Me?"

"I found this shoe when doing the rounds of the road, which I was doing because you were sidelined by your *coccydynia*. Without the blue shoe I would've had no artifact to convince the gullible intruders that the moai was a time portal through which I could communicate with dead Elvis. And because people believed that I was channelling the King, you and I went viral. Our mugs were beamed through all the cyber spaces, whereupon Brando's son beheld my face after a lifetime of wondering who in the heck was the skinny Indian guy standing beside his super-gorgeous celebrity father. If Brando's son had not found my cyber-face he could not have sent us e-tickets and we would not be standing here-and-now at the foot of these fifteen splendiferous crazy moai men, fulfilling your lifelong dream of coming to Easter Island."

Villis held out his hand for the shoe. Then he stooped and scrabbled in the rubble at the base of the biggest moai. "I think we should bury this in honour of the asshole. Elvis 1. Roland, I mean."

Bipin grinned in a self-satisfied way. "I am struggling against smugness."

Villis sighed, but not ironically. "I'm sorry for what happened, for the accident. But I'm not sorry about the rest. If the asshole – Roland, I mean – hadn't come into The Pearl on his machine, I wouldn't be here."

"Fact: the asshole was the grit in your oyster," Bipin said, waving his hand along the towering row of moai. "And *this* is your string of pearls."

Villis stood up, shuffled a few more stones over the blue shoe with his toe. Then he took in the fifteen moai, one after the other, left to right, thinking that he had come a long way from Camp TTK-6. Wouldn't Juozas, Janis, Gregori and Endres, those northern boys with their big plans, be pleased to see him here?

String of pearls. All of them.

Villis smiled, thinking, wouldn't those fifteen moai look even more adorable in Ray-Bans? Especially broken ones held together with tape?

Bipin came up and stood beside him. He had pulled out the GPS and was peering intently at its bright, tiny screen. "Holy cow, will you look at this, my smiley chum? It's a satellite image of Easter Island. It seems there *are* trees on this island, after all." He pointed at the screen.

Villis bent to look. Amazing. Easter Island from outer space. It looked predominantly brown and grey and smooth, but there were a few scattered patches of feathery green rising up like hopes. Bipin was right. Had to be woods. Small. But there. Villis squinted at the image, checking to see if he might find his and Bipin's heads, dot dot, like two particles vibrating amid a larger universe. Wouldn't it be cool beans to see himself from above, while at the same time looking up from below? He was an old fool. What did he know? Still. Who could say otherwise?

He handed the GPS back to Bipin. "Let me have that notebook. I want to write something in it."

Bipin handed him the notebook and a pencil.

Villis flipped to an empty page and wrote: Blessing Number 1, September 23, 2011 – *Thank you for everything.*" Then he read his own words back to himself. *Thank you.* But to whom? He smiled again. To whom? It didn't matter.

Fact: believing or not believing did not change the truth that (mostly) life was good.

ACKNOWLEDGMENTS

The Last Year of Confusion is a novel that is, literally and metaphorically, close-to-home. Home is, therefore, a fitting place to begin these acknowledgments. As before, as always, my biggest barrel of thanks go to my husband, Mike Myers; daughters, Stephanie Myers Todman and Ella Myers; sons-in-law, Steven Todman and Rhett Fester; and my parents, Joan and Charlie Turpin. You are, all of you, my champions, my motivation, and the oasis from which I draw my strength.

I would like to extend special thanks to Maureen Whyte, Publisher at Seraphim Editions, for taking yet another chance on my work and publishing this second novel of mine. I'm also honoured that *The Last Year of Confusion* is being released during the 20th anniversary year of Seraphim Editions. Congratulations to you, Maureen, for your impressive and inspiring contribution to the literary arts in Canada.

Huge thanks, as well, to the dynamic duo, George and Trudi Down of The Book Band, for all the excellent work you do in support of Seraphim titles, and for backing me up in my writing adventures. I would particularly like to thank you, George (again), for your exceptional editing skills and to express how much I enjoy working with you.

Thanks, also, to Rolf Busch for his excellent design work and wonderful cover art.

Many thanks and much love, as well, to the best writer-friends a writer could ever want; the members of Vermillion: John Bandler, Valerie Burke, and Steven Jacklein. Here we go again, guys ... novel #2! Who would've thunk it?

And, of course, I become teary-eyed when I think of my posse of diligent manuscript readers, all of whom have provided me with honest, insightful, utterly helpful suggestions and observations which were invaluable to the well-being of this novel. Heaps of gratitude to: Stephanie Myers Todman, Ella Myers, Rhett Fester, Barbara Ackerman, Anna Schantz, Loretta Bailey, Stephanie Oldfield and Karen Jones. Special kudos to Stephanie Todman, who was the first person to read the manuscript, and who did so while on vacation in French Polynesia (no less), curled up beneath a mosquito net, on an island that wasn't 'too far' from Marlon Brando's island.

As well, a tip of the hat to Yogi and Magnus – two entirely interesting gentlemen who have walked with me in the woods of Cedar Springs sometimes, and talked to me about spirit and dying, the beauty of trees and the benefits of keeping fit into one's old age.

And ...

... since a ribbon of yoga flows through this novel like a deeply drawn *ujjayii* breath, I must also thank my exceptionally gifted yoga teachers, Sjonum A'Walia St-Cyr, Phil St-Cyr and Soek A'Walia (and my entire yoga-family at Rejuvenating Spring) for nourishing me for years now — body and soul — on yoga, greens-juice and affection.

And finally, last but certainly not least, I give a great group hug to the entire Cedar Springs Community, who have proudly and stead-fastly protected the precious Niagara Escarpment lands that we have shared and loved for ninety years, keeping these beautiful lands green and pristine. Thank you, also, to my fellow Springers, for steadfastly supporting — with enthusiasm, friendliness and faith — Janet-the-writer, for as long as I have lived in this remarkable community.

Janet Turpin Myers
Cedar Springs
April, 2015